Crossings

Battle Lines
Part 1

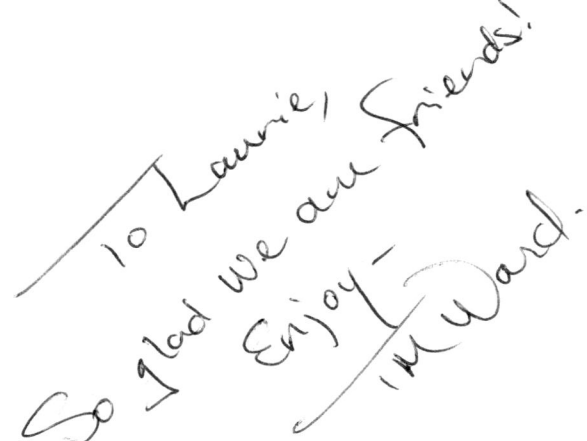

To Laurie,
So glad we are friends!
Enjoy—
TM Ward.

T. M. Ward

ISBN 978-1-64515-636-9 (paperback)
ISBN 978-1-64515-637-6 (digital)

Christian Faith Publishing, Inc.
832 Park Avenue
Meadville, PA 16335
www.christianfaithpublishing.com

Printed in the United States of America

To all who have ever been or ever felt orphaned

Acknowledgements

I could not have developed a vision for this story without the knowledge, support, patience, and love of my four beautiful children, my brother, all of my pastors, and my friends – and they know who they are. I thank God for all of you.

Special Tributes

Bern Miller: Were it not for Bern, I doubt seriously I would have known to give character development to any horse, let alone the Morgan. It was through my discussions with Bern that I, too, developed a passion for the Morgan, and that's coming from someone who previously knew little of horses. He is an educator, and his candor struck me swiftly and deeply such that I immediately shifted direction in my research and added to my content a significant place for horses with special emphasis on the Morgan. Though I am far from being an expert, and I hope for grace if I fall short, I am changed by how Bern inspired me and by what I've learned of the use and care of horses in America. I hope you will be inspired too.

Jeannie Mellin Herrick: I had the privilege of speaking to Jeannie on May 4, 2015, when I called her while conducting research on the Morgan horse. She joyfully and selflessly gave of her time without limit to talking with me about her love for this breed. She shared her deep concern for the potential loss of this breed to cross-breeders and urged me on to represent the beauty of this horse and, if at all possible, contribute to its preservation. She spoke of the horses she still had, and there was no mistaking the joy in her heart at the mention of them and her years of breeding, training, and showing her horses. We discussed the possibility of me visiting her, and she openly welcomed the idea, but time would not permit it. Jeannie passed away on November 21, 2015. Her beautiful legacy is well-documented.

Rita Sailors: personal editor, content and context evaluator, and friend.

Joyce Parker: she knows why.

A Brief Explanation on Content and Context

I asked myself repeatedly where and when to start this novel. Starting in the mid 1850's moved back to the 1840's and then again to the 1830's. And the 1830's could have easily moved to 1812. And how easy it would have been to go back another hundred years. There is just so much great history in this nation. Edward Coles became the marker for the starting point because his story is severely under-told, and his life crossed so many other incredible paths.

But the story is not directly about Edward Coles or any other real character or event in this novel. It's about Sam, a fictitious character who gives us an internal and external view of what walking in his shoes would have been like. Each real character helps us see more of Sam's character and more of the times of his life, good and bad. It was difficult not to bring in other figures and not to give full exhaustive attention to each event, but such is not within the scope of this effort, and the research conducted is limited thereto. The scope does, however, aim to entice the reader to want to know more and perhaps even write about it.

Certain liberties are taken for timing and storyline pursuits.

Introduction

*B*attle line: "a line along which a battle is fought" (*Merriam-Webster Dictionary*).

When I was in graduate school, I did some research on some of the early decisions made at the founding of our country. Along the way I met Edward Coles, and I was a bit surprised and very ashamed that I had not heard of him before. Authors Kurt E. Leichtle and Bruce G. Carveth painfully describe in the epilogue of their book, *Crusade Against Slavery; Edward Coles, Pioneer of Freedom* (2011), how Edward Coles is not represented in history as among the worthies, which until their book came, certainly appears to be the case. That made me think about how much of our great history is undertold. For example, Abraham Lincoln said that some of his fondest memories are those from his military days. Yet so few know anything about his military days. Emphasis placed on this great man's life is not about what interested him most but what we think should be most interesting: the Civil War, emancipation, and his horrifying death, each of which is meaningful and monumental, to be sure. But if he were watching our reflection on his life, I wonder if he would be thinking, "Can we please talk about something else?" And Chief Black Hawk might be thinking, "Can we please talk about it, at all?"—namely being the flawed Saint Louis Treaty of 1804 that forced him and the Sauk nation off ancestral lands.

There are countless other historical figures and events that have been shelved or not found worthy of fuller representation. As such, I took to reaching for those somewhat forgotten pieces of history to dust them off. I say "somewhat forgotten" because I am not naïve; I know that many historians and historian wannabes like me are in the know, at least to some degree. When I have the privilege of speaking to these groups about treasures in our history, we see the tragedy of the under- or untold stories. Look at what our generation is missing! Perhaps the biggest tragedy for me is having to choose between which stories to dust off while constructing *Crossings*.

On one of my first research trips for *Crossings*, I met Bern Miller who runs the Pioneer Trails Museum in Bridgeport, Nebraska. On this unexpected museum stop en route to Fort Kearny, Nebraska, still miles away, I thought I would be there for only a few minutes, but he and I talked for over an hour about horses on the frontier. The conversation proved pivotal for me. He explained how it is impossible to examine seriously westward expansion without giving meaningful consideration to the horse, in particular, the Morgan.

Home again, I continued with research on the Morgan horse, and it led to my calling a horse trader, Jeannie Mellin Herrick, who had been a Morgan breeder in upstate New York for decades. Her appreciation of and passion for the Morgan was profoundly moving, and out of respect for that and what I had already learned from my friend in Nebraska, I was joyfully swayed to make the Morgan important to my storyline.

History is commonly examined from a cause and effect, or consequential, viewpoint. Life's choices should be as well. *Crossings* explores this in many ways to include what it means to be fatherless. From friends who run ministries engaging the fatherless, to even the slightest glimpse of communities across our nation where fatherlessness is prevalent, to acute awareness of a home where both parents are void of parenting skills, to personal experience of father abandonment, my observations are that the results have a common thread for those impacted; they are orphaned. A child who grows up without a father, with a present father who is otherwise absent, or with an abusive father is left deprived of protection and/or advantage, which is defined as *orphaned* (Merriam-Webster). Being orphaned can happen at any age. An orphaned condition places the person at high risk of serious problems throughout life.

Someone very close to me teaches state-mandated parenting classes to both men and women, and he also ministers to both men and women in prison. When asked what's missing and what they truly need and desire, a common answer from these students and prisoners, regardless of age, is their father's approval, recognition, and love. Most of these men and women never received it and never will. When Jesus explained to his disciples in his final hours that soon he would be leaving, it left them confused and worried. He provided the ultimate solution to comfort and assure them when he said, "I will not leave you as orphans; I will come to you" (Jn. 14:18, NKJV); therefore, we can always choose God to be our Father.

And, of course, *Crossings* also explores love; it "bears all things" (1 Cor. 13:7, NKJV), and "bears it out even to the edge of doom" (Shakespeare, *Sonnet 116*). A one-time read of the *Song of Solomon* will leave a wanting on anyone who is not emotionally and spiritually dead. Love like that is not casual or accidental. It is calculated. It is passionate. It is intentional. It is longsuffering. It is forgiving. It is divine. On the other hand, love's ungodly antagonist, hatred, is an intentionally, passionately, destructively, and tragically self-centered contrast. Humanity has only briefly known one without the other, which was before evil entered the world.

Especially, *Crossings* deals with idolatry, which is a constant in history. When we think of idols, which are objects of worship, we commonly think of things like money, people, possessions, gods, etc. More accurately, however, idolatry comes from the need for control, approval, comfort, and justice. With the worship we give these things, we *then* pursue money, people, possessions, gods, etc. We are slaves to whatever we worship. When we don't get the results we want or what we perceive that we need, it leads to secondary responses, such as anger, fear, hopelessness, self-righteousness, revenge, hatred, selfishness, and more. What we worship is rooted in what we believe, and what we believe defines who we are, which is where we draw the line. Where we draw the line is also where the battle is fought, sometimes physically but always mentally, for we will not fight a battle physically unless we have submitted to it mentally. So where exactly does the battle begin? In the mind.

13

The most defining and demanding line in human history is God's first commandment: "You shall have no other gods before me" (Ex. 20:2, NKJV). Of all the battles fought involving this commandment, perhaps none is as critical as the one fought in the mind. The apostle Paul guides us in 1 Corinthians 10:4–5 (NKJV) on how to protect our minds from thoughts that lead to idolatry when he said, "For the weapons of our warfare are not carnal but mighty in God for pulling down strongholds, casting down arguments and every high thing that exalts itself against the knowledge of God, bringing every thought into captivity to the obedience of Christ." When we don't do this, confusion and chaos abound, and one deviation is all it takes to cause a storm.

Now, if you please, meet Sam Callahan, who, at first glance, is an orphan who loves and is loved; he hates and is hated; he is lost and is in bondage. His story is caught up in under-told history, horses, and idols while he struggles to decide what defines him. Upon second glance, there are only two powerful words: but God. If you take this read on, you might be moved to increased compassion for the broken, the lost, and the hopeless. Or you might be moved to greater introspection, drawing strength from Sam. Or you might even say, "I need no introduction. I know him well."

Chapter 1

S am did not smile. Upon arriving to Edwardsville, Illinois, in January of 1830, his father called him and his brother Amos into his freshly arranged study to set strict ground rules for their new home. Sam had no particular attachment to the home they left in Washington, DC, but he had mastered the environment there, such that his father eased up enough on him and Amos for them to know how and where to find some joy in their smothered lives. There were random occasions of displaced discipline, but things had been otherwise stable. Now, though, things were not stable.

Sam's mother Charlotte sat quietly to the side, which had become her strongest skill. She was very intelligent and could be quite loving, but she took one wrong turn early in her life, and that was marrying Bishop Callahan. Though he showered her with comforts, gifts, and what he said was love, none of it was free. He demanded her full and undivided attention, which had pulled so much life out of her that it left her little to give to anyone else. Her eyes were dull resulting from learned helplessness, which came with the arrival of her children. She loved Sam and Amos, but only in secret, because Bishop would not allow her to share her affection with anyone else, not even her children.

As she sat there watching Bishop rant in front of the boys, her mind jumped across the memories she had of rare moments of being a mother to her sons. Soon after Sam was born, Bishop hired nannies and housekeepers, which he said was to ease her burdens, but she soon learned it was to separate her from all distractions. He forced her to be consumed with only him, and she learned not to resist.

One day, she was reading and laughing with Sam. Bishop walked in just as she embraced him and said, "Samuel, I love you very much." She was startled and horrified when her child was ripped from her arms by Bishop and taken behind closed and locked doors. Charlotte heard the screams but could not get to her son or even comfort him after, as Bishop called on the nanny to calm Sam down and wipe his tears.

She was sad the day Amos was born. Still, she looked for ways to protect her children. She would wait for Bishop to leave for work, and she would school them, nurture them, hold them, pray with them, and certainly love them. Until one day, she saw Bishop interrogating the servants, and then he took the boys behind closed and locked doors.

Her last attempt involved late-night visits to her boys. After everyone was asleep, she would quietly sneak into their room, wake them up, and hide in a closet with them. There, for several years, she taught them by candlelight about love. They learned through her stories, her books, her hugs, her eyes, and her love for God. Until one day, Bishop opened the closet, and then he took her boys behind closed and locked doors; this time he was particularly furious. From then on, Charlotte decided that the best way to protect her children was to ignore them.

Now, Sam and Amos stood at near attention before their father's desk in view of an open cabinet door where various leather straps hung as Bishop established new codes for their new environment. Sam was eighteen; he knew he could avoid his father's wrath, and so did Bishop. Bishop's answer to that was to transfer Sam's punishment to Amos, leaving Sam trapped.

"You will be exposed to the wild and untamed side of this territory. Any evidence that either of you is being corrupted by it will be met with a swift response," Bishop said sternly as he paced the floor in front of them. He looked in their direction only at times when he wanted to pound in his message, and he spoke with his chin pulled in, which emphasized the weight on his face. He was easily six feet tall and carried much of his 275 pounds in his midsection, which caused his back to arch. He grayed early and groomed his wiry hair as best he could, but never did it look tame, which only further personified his temper when it flared. As the list of constraints and tolerances was delivered, Sam was already calculating a strategy for surviving his new home. "I expect full obedience to my wishes for the entire duration of our stay here. Do I make myself clear?"

"Yes, Father," both boys said in unison.

Neither Sam nor Amos resembled their father. Sam was five feet eleven and wore his brown hair short, parted to the side and combed back, which revealed his strong square jaw. His green eyes and full lips were finishing touches of the seemingly perfect creation that Bishop had both helped to make and come to resent.

Amos was fourteen. His hair was longer and darker, which made his deep blue eyes stand out. It was Amos's disposition more than his appearance that made him so attractive. He maintained a reliable, jovial mood that reduced Sam's protective nature to something seemingly unnecessary. In fact, Sam grew to depend on Amos's stable response when times were particularly dark, like now.

Bishop was part of the political undercurrent largely responsible for shaping the young nation at the time. The balance of land rights, the balance of slave states, and the balance of public perception were among what he considered his specialties. He was wealthier in money than in status, something he was determined to change as revealed in his ongoing intent to establish sufficient distance between himself and what he called the Irish filth he was raised in.

Bishop's family emerged from a line of Irish immigrants from the colonial days that escaped poverty in Ireland in exchange for poverty in the New World. Their passage was paid for by their indentured servitude, which took seven years to pay off. After the War for Independence, some poorer Irish struggled so hard to integrate equally that they wondered if slavery wouldn't have been more fruitful. At least then they would know when their next meal would come. Bishop's father could not read or write. Therefore, he found only jobs with high mortality rates; even then wages were pathetic, ensuring that the Callahans would be stuck in poverty indefinitely. Bishop decided early on to part ways with that life, and there was no going back. He was bent on creating a new image for his Irish heritage, one that would place his family among the elite. His wife and children would display themselves as refined at all times to satisfy the outward appearance that he longed for. As such, Bishop Callahan ruled his boys so tightly that it was difficult for them to breathe.

The Callahans made an abrupt move from a posh Washington, DC, setting to rugged Illinois upon Bishop's assignment to help engage the Sauk and Fox Indian problem, which was growing in tension over treaty interpretations. While Bishop was all too happy to contribute to moving Indians west of the Mississippi River, he loathed settlement in progress and the undefined social structure that came with it. He took the assignment with resistance but also with just enough compliance to worm his way back East as soon as it could possibly be arranged.

Edwardsville was the seat for Madison County, which drew a steady flow of political traffic in and out of the small city. A likely location for Bishop's post would have been Vandalia, the capitol, but he argued successfully that Edwardsville put him closer to tensions and within reach of the state's Indian agents who were focused on the crisis. None of that was true and everyone knew it. The cold fact was that nobody in Washington, DC, cared where Bishop went, as long as he went, and if he managed to get himself in the middle of an Indian battle where he took an arrow to his narcissistic heart, all the better. Both Bishop and his political peers knew he had worn out his welcome, which forced Bishop to consider new strategies for maintaining, and perhaps even elevating, his standard of living and status.

Though Bishop saw himself as sly, it was no secret that he couldn't care less about the Indian crisis. He knew little about it and spent the majority of his time avoiding it. His motives for living in Edwardsville were linked to something else. Unlike Vandalia, Edwardsville had Edward Coles, the former governor of Illinois who had, at this point, removed himself from politics and settled on his farm, Prairieland. Bishop intended to bond somehow with Coles because he came with uncommon value. Coles was wealthy in assets with mass acreage in Illinois as well as properties in Philadelphia, Missouri, and elsewhere. More important, though, was that Coles maintained significant status back East and had a history with many of the nation's founders including Jefferson and Madison. In fact, his family's vast property bordered Jefferson's, he had worked for President Madison, and Dolley Madison was his first cousin. Those were just the beginning of Coles's connections, and Bishop wanted those royal relationships extended to himself.

He did not share Coles's sentiment for slaves, though. He was disturbed, perhaps even disgusted, that Coles was the catalyst behind making sure that Illinois remained a free state in spite of aggressive efforts by proponents of slavery to change the state constitution, thus legalizing slavery.

If that wasn't enough, Bishop found it preposterous that Coles exposed an abolitionist nature when he snuck his seventeen inherited slaves out from under his family's Virginia settlement to Illinois only to free them along the way and set them up on their own farms. Bishop was among many who saw Coles's decision to free his slaves as nothing more than throwing away one-third of his lucrative inheritance, which was blatant disregard for that which his parents had worked so hard.

"What's the difference?" Bishop would laugh. "Being a slave in Virginia or working on a farm in Illinois from your former master?" Black codes were springing up all over the place to control movement, employment, and assembly, which diminished any hope of equality, and appropriately so, according to Bishop. Anything he could do help in that effort was worth the sweat.

Coles travelled often and placed the affairs of his estate in the hands of several people. By now, Robert Crawford, who was freed by Coles, managed Prairieland. He was well-liked by everyone such that he was often called Uncle Bobby, yet without losing authority in his position, which furthered Coles's confidence in his decision to put Crawford in charge.

Others managed Coles's enormous range of properties, and Adrien Pruitt was in the mix, handling some of Coles's local interests and frequently traveling to St. Louis on his behalf. When Coles put Bishop in a position to have to deal with Adrien, things did not go desirably for either of them.

Bishop burst into Adrien's office and said, "I've come to see about employment for my son, Samuel."

"What made you think to come here?" Adrien remained seated and continued with his work, intent on returning Bishop's rude behavior.

"I asked Governor Coles about a position, and he sent me to you. Now what are you going to do about it?" Bishop demanded as he noted Adrien's dismissive attitude.

If Governor Coles spoke to you at all, it's because he does not yet know you for the horse's ass that you are, Adrien thought. But he only said, as he finally came to his feet in defiance, "Nothing. Robert Crawford does the hiring at Prairieland. Perhaps you should see him." Adrien hit below the belt with that suggestion, knowing that Bishop would never deal directly with a colored man.

Bishop moved past Adrien's desk and walked into the next office. Adrien was stunned by his audacity.

"Why not here?" Bishop tried to command.

"Mr. Callahan, in case you did not notice the sign over the door, it reads, 'Adrien Pruitt: Assets Manager.' Mr. Coles does not own this operation. I do, and I have no position for your son. Now if you'll excuse me, I'm very busy."

Bishop thrust forward a note written by Edward Coles. It read, "Position for Sam Callahan, see A. Pruitt."

"It seems my son will be one of Mr. Coles's assets that *you* will manage. The farm will do for now, if that's all there is." It was not Bishop's intention to get his son's hands dirty on a farm, especially if it meant working for and alongside Coles's former slaves, but one foot in the door at a time, Bishop thought.

Adrien looked at the note, and he slowly raised his eyes with scorn until they met Bishop's. What was Bishop up to? Whatever it was, his son would pay the cost, and Adrien tried to expose that cost. "Does your son have any experience on a farm?"

"What does it matter?" Bishop asked, but he was not interested in an answer.

"The job is very demanding. Long days, dirty work. What of his studies? Is he not preparing for college?" Adrien asked in hopes that he would come to some level of reasoning.

"That's none of your concern," Bishop said and raised his head, attempting to look down his nose to the equally tall Adrien Pruitt.

Adrien could not prevent giving the assignment to Sam. Under the circumstances and against his better judgment, he conceded. "Very well. Have your son report to me Monday, eight o'clock."

Chapter 2

Sam's first church service was nearing its end, and he was hanging on to every minute, but he didn't hear one word of the sermon. He pretended to stretch his neck as he turned repeatedly to get another glimpse at perhaps the most beautiful creation he had ever seen. But who were those men beside her? Her father, no doubt. And the other? He could be her brother, God willing. When her eyes finally met his, he turned forward quickly and simultaneously felt his mother's nails press into his knee to inspire him to behave. He winced. Upon leaving the church, he heard the reverend call her Jane.

Meeting Mr. Pruitt in his office that first day of work was far from inviting. Sam had already received expectations from his father, and now he was hearing more from the boss, who made it known he was not thrilled to be giving Sam a position, nor should he expect any special treatment. Sam was under a lot of pressure at his tender age to accomplish his studies around his work schedule. Poor performance at the farm would mean failure to be elevated in Coles's eyes, which would also mean stern discipline from his father. But most concerning, it would mean failure with Mr. Pruitt, which was unthinkable to Sam; Mr. Pruitt was Jane's father.

Adrien was steady with only rare exceptions. He was honest and very firm yet gentlemanly, and he walked a straight line visible for all to see. He was tall and lean with sharp features, and his deep-set dark eyes were emphasized by his straight dark hair. Altogether, he projected high standards, dignity, and wisdom. Everyone who crossed his path could see he was a man of high and clear ideals, even if they didn't know him. Sam was intimidated by him.

The Callahans had only been in town a few weeks when Sam started work on the farm. Adrien assigned Sam to Buck Saunderman, who was a bit of a mystery. Saunderman was white and left everyone connected to the all-black Prairieland Farm with the perception that he was just passing through. He had done odd jobs for Prairieland off and on but had yet to leave. He seemed to be skilled at just about everything, and he shared his knowledge freely, which made his stay more tolerable. He had no authority on the farm; he simply came each day, worked, and left. No one even knew where he lived, and no one ever really knew whether his next day would be his last. Even with that, everyone believed Saunderman would be there longer than Sam.

Sam was acutely aware of his own ignorance of farming, which he tried to hide, but Saunderman saw right through it and gave Sam tasks that he knew he could not complete, putting Sam in a state of crisis. He was face to face with failure and noticeably sinking in fear.

After watching Sam struggle for several weeks, Saunderman shook his head and wondered why he had not quit. He called Sam over to the shed where he was repairing spokes on a wagon wheel. "You don't know the first thing about what you're doing, do you, son?" Saunderman asked and pushed his hat back with a pair of pliers.

He wasn't old, but his skin was leathery from years of being outdoors; this produced a rough appearance that led Sam to presume the worst. Furthermore, Saunderman made himself unapproachable with cold expressions and meaningless guidance. Asking for help seemed futile to Sam, and he had little more respect for this man than he did his father.

Sam surveyed a list of potential answers, and after a moment, he settled on the truth. "No, sir. I have no knowledge of farms or farming." He struggled to hold his eyes on Saunderman's. He saw himself as a failure and began to picture his father's rage, but Saunderman saw something else, and after a moment he laughed, which lightened the tension in the air. Sam was confused.

"Well, I admire your honesty," Saunderman said, looking around the farm. "I tell you what, kid, just do what I say. I won't let you fall."

Sam couldn't understand it, knowing his privileged lifestyle was not welcomed on the farm by anyone. "Why are you helping me, Mr. Saunderman?"

Saunderman had Sam figured out, and it showed in his changed demeanor. "It's not your fault your father is...well...your father."

Sam was surprised by the observation. If his father could be so accurately assessed by Saunderman, who else took notice? Saunderman wondered how a man could deliberately set his own son up for failure. He even wondered how Adrien could dump Sam on the farm unless he, too, wanted Sam to fail. It was like feeding Sam to the wolves. True perhaps for Bishop, but Adrien must have had other reasons. Saunderman couldn't care less what Bishop thought, but he knew that Adrien was fair, and if Sam carried his weight, Adrien would make concessions.

Saunderman quickly broke from the growing intimacy that was not necessary for his role. "Follow me and pay attention," he said, and he and Sam worked closely together for months.

*****

Adrien pulled his eyes away from the portrait of his wife, unsure of how long they had been stuck there. He was widowed. His wife died in childbirth with their third child, who also died. The unexpected pregnancy came later in their lives, and the delivery came so abruptly that there was no time for a midwife or doctor. It all proved too much for Mrs. Pruitt. Jane and her brother Nathan joined their father in a frantic effort to aid Mrs. Pruitt as she suffered the failed delivery to her last breath, leaving them all stunned in joined helplessness. Adrien wept for months, during which time he was barely able to meet the demands of his livelihood or the needs of his children. He had yet to remarry.

Jane's father had come from inner circles of city life, and her mother was from the country. Jane, therefore, was shaped into being a sophisticated homemaker. Her father exposed her to elite settings in Illinois, but only cautiously in fear that too much would lead to corruption. In contrast, her mother taught her to sew, prepare and preserve food, clean and nurture the home, and also manage household schedules, supplies, budgets, and finances. Jane compensated for the gaping hole in her life left by her mother's death by assuming her mother's role.

Nathan was the spitting image of his father and well on his way to success. He was close to his father and sister but was being pulled toward influences uncharted by his rearing, which was disturbing to Adrien who couldn't quite put his finger on where it was taking his son, except to observe that it was taking him far away. Nathan was confident, refined beyond his years, the future hope of nearly every girl in town, and even some in other towns. Adrien had recently arranged for Nathan to meet the daughter of one of his close friends, a lawyer from Quincy named Jack Donovan, and Nathan saw her only on rare occasions due to the distance between homes. There was no question that Elizabeth Donovan was a catch, and Nathan displayed overt interest, such that it justified his growing unavailability at home.

Over the years, Adrien hired servants to help several days a week to ensure stability in the home and to lighten his wife's load. None of Adrien's servants were indentured; all of them were well-paid and came from within communities where many freed blacks had migrated to be among those like-minded and in like circumstances, such as Edward Coles's freed slaves. Pierre and Esther Hays were free and had been regular hired cooks to several families in Edwardsville but came under full-time employment with the Pruitts following Mrs. Pruitt's death. The closeness between the Pruitts and the Hays was like that of family.

Adrien saw to it that both of his children were well-educated regardless of living on the frontier, where they had lived for many years before Illinois became a state. In addition to lessons permitted for ladies at the time, Jane had become a near master on the piano. Nathan was being tutored on many topics to include the history of the world so that he might become influential in ensuring history would not repeat itself. Adrien, however, also personally schooled both of his children, often during mealtime, through conversation about books, events, and the nation's leaders, finishing each discussion by examining what God might have to say about it.

*****

Nathan and Sam had the same tutor in preparation for college, both of whom suffered setbacks for admission brought on by family constraints. Nathan was studying for entrance as a freshman while Sam was expected by his father to enroll as a sophomore, which demanded successfully passing extensive entrance examinations. The two quickly became friends, and Sam shared that relationship with Amos as often as he could. Nathan was intuitive and somewhat aware of the burdens belonging to the Callahan brothers, though Sam and Amos never spoke of them. The three boys were inseparable as far as liberty would permit.

As soon as the tutor left them alone, Nathan sat back in his chair and looked at Sam, who was across the table engrossed in his studies. Sam glanced up briefly but remained committed to his book.

"Enough, already!" Nathan laughed. "He's gone." Sam kept his head down. Nathan sighed, knocked his knuckles on the table to gain Sam's attention, and said, "Sam!" Sam gave in and closed his book. "You work so incredibly hard. Why?" Sam had an answer; he just didn't want to give it. And Nathan already knew, anyway. "Ten minutes. You can afford that. Then we will get back to work." Sam nodded.

Nathan came to his feet and looked around the tutor's scholarly study that was filled with fine furniture, fine art, and fine books. He started to think about what college would be like, but he only had ten minutes and wanted to make better use of them. "What are your thoughts of the picks?" Nathan asked. Then he sat on the edge of the table waiting for Sam's input.

"William and Mary is my first choice. Harvard is beyond—" Sam began, but he was cut off by Nathan.

"No, no, no! I mean women! You've been here long enough to have made note of your surroundings," Nathan ventured, smiling. Sam laughed a little. Then he, too, stood up.

"I have no time to make note of anything but what this book says," Sam lied. There was time for one woman, but her relative proximity was too close for this conversation. He simply clung to his brief glances of her during sermons. "You, however, seem to welcome the distraction. You do have one in mind, do you not?" Sam asked.

"One? No. Many? Oh yes!" Nathan laughed and raised his brows.

"Come on. What's the point? You're leaving soon," Sam stated.

"Well, I'll believe that when it happens. Until then, I'm here, and so are other opportunities," Nathan slyly suggested.

"What about Elizabeth? I thought that was all settled." Sam said. Nathan glared in protest. "What could you possibly want in a woman that she does not have?"

"Nothing. She has everything a man could want. She is beautiful, smart, and would do anything for me. She lacks nothing"— Nathan smiled, insincerely—"except one thing: my love for her. Still, as long as I am here, there will be assumptions about our future together."

Sam did not miss Nathan's confession but moved quickly past it. "Why are you still here?" During Nathan's pause, Sam explained his own situation. "I'm delayed a second year now because of my father's political aspirations. He both insists that I attend a good college and prevents me from doing so. It's a rather vicious game he plays. Like you, I'll believe it when it happens."

Nathan walked around the table feeling the grain of its wood with his fingertips while he listened to Sam. He silently acknowledged that Sam's delay was a tragedy like his own, and he decided to give him an inside look, as well.

"About three years ago, my mother passed away during childbirth. It was believed that she could have no more children due to an illness, so we were all taken aback by the news of her pregnancy. She became rather frail during the months of carrying the child such that it was very concerning. Her labor was sudden…and brief."

Sam became uncomfortable, not only because of the sadness behind Nathan's story but because he had no idea what to say or do. What if his own mother had died in his youth? Would it have mattered? Would he have experienced the same grief that even three years later was dominant in Nathan's voice? He realized that he didn't even know his mother.

"Father might as well have died, too, that day," Nathan continued. "College was still a way off, but I wanted to leave as soon as possible. Father rejected the idea. When it finally came time, Father asked me to wait a year. He felt we all needed to remain close to home for a while. I was given a sizable role in his business, and Jane took over everything my mother did in the home. He's better now." Nathan looked at Sam and smiled softly. "And Jane is seventeen now. Neither of them needs me as they did before, hence my resumed studies. It has all left me wondering, though…" Nathan's voice dropped off.

"Wondering what?" Sam gently pressed.

"About love. She was such a part of him that when she died, it stripped half of him away, nearly destroying him. Love did that to him. So, I wonder, is it all worth it?" Nathan looked very intently at Sam.

Before Sam could form an answer, the tutor walked in. Sam was both startled and relieved, but Nathan hardly acknowledged the interruption as he remained focused on Sam.

"Gentlemen! Must I govern your every moment?" the tutor snapped. Nathan hid his smirk behind his hand, and the two took to their seats and their books. The tutor shot them an intimidating glare before leaving again.

Nathan whispered, "Come to supper tonight."

Sam shook his head as he leaned into his book. As much as he wanted to meet Jane, it came with risks. He declined by saying, "I should see to my brother."

"*Bring* your brother," Nathan insisted. "Yes?" he pushed some more. Sam gave a hesitant nod.

*****

Pierre opened the door and greeted Sam and Amos. Both of the Callahan boys were well dressed, perhaps a little too well. The Pruitt home was modest yet of a certain quality that left guests in the dark on Adrien's status. Did he have money or not? Adrien made it a point of leaving people guessing.

Adrien and Nathan welcomed the young men into their home, and Nathan quickly swept them away until supper was served. He showed them around the house and the property and described select and dramatic experiences from his upbringing. Nathan seemed thrilled to have company as most of his friends had already left for college. When they entered the dining room, the table was set, and Jane was placing the meal on the table with Pierre and Esther. Adrien watched and waited, standing tall with his hands behind his back.

"Jane," Nathan called as Pierre and Esther returned to the kitchen, "meet Sam. And this is his brother Amos."

When Jane turned around to Sam, she was noticeably struck. She brushed her hands down the front of her dress and over her cheeks as if concerned about a labored appearance, which did not exist. Sam's chest began to rise and fall with shallow rapid breathing. Then they both broke into a smile and stepped forward to greet each other, and Sam delivered a kiss to her hand. Everyone noticed the obvious affection, but Adrien noticed it the most and was in a panic.

"Very nice to meet you, Miss Pruitt," Sam said as he lifted his lips from her hand and planted his eyes on hers. She was blushing. So was he.

Adrien stepped forward and interrupted, "Mr. Callahan." Then he cleared his throat. Sam immediately and obediently diverted his attention from Jane and to her father. "The table is yours. Please choose your seat."

Jane and Nathan looked at their father with confusion. This was unexpected, and Sam glanced quickly at the others in the room before complying with Adrien's order. Sam observed a long oval table with eight chairs, three on each side and one at each end. He also observed that there were seven place settings. After the Pruitts, Sam, and Amos, two seats remained. *For whom?* he wondered.

This was a test, no doubt about it. There was no mention of being the guest of honor, so Sam stepped forward and placed his hands on the back of one of the middle chairs, a neutral choice. Then he protected and honored his younger brother by signaling him to take the seat to his right. His choice could not have been any humbler.

Adrien was surprised. He stood at the head of the table, Nathan at the other end, and Jane directly across from Amos. She was about to sit down, but her father stopped her. "We'll wait," he said. Jane and Nathan were again confused. They were unaccustomed to this etiquette in their own home. What had gotten into their father?

After a moment, Pierre and Esther returned with the last of the food, and Adrien gestured for everyone to sit. He watched Sam and Amos watch Pierre and Esther sit down next to Jane. Amos looked around slightly, but Sam concealed anything he might be thinking. Sam handled himself prudently in this first round, much to Adrien's dissatisfaction.

Sam was careful not to be too attentive to Jane, which disappointed her. Even Nathan was steering conversation to include Jane, which annoyed Adrien, who was determined to turn off Sam's interest in his family, especially Jane. So it came: round 2.

"The news from Alton this week was bittersweet," Adrien blurted out. That gained everyone's attention, as planned. "A band of runaway slaves crossed the river, seeking refuge. Several found it or got away, but several more were met by slave hunters, eager for their reward. Two runaways died trying to escape." Adrien stopped there, giving no indication of his opinion on the news. He simply turned his attention to Sam and waited for a response.

Sam felt some blood rush to his face. This was another test, and he thought quickly as he looked into the eyes of all those looking at him. Adrien worked for Edward Coles. Edward Coles emancipated his slaves. Therefore, this news from Alton was bad. Plus, Adrien's colored servants dined at the same table with the family. Sam was running out of time. Adrien raised his brow to push Sam for an answer.

Nathan was becoming angry with his father, but Jane was beginning to understand what was going on. She waited too. Pierre and Esther looked back and forth between Sam and Adrien. Amos was lost and thankful that no one had placed any demands on him.

Sam wiped his mouth with his napkin and began by speaking directly to Adrien. "How disappointed the bloodthirsty slave hunters must have been to learn that they would not receive money for the two that died." Adrien wasn't quite sure what that meant regarding Sam's position on slavery. He squinted. Sam took a drink of wine to appear calm under fire, yet he had to make every effort to hide that he was shaking in his boots. Adrien was about to speak, but Sam continued, and this time he gave his attention to everyone. "I imagine it would be hard to know the thoughts of those being returned to their masters. The two who died are now free. Arguably, they have it better than those who were caught. It's a grim ending either way. Still, bravo to those who got away." Sam paused his focus on Adrien briefly. Then he turned to his plate and took a bite of food to show that he was finished, and he thanked God that he had been forced to study Greek philosophical essays on reason and argument.

Adrien was confused. *This* was Bishop Callahan's son? He stared at Sam, not sure if he was being honest. Sam wasn't sure either until he allowed his eyes to breeze over Jane's approving expression. If opposing slavery meant winning Jane Pruitt, so be it. But Sam began to realize that it took no effort for him to do so. He had never really understood the mentality of slave owners. He had often wondered, *What right did any man have to own another man?*

"Indeed," Adrien conceded. "Well-spoken, Mr. Callahan," it pained him to say.

To everyone's relief Nathan took over the conversation, but he could have watched Sam in action all night. Adrien, though, was finished, and rather than enable Sam with another chance to match him, he cut the night short by saying that he and Nathan had a challenging day ahead. Sam was relieved but only in part. Nathan's frustration showed. Jane was experiencing a longing she had never before known, and Sam hadn't even left yet.

The Callahans were seen to the door with Pierre and Esther. Jane handed Esther a prepared and wrapped plate of food and said, "Esther, please give this to your son, and tell him we would love for him to visit sometime. We miss seeing him."

Sam bowed slightly to Adrien and said, "Thank you, sir, for a pleasant evening. And thank you, Miss Pruitt, for the delicious meal. Amos and I are grateful for your hospitality." Adrien simply nodded. Jane glowed.

As Sam and Amos mounted their horses, Nathan said, "Again, Sam. And soon!" Sam agreed and tipped his hat to Jane, who smiled and waved goodbye. Adrien shut the door somewhat prematurely.

"Father!" Nathan and Jane exclaimed simultaneously.

"While I have not forgotten my station, sir, I daresay that you were so rude to my guests that I am embarrassed," Nathan asserted.

Jane contributed, "I have never seen you so brash, Father. You tried to crush him."

Nathan's senses heightened. Jane was right. "It's true, Father. You did try to crush him, and in a very determined way. Why?"

Adrien had to contend with his pride as he took his first real rebuke from his children. "You know who his father is! You *know* it! Yet you invited him into our home, anyway. Apples don't fall far from the tree, Nathan."

Nathan was furious. "Yes, I know who his father is. Forgive me for exercising the virtue of leaving judgment to the Lord!" Nathan crossed his arms.

"Watch your tone with me, young man!" Adrien demanded with a pointed finger.

Nathan continued his challenge, "I *am* watching my tone, Father. I most surely want you to know how deeply, for the first time in my life, I think you are wrong." He stormed off toward the stairs to go to his bedroom, but he shared one last thought before ascending. "What you don't seem to understand is that I invited him to our home because of who *my* father is." He pounded his feet in anger as he climbed up the staircase.

Adrien closed his eyes and pursed his lips. He didn't want to be wrong, but he knew he was, which was foreign to him. He became angry with himself as he allowed Nathan's words to sink in, and he realized that he had let his son down. Adrien was a good father, a blatant contrast to Bishop Callahan that should have stood out, but the opportunity was lost.

Jane continued carefully. "You like him," she said. Adrien did not respond. Jane poured a glass of wine and handed it to him, and he took it. "He held up to you remarkably well. I know of no one else who could have done as well. Admit it, Father, you like him."

"*No*, Jane." Adrien held his eyes on his daughter. "*You* like him. If we are calling for honesty here, then *you* admit it." Adrien handed the glass of wine back to her and left the room to go upstairs. Jane was shocked.

Adrien tapped on Nathan's door before entering. He kept his hand on the doorknob with intent to be brief. Nathan was standing over his desk looking at nothing in particular. He glanced at his father, but his anger was still boiling.

"You were right. I was wrong," Adrien said. Nathan looked at his father, somewhat surprised. "Invite him back. Amos too. Good night." Nathan hardly had time to nod before his father left.

*****

It was a quiet trot on the way home until Amos asked, "Are all fathers the same?"

Sam could see that Amos was struggling with dark and confused thoughts. "No, Amos. Actually, all fathers are different and manage their homes and families as best they know. Mr. Pruitt is stern, not mean." Sam slipped. He knew Amos would make the comparison.

"Why does he need to be stern?" Amos asked.

Sam retraced the events of the evening in his mind in an effort to try to answer Amos's question. Everything seemed fine until... until Jane came in the room.

"He's on guard, Amos. If you were the father of a smart and beautiful daughter, wouldn't you be on guard?"

Amos thought about it for a minute. "Ah!" He laughed. "He doesn't like it that you like Jane."

"Wait a minute!" Sam protested. "Where did you get that idea?"

"Honestly, Sam? 'Very nice to meet you, Miss Pruitt,'" Amos mimicked Sam, and he reached his hand out to be kissed as he made several smooching sounds. Then he raised his eyes to heaven as if in a daze.

Sam was embarrassed and lowered his head, smiling. "It was obvious, wasn't it?" He admitted. He looked at Amos who was smiling and nodding up and down. "And what about her?"

"What?" Amos asked.

"Well, you know, did she seem…" Sam hoped Amos would catch on.

"Seem what?" Amos purposely offered no help. Sam dropped it. Then Amos said, "Sam, she couldn't stop looking at you."

Sam smirked and gave his horse a kick.

Chapter 3

Sam's occasional suppers at the Pruitt home pleased Bishop because he thought that they aided his plan. But for Sam, it only meant occasional exposure to Jane. They were attracted to each other in obvious friendship. Adrien continued to worry it would lead to more, but Sam and Amos brought something with them that had been missing in his home for some time, and that was the return of happiness. He saw his children come back to life, which was a pleasant reminder of how things once were.

But it was Sam and Amos who really benefitted from the bond. They saw the workings of a beautiful relationship between a father and his children, which bled over to them while in the Pruitt home. The Callahan boys were drawn to it strongly but were also careful not to overdo it in fear that their own father would sabotage the one thing they longed for.

The months on the farm took a toll on Sam's affluent appearance. Not only did the work bring out a roughness in him, Saunderman's influence left a permanent casual mark. Saunderman did his job well, and he knew it. He didn't care what anyone else had to say. Sam admired that he was happy with who he was and made no effort to impress others. And the other farmhands, most of whom were Coles's former slaves, got along well with Saunderman. What Sam was witnessing on Prairieland and in his relationship with the Pruitts was new for him—equality in action.

Some things on the farm came slowly for Sam. He was no good with animals. He grew up understanding that they were no more than a means to an end, and the animals on the farm seemed to sense that. Sam was constantly getting bit or kicked or chased, and Saunderman just laughed at him. One time, Saunderman walked by Sam and told him to clean the hooves of all the horses. Sam was in the middle of mending a fence gate, and he hated the idea of locking himself in the stalls with those beasts.

"Now," Saunderman said as he kept walking.

"Shouldn't Danny do it? I'm not finished with this fence." Sam was nearly prayerful. Danny usually cared for the horses and seemed an obvious choice for the task.

"No. I said you," Saunderman hollered, now farther away.

Sam looked at his half-finished work, and he threw his tools down. He whispered foul resistance under his voice and made his way to the stable.

Danny was also surprised by the order. He intercepted Saunderman and begged him to keep Sam away from his horse. It wasn't his horse, really. Danny had taken responsibility for a mare while she was pregnant. When it came time for her to give birth, Saunderman and Danny were there deep into the night. When her foal was born, Danny felt like a father. No one came near that horse if he could help it.

"You surprise me, Danny. Is your memory so short?" Saunderman asked.

Danny was slightly older than Sam and very competent on the farm. His dark-bronze skin tone and sharp eyes emphasized his chiseled cheekbones and jawline. His oval lips matched in fullness below his wide and perfectly straight nose. His voice leaned toward deep, depending on the topic. Danny pulled his lips in between his teeth as he pondered Saunderman's question.

"No, I remember," he said, fully accepting of the gentle rebuke. It was not that long ago that Danny was in Sam's place with the horses. Saunderman raised his chin toward the stable, signaling Danny to meet him there.

"Okay, which one of you wants to be first?" Sam asked the dozen or so horses with great apprehension. He took a breath and entered the first stall, and as he turned to close the gate, the horse became restless and bit him hard on the shoulder. He tried to mute his yell as he got out of the stall, but the pain was deep. Danny stood next to Saunderman just outside the stable entrance and had to cover his mouth to muffle his laughter as they walked in the stable together.

"They don't like you," Saunderman said.

"Well, the feeling is mutual!" Sam barked as he checked for blood on his shoulder.

"Danny, show him how it's done," Saunderman said. Danny nodded in understanding.

"Watch me," Danny said, wondering if Sam would be willing to learn from him. He removed his gloves and walked into the stall. He gently placed his hand on the horse's lower neck and rubbed it for a while, which the horse obviously liked. Then he took a handful of hay and fed it to the horse while he continued to rub his neck, chest, and withers. When the horse was completely calm, Danny faced him, whispered to him, and finished with a kiss on his nose. He came back to the side of the horse. With his hoof knife in one hand, he gently ran his other hand down the horse's leg, caught his foot as the horse lifted his leg, and then began scraping the mud out of the horse's hoof.

Sam watched Danny work as Saunderman explained what he was doing from hoof to hoof. Then Saunderman added, "Animals, especially horses, can tell if you're nervous. If you're uncomfortable with them, they'll be uncomfortable with you. Always approach a horse with confidence and take control but treat it like...well... someone you love. Keep your tone soft and your touch slow and agreeable. Feed it. Talk to it. Whistle softly. And learn its behavior. Every horse is different, so you have to act a little different with each one. But never be afraid. If they sense any fear, you will lose control. And never, ever beat an animal." Danny was finished and came out of the stall.

"You sure make it look easy," Sam said, showing no signs of superior demeanor, which eased Danny.

"It wasn't always so. I got bit plenty. I jus' did what Mr. Saunderman told me to, and now"—Danny shrugged—"it's easy. I even like it."

"Sam, take your knife, go to the next stall, and give it a try. When you're done, go back and groom each horse. Have them all done before you leave for the day," Saunderman said. "Danny, stick around and help him out if he needs it."

Sam walked to the next stall and stood there for a minute thinking about everything Danny did and Saunderman said. He took a breath, rolled his shoulders back, and entered the stall. He did exactly what he was shown right down to the kiss on the nose, and before he knew it, he was done with this horse's hooves. He made his way from one stall to the next, and when he came out of the last one, he found Danny grinning. Sam extended his hand, to which Danny hesitated initially but soon responded by delivering a firm friendly shake. Saunderman, watching from the distance, simply went back to work.

Danny and Sam became regulars with the horses for all associated care and maintenance. Saunderman even handed off to them the unsupervised responsibility of caring for the mares when pregnant and overseeing their deliveries. Sam's first experience watching a foal come into the world nearly took his breath away. They spent hours and hours together laboring with the mares. Danny passed on to Sam all that Saunderman had taught him, and it changed the way Sam viewed the world and people in it.

Sam became so interested in horses that he found himself reading everything he could find on them to the point that it interfered with his studies. He didn't care. Any and all types of horses and their origin captured his attention with a deep desire to reach mastery of their care, their training, and their breeding. But the horse that got his attention the most was the Morgan, a relatively new breed introduced by Justin Morgan of Vermont. The strength, endurance, and adaptability of this breed convinced Sam that the Morgan was the horse to own. *Someday*, he thought. And everything he learned, he shared with Danny, whether Danny wanted him to or not.

"My parents say some pretty nice things 'bout you," Danny said one night while waiting for a mare to deliver. Sam looked confused. "My ma and pa work for the Pruitts," Danny said as he glanced at Sam out of the corner of his eye.

"Pierre and Esther are your parents?" Sam asked, surprised.

"Yeah, you know 'em," Danny stated.

"Yes, I do," Sam said. "I see them often. They're very kind." Danny looked at Sam curiously. "Nathan and I are friends, so I visit sometimes and have supper," Sam continued, trying to explain himself.

"Uh huh," Danny said accusingly. "Often, sometimes…which is it?" He laughed and shook his head.

"What?" Sam asked, laughing.

"Look. There's only one Jane Pruitt in this world. Ain't no one else like her. Her father knows it. He won't like it that you know it too."

Sam agreed by saying, "He's made that clear." Then Sam changed directions and said, "There's nothing like her cooking, either."

Danny smiled and said, "Got that right. Mama scolds me for askin' her to bring me home a plate."

A blank stare crossed Sam's face. Danny dropped his smile and asked, "What's you lookin' at?"

Sam looked away when his eyes became overly serious. "Danny"—he shook his head—"I, uh, I just want to say thanks. I don't know…" Sam struggled so hard to speak that he laughed.

"What?" Danny asked. "You don't know what?"

Sam pulled it together and was honest. "I don't know how two friends like us are going to make it in this world, but we *will* find a way."

Danny swallowed through the impact of Sam's unexpected comment and kept his answer short. "Fair 'nough."

As the months went by and with Saunderman's help, Sam overcame many of his challenges. Saunderman was consistent about telling Sam how it was, and he never lost his temper. If Sam performed well, he performed well. If not, he was told so and had to do the task again. For reasons Sam did not understand at the time, Saunderman rotated him around the farm, giving him exposure to all the components required to keep the farm up and maybe even make it profitable. He had already done the same with Danny under the request of Robert Crawford. Sam touched everything from minor to major repairs and construction, management of livestock, combating wildlife, planting, pruning, harvesting, ordering supplies, maintaining tools, and planning schedules. But as with Saunderman, people were off-limits. Saunderman, knowing enough about Sam's father, was very careful never to let Sam think he had authority over anyone. But it did not take long for Saunderman to realize Sam needed no such supervision.

By the end of his first year, Sam's work ethic had become strong largely because he loved his job and his boss. He learned to carry more than his weight, which cut both workloads and work time down when he was paired up with someone. The other farmhands' resentment toward him diminished, and consequently, Sam's circle of friends grew to the point that they would sometimes fight over having him work with them. Danny fought the hardest and usually won.

When Sam wasn't being claimed by Danny, he was being claimed by Nathan. Nathan's father felt his son pulling away even more, and it grieved him like another death. He often asked him to dine with him or meet after work at a tavern to talk business or politics or anything, but Nathan was always too busy or too tired. Adrien accepted defeat and settled for sharing his son with others, which often meant hosting the Callahan brothers.

And like Nathan, Sam avoided his father, though for very different reasons. Bishop rarely saw Sam immediately after work, which gave Sam time to restore himself to his father's standards for appearance. Increasingly, though, Sam felt confined in a coat and tie, and as soon as he was out of his father's reach, he removed them. Even the Pruitts dressed casually when at home, so there was no shame that Sam dressed down when having supper there. This time, he wore a white shirt open at the neck, a blue vest, and mustard trousers tucked into his black Wellington boots. No coat. He was eager when he opened the door to leave his home, but then he stopped himself and closed it. He found Amos and told him to hurry if he wanted to come. Sam wanted to be gone before his father got home.

When Jane took one last look in the mirror before supper, she dropped her eyes, disappointed that this was her best. She did not see herself as attractive, certainly not in a competitive way, and no matter what she did with her humble wardrobe, it was still a humble wardrobe. The Pruitts were not poor, nor were they rich, at least not like what she knew the Callahans to be. Jane resented her own awareness of her status among those more privileged.

In truth, though, Jane was lovely. She had a strong appearance for such a young woman, one that most would attribute to her father, had they not known her mother. She had auburn hair, very long and with loose natural curls. She parted it down the middle and pulled it back loosely to allow for fullness, leaving a few ringlets to hang at her temples, ears, and neck. The length was gathered in a thick cross bun in back, within which she inserted a decorative comb. Unlike her father, her eyes were blue and wide and made her look as though she missed nothing. She was almost goddess-like. Any man who knew her deepest thoughts about herself would think she was mad. She tried to dismiss her concerns as she reminded herself that Sam had never made her feel inferior in any way. They were friends. Her bigger concern was how to make their friendship something more. One last breath and she carried all of her hopes with her to the dining room.

During dinner, Nathan asked Sam how things were going on the farm, and Sam's confessions had everyone, including Adrien, rolling in laughter. Sam offered to show scars, which caused Nathan nearly to choke on his food. Jane looked like she was listening, but she was so preoccupied with just watching him that she could hardly hear. Then Sam became a little more serious as he described how Mr. Saunderman had been teaching him his way around the farm, and he was finally becoming useful. Adrien became very attentive to Sam's details, especially ones about his respect for Mr. Saunderman and the other farmhands and how he had come to love the horses that had left him marked for life.

After supper, Jane played a few songs on the piano, and Sam watched and listened in awe. He didn't know she played until now, and he realized that there was never any music in his home. A casual supper, friendly conversation, music—being at the Pruitts' home soothed Sam's soul. He glanced at Amos and sensed a mutual sentiment.

Nathan commented on what a perfect day it had been as he observed the sun that was beginning to set. They all walked outside and eventually found themselves on the lawn talking back and forth about things of interest to young people of that time. Jane was sitting with one hand down for support and the other playing with the layers of her dress. Sam and Nathan were on their sides on one elbow, facing Jane. Amos sat cross-legged next to Jane quietly listening, watching, learning.

The glow of the evening sun revealed tiny bugs flying between bits of floating pollen. The increasing sound of distant crickets hinted that the sun was near finished for the day, but the four of them held on as long as they could.

"Annabelle!" Sam said, out of the blue. "Will she be the one to win your heart?" Sam stared at Nathan.

"Good heavens, no!" Nathan laughed in disgust and Jane followed, knowing Annabelle was no match to Elizabeth. Amos only smiled, not sure what Sam was talking about. Nathan, though, knew exactly what Sam was talking about and pointed it away from himself. "She is horribly indiscreet! She makes advances on me. Then when she thinks I am out of sight, she makes advances on others. It's not me she's after. It's any man. She has even tried to catch the eye of Sam, here."

"Is that true?" Jane asked Sam through her full smile, intent on hiding any threat she felt.

Sam was spinning a long blade of grass between his fingers. He shook his head at Nathan's affront because it was, in fact, not true. Then he looked at Jane, whose smile and big blue eyes were waiting for his answer. Sam's expression fully exposed that he was thinking, *God, she's beautiful,* which made it hard for him to take his eyes off her. Nathan made note of the growing attraction between his sister and his best friend.

"Clearly, taste is not her dominant quality," Nathan said of Annabelle before things became awkward. And they all laughed again. Nathan rolled over on his back and looked at the sky and its emerging stars. "The problem, you see, is that I love them all."

"Oh, my goodness, Nathan! You're a Romeo!" Jane exclaimed.

Nathan rolled over on his side again, came up on his elbow, and said, "I'm afraid you're right! But until I find the one for whom I'll drink poison, I'll remain a bachelor!"

Adrien could hear the four of them in constant laughter, and it comforted him, but only to a point. He wanted to like Sam and Amos, but his contempt for Bishop made it hard. He saw Bishop as a rude, pompous mass of flesh with an endless need for superiority and entitlement, and he was concerned that Jane would suffer in a relationship with Sam who, he believed, could not have possibly escaped the influence of his father's harsh disposition. But he took comfort in knowing that the Callahans' time in Illinois would be short-lived, and the problem would take care of itself.

In contrast, when Bishop became suspicious of Sam's attraction to Jane, he was furious. He ordered Sam to end his association with her at once and threw threat upon threat with his order. He announced that he had other plans for his son, ones that did not involve a lustful opportunist that would ruin his son's future. Sam's silence to the order did not equate to the submission that Bishop demanded. As such, Bishop concluded that Sam's interest in Jane explained why no meaningful relationship had evolved between himself and Edward Coles. He blasted Sam, saying that he failed him and consequently, the family would be returning East sooner because of Sam's worthless contributions to his employment, which his father went to great pains to arrange. There was nothing to gain by remaining in Illinois any longer than absolutely necessary. In the meantime, except for his job, Sam was kept very close to home and forbidden to entertain any further ideas about the substandard distraction named Jane Pruitt.

Jane was lost in pain, the kind she had not known since her mother died. Sam's abrupt halt to visiting created a void that consumed her to sickness. He didn't even look at her in church, at least not when she was looking at him. She only now realized how she had come to be dependent on his company and affection, and she faced the truth that she was in love with him. She had been hoping that somehow before he left that they would arrive at some kind of commitment. That hope was being robbed of her now, and the only shred of comfort she could find was in prayer. And she prayed a lot.

Sam was frantically trying to catch up on his studies. Greek, Latin, Hebrew, mathematics, philosophy, rhetoric, politics, economics, science, geography, and architecture filled nearly every waking moment he had except for his time on the farm and when he wasn't distracted with thoughts of Jane. But he was always distracted with thoughts of Jane. Comparing Aristotle's ethical theory to Plato's took numerous reads due to his inability to concentrate. In frustration, he flipped back several pages and began to read again; then suddenly, he closed the book and shoved it away in favor of a book on architecture. Moments later, the housemaid interrupted him by saying that he had a visitor.

Weeks had passed since Nathan had talked to his friend, and he made an unannounced visit to the Callahan home, which was a breath of fresh air for Sam. He broke from his academic commitments to accommodate his guest. Amos joined them for a while, but then he left the two alone upon Nathan's request, at which point he exposed his sister's grief to Sam.

"She prays constantly. She wants to understand. She wants you to notice her. Even a glance would suffice. Honestly, Sam, if it was something she did, she has a right to know," Nathan declared in defense of his sister.

Sam looked away as he contemplated how to make Nathan understand; then he whispered his answer, "Father has forbidden me to see her or have any contact with her whatsoever. I am pinned to the wall, Nathan. And when I say pinned, you must believe I mean it. I have run every thinkable scenario through my mind on how to get around it, and nothing I consider ends well," Sam said. Then he looked at Nathan with distraught eyes. "I don't want Jane hurt by my father's opinion. He doesn't even know her. But he did not choose her, and therein lies the problem. My objective is to buffer her from him. He will degrade her if he gets the chance. Please tell Jane I think of her day and night. I can't very well ask her to wait as I have no solution to my problem at present. But on the day that I find one, if she has not been swept away by another, then there is evidence that God truly listens to my prayers."

Nathan blinked a few times. "Perhaps a letter," he suggested.

Sam looked at Nathan as though he had not heard a word he just said. Nathan studied Sam's expression, studied Sam's genuine explanation, and shared in Sam's helplessness. Even Nathan, at such a distance, knew there was no combating Bishop, and he yielded.

"I'm curious," Sam countered Nathan, "for someone who avoids the effects of love as you do, I find it interesting that you invest so much in it for others. Why is that?" Sam stared at Nathan until he was able to convey that he knew Nathan resisted love with all his might, even the perfect love that came from Elizabeth Donovan. And Nathan knew that Sam saw him clearly, that he was at no risk of drinking poison for anyone because no one would ever get that close to his heart. The idea that it was better to have loved and lost than never to have loved at all was all backward, according to Nathan.

Nathan looked down at Sam's open book on architecture and began flipping pages as he tried to construct his answer. He closed the book; then he reached for his hat and cloak and said, "What kind of a man would I be if I ignored my sister in her time of distress?" Nathan stood before Sam in obvious defiance, and then he said abruptly, "I must be off."

They parted not knowing when they would see each other again, and Sam returned to his studies, but all he could think of was Jane. Even his books on horses could not prevent his mind from wandering to her.

Bishop's return home crossed paths with Nathan's departure. Nathan tipped his hat in respect as he rode past Bishop's carriage. Sam's focus was further distracted when he heard the front door slam followed by a brief pause before he heard his father order him to his study. Sam was confused by his father's anger as he stood before Bishop's shouts about his disobedience.

"Nathan and I are friends, Father. This has nothing to do with Jane. I've done everything you've asked of me. You told me to distance myself from her, and I have!" Sam spoke only the physical truth.

Bishop's logic was distorted as he tried to justify his anger. Nathan was a direct link to Jane, which equated to blatant noncompliance from Sam. Or was it that Bishop realized that his chance to lock arms with Coles was officially gone? It was all the same to Bishop, and he threw open the cabinet door holding his leather straps.

"Choose one!" Bishop demanded.

Sam stared in disbelief. *He must be joking*, he thought. But Bishop never played games. Once he started something, he finished it. Sam, who was now twenty, believed he and Amos were both worthy of manly treatment. For the first time in his life, he refused to obey an order from his father and maintained a firm stance in the middle of the study. Bishop walked to his study door, opened it, and yelled for Sam's replacement. Sam's eyes grew large and full of hate.

"Very well, Father!" Sam stormed across the room and pulled a strap from the display. "I choose this one!" It was thin, and Sam's experience reminded him that it was sure to leave the worst degree of pain, which was Sam's message to his father that he could take anything he could throw him. Just then, Amos reluctantly entered

"Amos, sit down," Bishop ordered. Amos took a seat, certain that he would be forced to witness Sam's punishment as a stern message not to repeat his mistake, whatever that was. The next moment happened too fast for Sam to respond. Bishop rushed him, forced him out of the room nearly knocking him off his feet, ripped the strap out of his hand, slammed the study door, and locked it.

As Sam regained his balanced, he realized what was about to happen. He tried aggressively to open the door, but it was no use. He slammed his fist on the door several times and yelled, "No!" He wept in helplessness against the solid wood barrier as he heard his brother taking lashes not meant for him and with the strap of Sam's own choosing. Sam's skin crawled as if he could feel the sting that Amos absorbed with each lash. Then it stopped.

Sam returned to a full stance as the door to the study opened. His face was wet and swollen from the trauma. Before he could speak, Bishop placed his oversized hand on Sam's shoulder with his thumb crossing his throat.

"Disappointing me has consequences," Bishop said. He stepped back to give room for Amos to leave. Sam's expression reached for Amos's forgiveness as if thirsting for water in a barren desert. Amos was red, and he was clearly in pain but without tears. He winked at Sam as he passed, and Sam's eyebrows met in confusion. He then looked up the stairs as he heard the door to his mother's room gently close. He looked back at his father with contempt, and Bishop closed the door in his face.

*****

The weeks that followed Amos's beating were tense for everyone but Bishop, who acted as though nothing had happened. Christmas had come and gone with little to no appropriate level of joy, and the New Year that was supposed to provide a fresh start was met with dullness. The Callahan family didn't even attend church. Plans to return home were in full motion, and the household was being packed in preparation.

Sam's work schedule would see him through to the last possible day, in accordance with his father's orders and as approved by Adrien. As Sam's time was drawing near the end, Adrien expressed praise to him for his efforts, calling them impressive. Sam credited any achievement he reached to Saunderman and Danny, much of which was true. Still, Adrien could not deny his admiration over Sam's regard for his supervisor, and he told Sam that his departure would leave quite a hole in the operation, one that would be hard to fill. While Adrien was being honest, he was also glad to see this chapter close, as the drama of Sam's home life was disrupting the harmony in his own.

Like everything else in the Callahan household, suppertime was confining. Conversation was limited to responding to Bishop's contributions. But Sam was out of time. He took Adrien's words seriously and sought to capitalize on them because he had come to love his job and had difficulty parting with it. But it was more than his job that he had come to love, and any fool could see it.

The only sound in the room was that which came from the noise of clanking silverware and eating. Sam was nauseated and deliberately did not touch his food to ensure his father would inquire, thus opening the door to discussion, which he already knew would backfire, but he could never have foreseen just how badly. Bishop looked up from his aggressive consumption and saw that Sam was making no attempt to eat.

"Mind your manners, boy. Eat your supper," commanded Sam's father.

Sam was hoping for a question to answer, but it did not come. He was still forced to break with code by speaking before being spoken to. How could he pose all of his thoughts in one statement, knowing he would not get subsequent chances? Sam took a deep breath of preparation.

"Father, Mr. Pruitt expressed that my departure will strain operations at the farm. I would like to discuss staying here in my current position to gain more experience, and I will follow you home next year."

Bishop kept eating as if he had not heard his son's request. Charlotte stopped eating with her fork suspended in midair while staring at her plate. Amos looked back and forth between Sam and Bishop, very aware that Sam had entered into dangerous territory.

Becoming more nervous, Sam cleared his throat and tried again. "Father...," Sam began, but Bishop made one pound of his fist on the table, jarring all the dishes and startling his wife and sons.

"Damn it, boy! I have spoken. Yet you question me still. This is not about the job. It's about that tramp you cannot forget. So I will give you a choice. You can drop this, never mention it again, and come with us, or you can stay here with your aspiring trollop and consider yourself cut off from this family."

Sam's thinking was hung up. What did his father call Jane?

Charlotte was stunned by the ultimatum. It was particularly brutal, even for Bishop. She tried to speak, but Bishop's scowl swiftly muted her.

"Father! I have prospects here that I want to explore! Please indulge me a discussion and your advice!" Sam pleaded with Bishop. He was reaching for a parent that did not exist in his home, but rather one he had found in the Pruitts' home.

Bishop removed his pocket watch from his vest, flipped it open, and looked at Sam. "You have one minute," Bishop warned.

Sam's mother was consumed with horror. She turned to Sam, turned to Bishop, and turned back again with her shaking fingers delicately covering her parted lips. The ticking of the watch was like a bang in a bell tower, complete with the echo.

Sam stared at his father as his chest tightened, and his breathing became heavier. Amos did not know how it would end but concluded that no outcome would be just. He watched in anticipation.

"Thirty seconds," Bishop warned again, still chewing his food.

Sam did not take his eyes off his father, and years of hate surfaced in every fiber of his being. The question of why rose, but Sam suppressed it, knowing there was no point in asking.

"Sam!" his mother cried in a pleading tone. She knew she would never see him again. Sam knew it meant losing everything: his family ties, his college opportunities, financial support. He remained fixed. Bishop closed his watch and wiped his mouth.

"You have disappointed me for the last time," Bishop said, oozing with arrogance as he carefully pronounced each syllable of each word. "I permit you to pack all you can carry. You may take your horse. I have no use for it. And I will give you time to say your goodbyes to your mother and brother. Ten minutes should be sufficient." He excused himself from the table and retired to his study.

"No, no, no...," Sam's mother repeated as she sobbed feverishly.

In some small way, Amos took Sam's decision as a sacrifice made to open the door for his younger brother's future departure from the hell they grew up in.

Sam looked at his mother and brother, and he began to tear. He blinked a few times to clear his eyes. He removed his napkin from his lap, placed it on the table, and went to his room to gather what he could from his already packed belongings. Amos followed to help.

Meanwhile, Charlotte regained her senses, wiped her eyes, and rushed to her bedroom. She threw open one of her trunks and dug out a box filled with jewelry. She removed as many pieces as possible that Bishop might not notice as gone and wrapped the most precious items in a kerchief with her initials sewn into one corner. Then she wrote a note, placed it in a book, and rushed down the stairs. She waited for Sam in the entryway as he and Amos descended the stairs together. Sam had a satchel over his shoulder and one bag in each hand. He slowed his pace upon seeing his mother, trying to prolong the parting from the woman he had longed to know all his life and now would never get the chance. He dropped his bags at her feet and threw his arms around her.

"Mother," Sam said as he wept in her arms, taking in any final moments of nurturing that time would allow. She embraced him tightly yet briefly, knowing Bishop was counting the minutes. She pulled his arms from around her and placed the parting gifts in his satchel.

"Take this," she said as she tugged on the satchel strap. "Sell it all. There is no sentiment attached to it, but it is all highly valuable. It will give you a start. And here." She slipped some money into his pocket that she had hid over the years of her marriage to protect herself if ever she faced the same fate as Sam. Finally, she placed her hand on his face and provided him a look confirming her love, which he desperately needed.

Sam turned his attention to Amos. A handshake turned into a brief brotherly embrace. Upon release, he displayed his regained manhood and said to Amos, "I'll be waiting for you."

"You won't be waiting long," Amos assured. One last heart-wrenching look was shared. They all heard the door to the study open. Sam nodded, picked up his bags, and then he was gone.

Chapter 4

S am could have gone to the Pruitts'. He would have been welcomed, at least somewhat, but he thought better of it. He stopped on the corner of the road that led to town, looking. It was a cold January night, and the breath from him and his horse was very visible even in the dark. He had the urge to just ride out of town, wondering if disappearing would be ideal, but there were other ways to do that. His choice was well-considered—one that would place him in hiding a day or two to give himself time to think.

Rose answered the door to her boardinghouse and looked at Sam curiously. "Yes?" she asked.

"I need a room, if you have one to spare," he said, looking down in shame as he realized that he was officially homeless. He was cold and nervous.

Sam was a Callahan, which made Rose hesitate initially, but she observed that the young man on her doorstep had been broken, and she knew the source. The familiarity led her to believe God had brought him to her.

Rose McGregor was in her late thirties, but she looked a little older. She had red hair and ivory skin. Leisure did not exist in her life, and she was a little worn out. When her husband died early in their marriage from yellow fever, she turned their large home into a boardinghouse to sustain her financially and to keep her close to him spiritually. Her level of independence was unusual for a woman of her time, and she was not regarded by some of the townspeople, especially Bishop, with much esteem. She should have remarried by now, they thought. She was handsome enough, and there was no excuse. The comings and goings of people under her own roof made her a bit unclean in their eyes.

She knew the thoughts of those around her, and it hurt sometimes, especially on cold nights when she was alone with her memories and broken dreams. At one point, the talk and pressure from neighbors traumatized her to the point of closing her doors for business and closing her drapes for privacy for an entire year. But later, she realized that they did not know her, nor did they want to, which made forgiveness easier. She went to church each Sunday, but not for appearances. She went to worship genuinely, to thank the Lord for what time she did have with her husband, and to look forward to a time when they would be together again.

She recognized Sam from church, and though she recalled no ill experiences with him, such was not the case for his father, who often looked her up and down and huffed in disgust as he walked off. Little did she know that she reminded him of the Irish roots from which he had cut himself years before. She counted the days until his departure, and she hated that he was able to stir such dark feelings in her.

Adrien saw Bishop's treatment of Rose one day and rushed to her side to tell her how delightful it was to see her again. He asked her how she was getting on, how business was, and would she please come by for tea? Adrien knew that his compassion for her would be misinterpreted by some in the church and town as affection. They both were widowed, after all. But he didn't care. He could not bear the thought of leaving her crushed by Bishop's brute force, and he happily risked his reputation to restore this woman's worth to its rightful place. She would never forget his kindness that day.

After a moment of contemplation, Rose answered Sam invitingly, "I do have one to spare. In fact, I have several." She was intent on helping him to settle him down. Rose's voice was deep but feminine and confident. "The house is empty, so you can have your pick. Take your horse around to the barn. I'll open the back door for you." Sam was good at doing what he was told and followed her instructions. "You're one of the Callahan boys, aren't you?" Rose asked as Sam entered the house, and she led him upstairs to look at rooms.

"Yes, ma'am," Sam answered, thankful she asked only after committing to renting him a room.

"I thought you were headed back to Washington."

"My family leaves the day after tomorrow," Sam stated.

Rose easily saw what was going on, but she pushed anyway. In her line of work, she had seen a lot of people endure transitions in life, and escape was one of the more common reasons. "But not you? You're staying?"

"That's right." Sam volunteered very little except to add, "And I would like to keep that private."

Rose stopped her ascent up the stairs and looked at Sam for a moment; then she nodded and continued her climb. "Well, you're not a boy anymore. It's probably time to start taking charge of your own life." She had mastered stating truths that helped her tenants face their circumstances.

At the top of the stairs, she opened several doors that went to rooms she rented, and she had him look around. One of the doors did not close properly because of a broken hinge, and she apologized.

"I'll take this one," Sam said of the room with the broken hinge. It was a simple but comfortable room with a bed for two, a dresser with a basin and pitcher, a small table and chair, and a wardrobe. The window had heavy drapery, capable of blocking all light. Rose handed him the key and showed him around the rest of the house.

"How long will you be staying?" she asked while discussing rent and meals.

"I honestly don't know. Is there a limit?"

"No." Rose laughed. "Stay as long as you like. But if you're going to be here for a while, I have a proposal." Sam looked at her inquisitively. "I have some work that needs to be done around here, and if you're willing, I'll take it off your rent." Sam didn't have an answer because he didn't know what tomorrow looked like, let alone long term. He didn't even have a job anymore. Rose continued, "It's not easy, you know, not having a man around. You think about it and give me your answer soon so I know what to charge you." Sam nodded.

Sam went to his room and looked around his new home. He lifted his heavy satchel over the table and dumped it out. After staring at the treasure for a moment, he looked around his room as if concerned that someone else might see it. He pulled the money out of his pocket and counted five hundred dollars. He dropped into his chair and lost track of time while wondering at the cost his mother would have to pay for what she did. He stored everything in the satchel, including the money, and searched the room for a hiding place. Drawers and wardrobes could be opened by anyone. Under the mattress and bed? Too obvious. As he held the satchel to his chest and continued to think, he looked down and noticed the seams between the wooden floor planks. He put the satchel down, quietly moved the bed, and rolled back the rug. Then he retrieved his knife, worked loose a plank from the floor, and secured his future beneath.

Once the rug was rolled out and the bed put back in place, he wiped his forehead and sat back down. Then he picked up the book his mother gave him. It was a collection of Shakespearean tragedies, which confused him. When he opened the book cover, there was a note from his mother. His tired and bloodshot eyes read her words:

> Samuel, my beautiful son, Shakespeare's trage-
> dies are centered on love, yet they confirm that
> we each have a tragic flaw that can destroy it.
> Discover yours and see that it does not destroy
> you and the ones you love. See that you tame it
> such that, through you, God can love all the ones
> you love, especially Jane. Remember the nights
> in the closet. Remember what I taught you and
> teach it to your brother. At all costs, obey Christ,
> and your steps will be firm and stable.
> All my love, all my love, all my love, Mother.

He immediately missed her and realized that he had always missed her, and he cried as a desperate desire surged through him to run to her. He looked around his room again, which was blurred from his watery eyes. Then he thought of Rose and wiped his face and mouth. Something about her made him realize he had come to the right place. She was just what he needed. She was honest and forward yet gentle, which told him what to expect. Within minutes of his arrival, she had him thinking about things that had never crossed his mind, like taking charge of his own life. There was never any time, never any room among Bishop's daily demands for his own thoughts about his own life, especially taking charge of it. He was Bishop's son, and he would live the life that Bishop gave him and planned for him. But not anymore, and strangely that left Sam feeling very insecure.

*****

Rose looked at the clock. It was after noontime, and Sam had yet to come downstairs to eat. She wondered if he was all right and was beginning to consider knocking on his door, but then he entered the kitchen. He looked tired and even old. What had he endured in his short life that should weigh on him so heavily?

He was a little embarrassed because of the hour. "I can't believe how late I slept. I'm not even sick," he said as a form of an apology.

Sickness has many faces, Rose thought, but for Sam's sake, she helped move him on. "Well, I saved your breakfast for you," she said. He went to the dining room and sat down. She placed a plate of food before him and let her hand slide across his back in a motherly way as she returned to the kitchen. Sam was not used to being touched, and he thought about that for a long time.

Rose brought out a tray of coffee for the both of them and sat down at the table.

"Will you see your family before they leave?" She knew her question would sink any existing joy, but she wanted him to become comfortable talking with her.

"No. I don't think that can happen." He revealed a lot to her with that answer.

"How did it come about that you decided to stay?"

How could he describe to her or anyone what had taken place? He was only now beginning to understand that while all his life he thought other families were strange, it was his that was not normal.

What did his staying come down to? "A choice," he said. "My father gave me a choice."

As Sam drank his coffee, Rose thought about choices, which she understood, and she asked no more questions. Sam was unaccustomed to relaxing, and he felt disturbed by the day's slow pace, but he took advantage of it and did little more than sleep the rest of the day.

Early the next morning, Sam rode to the outskirts of town to a place on the road where his family would be traveling. He waited so long that his horse became impatient. Upon hearing the sound of wagons and carriages approaching, he moved on to the edge of the road and watched his parents and brother drive by. Amos thrust his head out the window of the carriage and raised his hand to say goodbye. Sam raised his hand, too, and held it there until Amos was out of sight.

Later, he went to church, but not with Rose and not to the sermon. He waited at a distance for everyone to leave, and when he saw the Pruitts' carriage ride off, he longed to go with them but remained hidden.

He entered the church and looked for Reverend Hunt, but what he found instead was the cross. Sam realized that he had never really even observed it before now, although he had been in church nearly every Sunday since his birth.

"Sam," Reverend Hunt said from across the sanctuary. Sam turned to him.

Reverend Benjamin Hunt seemed young to be in charge of his rather large congregation. Yet he was completely confident leading his flock because he maintained an apostolic spirit to his ministry and had the passion and wisdom to see it through. In his mind, he was not leading anyone; God was. He was simply a willing and obedient vessel of the Lord. At first sight, he might be dismissed as frail. He was fair skinned with soft brown eyes and smooth dark blond hair that receded slightly, giving him a high forehead. But upon opening his mouth, he commanded respect and displayed authority in his pastorship.

"You've missed many services. Have you been ill?" the reverend asked.

"Yes, in a way, I suppose I have," Sam replied, honestly.

"And your father? I have not seen your family here either," Reverend Hunt asked as he returned hymnals to the shelves under the pews.

"I no longer have a father, Reverend," Sam said.

Reverend Hunt took a moment to consider how he would respond. "Let's sit down," he said and gestured to a pew. "You have no father, you say."

Sam confirmed hesitantly with a nod, and then he described his upbringing with long, descriptive details to the very bitter end as if confessing sin, none of which was his own. Reverend Hunt listened without a word, though internally, the images of Sam's suffering traumatized him in body, mind, and spirit.

"So I mean it when I say that I no longer have a father," Sam said. "It's painful to admit, but I must face the truth."

"Ah, the truth." Reverend Hunt looked up at the cross briefly. "Is that what you want? To face the truth? Be honest, Sam."

Sam searched his mind. What was Reverend Hunt implying? He became a little defensive over the notion that he was somehow in the wrong in his crisis. "Are you suggesting that my father and I can reconcile?" Sam asked.

"That is exactly what I am suggesting, Sam."

Sam tried to picture it but could see nothing. "I don't think you understand what has happened, Reverend," Sam said.

"I don't think you understand what I am saying, Sam." And Sam's look of confusion proved the reverend right. "Sam, this isn't about Bishop Callahan."

"Well, then who?" Sam asked. He was genuinely lost. Reverend Hunt waited. Sam did too. "Please tell me," Sam asked the still and patient Reverend Hunt. Then Sam remembered what he saw when he first entered the church. He looked at the cross and back at the reverend. "You mean *the Fa*ther." Reverend Hunt dipped his head and then raised it back up, confirming Sam's revelation. "You said 'reconcile.' Have I offended God?" Sam had lost his family, had no clear vision of his future with Jane, had no job, no home, and very little hope. Now he was hearing that he had lost God too. He was not sure how much more he could take.

"Let us focus on your pursuit for the truth. If you know God, you will also know the truth. Until then, you will be blind," Reverend Hunt said. Sam dropped his head into one of his hands as if the weight of it was too much to hold up on its own. "Sam, the truth is that you are not without a father. You will never be without a father if you choose to be God's son. That choice is the essence of freewill." Reverend Hunt paused and then asked, "Why did you come here today?"

"I don't know," Sam said.

"Surely, something was on your mind when you came in, knowing service had already ended," Reverend Hunt said.

"I don't know," Sam said again in distress. He became a little dizzy thinking about everything that was on his mind, and he struggled to speak.

"One thought at a time, Sam. Just say one," the reverend said.

Sam slowly lifted his head to look at the reverend and said angrily, "He's never cared about me." And he got up to leave.

"Sam!" Reverend Hunt called out to him as he walked out the door.

Sam rode his horse on the outskirts of town aimlessly for a couple of hours. It was cold, but his rushing blood kept him warm. He again stared at the church from a distance, and finally he walked back in as abruptly as he had left. He stormed down the center isle between the pews, turned and turned again to make his way through the church to Reverend Hunt's office. He entered without knocking, not realizing that his return was an answer to the reverend's prayers, who calmly came up from his book.

Sam asked very aggressively, "What kind of a god creates a man like Bishop Callahan? What kind of a god leaves a defenseless wife and her defenseless children in his hands? He's never cared about me. And now you tell me that I will never be without a father? Do you really expect me to believe that?" The reverend did not answer, purposely. "What kind of a god does that?" Sam yelled.

The reverend quietly asked, "How badly do you want to know the answers to your questions?"

Sam was thrown off a little by the reverend's response. It had not occurred to him that his questions could be answered. He gritted his teeth and turned around to leave, but he stopped himself. After a moment, he slammed his hand on the doorframe. The reverend stood and put his hand on Sam's shoulder to comfort him, but Sam jerked away and walked out again.

Rose saw that Sam's horse was gone. She came into her house and immediately checked his room, relieved to see that his belongings were still there. Near noon, the back door opened and it was Sam. He was noticeably upset, and he went straight to his room. About an hour later, he left again.

Sam walked back into the reverend's office and said, "I *do* want to know, badly. I want to know how in the hell anyone can explain God's ways. How in the hell…" Sam paused, and the Reverend Hunt watched and waited. Then Sam started to cry and almost collapsed under the weight of his grief.

Reverend Hunt moved Sam by the shoulders to a chair and sat him down, and he took a chair in front of him. He waited while Sam cried behind his hands. After Sam calmed down, the reverend revisited an earlier question. "I'm asking again, Sam, why did you come here today?"

Weakened, Sam answered, "I just feel…lost." The reverend nodded. "I've felt abandoned since birth." More tears fell. "I'm so alone. I don't know what I should do or where I should go." Sam's panic began to rise again.

"Do you *have* to do anything? Do you *have* to go somewhere?" Reverend Hunt asked. "Right away, I mean?"

Sam thought about it and said, "No, not really." He wiped his face.

"Try not to look so far down the road, Sam. Let's just go hour by hour, all right?" Sam nodded and felt his crisis subside. "So do you really want to know?"

Sam stared at the floor and said, "I think so."

"It will take some time, but you seem to have no shortage of that." Reverend Hunt smiled softly, and finally, so did Sam. "Are you willing?" Sam nodded, hesitantly. "Let's go back to the truth, Sam, and keep our focus there. Here is the truth: God loved you into creation not to abandon you but to father you. Try to picture that. Try to experience that in your mind. He wants to reconcile you to him. You are not an orphan. From the garden of Eden, we all have fallen short. That includes fathers and sometimes tragically so. In response to our fallen state, Jesus tells us in John 14:18, 'I will not leave you as orphans. I will come to you.' The important question, Sam, is how will you respond to him?" He waited for Sam to show signs of agreeing.

The reverend continued, "Were I to summarize your questions, it would sound like this: 'Who is God?' Would you agree?"

Sam didn't want to agree, but the reverend was right. He nodded.

"So you want to know who God is," Reverend Hunt concluded. He stood up and walked behind his desk while asking, "What are the four Gospels?" And he picked up a Bible and opened it.

Sam wiped his face again. "Matthew, Mark, Luke, and John," he answered.

"Choose one." When no answer came, Reverend Hunt looked up from the Bible at Sam and waited. In Sam's delayed response, the reverend said while lifting up the open Bible, "Sam, this is who God is. You said you came here today because you are lost. If you don't know who he is, you will never know who you are."

Sam took a breath and said, "Um, John."

The reverend smiled. Then he sat down again with Sam and handed him the Bible. "This is yours. I want you to begin with the Gospel of John. Pray before each reading. Read it as if you are one of Jesus's disciples sitting among all his disciples while he teaches. Each time Jesus says, 'I tell you the truth,' I want you to write down the verse, word for word, and meditate on it. Five chapters by tomorrow. Four chapters each day thereafter. And we will meet here each day at two to discuss what you have learned about who God is."

*****

Jane was so sad that she was useless. She wept in her room. No letter, no words. Nothing. "Why?" she asked. Esther held her like a child as Jane whispered, "How could he leave me this way?"

Adrien could see bitterness trying to take root in Jane's heart, and he asked her to dine with him. He got her out of the house for some fresh air and a change of scenery. In waiting for dinner to be served, he said, "I'm angry, Jane."

She lowered her head and said, "I'm sorry, Father. I've allowed my brokenheartedness to become a central theme at home. I'll pull back."

"I am not angry with you, dear. I am angry with myself. Why would you respond any differently? You learned from the best." Knowing he had her attention, he continued, "My prolonged grief over your mother's death was inexcusable, and I was not there for you and your brother as I should have been."

"Father, you don't have to—"

"I do have to." Adrien was firm. "I need to say this, and you need to hear it. My attachment to your mother was so strong that she became the most important person in my life."

"Well, shouldn't the most important person in your life be your spouse?"

"No, Jane. The most important person in your life must only and always be Jesus." Jane's brows tried to meet as she considered his point. "I raised you to understand that, but I forgot it. I'm not going to let you forget it too." Jane tried not to cry because she was in public.

"Jane, your attachment to Sam has dethroned the Lord from your heart, and you hardly even know him. Pray for him, of course, but make sure you remove him from God's seat." He placed his hand on hers. "Make Jesus the most important person in your life and trust him. One day, everything you are going through here will be made clear to you. Can you understand what I am saying?"

Jane dabbed the corners of her eyes and nodded while saying, "Thank you, Father."

That night, Jane traded her sadness and confusion for God's wisdom. She read, prayed, cried, repented, and began to release her situation to God. "I love him, Lord. Please protect him."

*****

Sam stared at his Bible. He had been schooled in the Word of God, but it meant no more to him than his math or language lessons. Faith was a task, not a condition of the heart and mind. It was something he did, not something he had. And as with the farm, he now felt out of place. He argued in his head that faith was just another form of slavery. But then he pondered the reverend's question: Why was he there? "Because I am lost, that's why," he confessed.

He opened his Bible and stayed the course with Reverend Hunt, reading and discussing the Gospel of John, grudgingly. But a few days into it, Sam lifted his head from his Bible. His mind raced. Everything he had learned in church since his youth was beginning to make sense.

By day 4, his discussions with Reverend Hunt were becoming livelier and expansive, and he jumped from book to book pointing things out. On day 5, when they finished their examination of the Gospel of John, Sam was uplifted as he made his way out of the sanctuary. But he was captured by the stained-glass windows. He stopped and looked at one after another and discovered in them stories he had never noticed before. From scene to scene, he saw God's history of the world glow through the sunlit colorful pictures. Then he looked to the other side of the church where the story continued, ending with the resurrection of Jesus Christ. Sam paused. He slowly moved toward the altar and imagined a sacrifice, which was something he never quite understood but now wanted to. Finally, he stepped behind the podium and looked at the Bible, which was opened to the Gospel of John, and he smiled a little.

His eyes glanced over the pages facing him, and the words immediately began to stir his soul. He pulled back a little and looked out over the pews expecting to see someone because he no longer felt alone. He looked over both shoulders where the cross was mounted high on the wall behind him, but no one was there.

He looked at the open Bible again, leaned in, and read a passage that he had read just days before: "Jesus, therefore, answered and said unto them, 'Murmur not among yourselves. No man can come to me, except the Father which hath sent me draw him.'"

Sam stepped away and turned his back on the Bible only to find himself facing the foot of the cross. He was trapped between God's Word and Jesus Christ, which he suddenly realized were one and the same. He felt a gentle weight on his shoulders pressing down on him, and he dropped to his knees and gave his life away. Observing from a distance, Reverend Hunt closed his eyes, lifted his head, and whispered thanksgiving.

*****

Sam was up early the next morning, and he met Rose in the kitchen. "Rose, if you make a list for me of things that need to be done, I will get started today." Rose agreed without inquiry.

Sam spent a couple of hours in the house making overdue repairs and the rest of the day in the barn, cleaning it out and grooming the horses. It was very cold, but he pushed through until it became dark. He tried not to think about his family, but he couldn't help it. What were Amos and his mother going through? Were they happy for him? Were they saddened by his absence? Or was Bishop taking his anger at him out on them? Whatever the case, Bishop made sure that there was nothing he could do about it. Or was it God doing that?

Meanwhile, Rose laundered and stored clothes and linen. She walked into Sam's room to leave him fresh towels. When she closed the door, she noticed that the door's hinge had been fixed.

Sam came back in the house with his arms full of firewood. He stacked it beside the fireplace, threw another couple of pieces on the fire, and warmed himself before the flames for a few minutes, unaware that Rose was nearby and watching in compassion.

He finished up a few inside jobs while Rose made supper. He was very hungry, and he tried not to overeat, but he enjoyed her cooking. Rose made herself a plate, too, and joined him at the table. They engaged in small talk, which was strategic on Rose's part; she knew what she was doing. Before long, she went a little deeper.

"Sam, I've been through some very tough times. It helps to have people near you that care. I want you to know that I do care, and I am here for you." Sam did not budge, so she came in through another way. "When my husband died," she began confiding, and Sam was soon engaging.

It was late when Sam said, "I'm exhausted. I think I will retire."

"You *should* be exhausted. You worked hard today," Rose replied, and they both seemed to know that his fatigue was emotional and spiritual, not physical. "Will you be going to church tomorrow?"

"No," he said. "Not yet. Good night, Rose." Though tired, Sam was awake for hours reading, seeking, and struggling to pray. "Father, I believe. Help me to see. I am willing," was all he knew to say.

He got up before dawn, lit a lantern, and began reading Genesis. Then he prayed before beginning his day.

Chapter 5

Adrien confessed to himself that he was thrilled to know that the Callahan family had left Edwardsville. He was not thrilled to learn at church and through the news circulating all over town that Sam did not go with them. Fearful and defensive, he sat his daughter down in his study to tell her that he had tolerated the affection between her and Sam because he knew it would come to a natural end.

"Had I known he would be staying, I would have put a stop to it long ago," he barked.

"Father, how can you say that?" Jane protested.

"Jane, this young man is damaged! Can't you see that he is his father's son, and it is only a matter of time before his father's influence will surface in his own treatment of you?"

"Father, you're wrong. Sam is not like that," Jane insisted. "And I heard you clearly the other night, but I think I know him better than that!"

"It's a game of chance. I cannot leave you at risk to that kind of misery. This has lifelong implications. No, Jane. I won't allow it." It was basic math in Adrien's mind. Why couldn't his daughter see it?

Jane struggled to maintain her composure as she bit her tongue to prevent her defiance, but she couldn't hold it back. "Father, I'm not sure that I am *asking* you to allow it."

Adrien's expression changed with the realization of what his daughter was saying. Nathan walked in like a knight moving to rescue a king in check.

"Father, forgive me, but I am compelled to tell you something." Jane lifted herself up from her chair to leave. "No, Jane," Nathan said. "Stay. I think you should hear this. It's about Sam." Jane sat back down, placing full curious attention on Nathan.

"Well?" Adrien demanded. His left eyebrow flinched upward. "What is it?"

"It's something Esther and Pierre were told by the Callahans' servants."

"Well, spit it out!" Adrien again demanded.

"It seems, Father, that Sam asked to remain here for another year to gain more work experience, and his father became quite enraged. He called Sam a liar, saying that he wanted only to stay for Jane. Then he gave Sam a choice to come with him now, or to stay and lose his family and all of his future security. Sam made the choice to defy his father and stay."

"Sam," Jane whispered as she placed her hand over her heart.

This was not the kind of information Adrien was expecting. While he agreed with Bishop, to his own displeasure, that Sam did want to stay for Jane, Adrien also knew he had influenced Sam by praising his work performance.

"There's more," Nathan said. "He's been staying secretly at the McGregor place and going to church this entire week receiving godly instruction from Reverend Hunt."

"So? Everyone runs to God when in a crisis," Adrien said. Jane's expression to Nathan begged him to keep making his point.

"Father, Sam is our friend. What he just endured was torturous. Surely, it speaks of his character *and* his will to be unlike his own father. If we do nothing, what's to become of him?" Nathan asked.

Adrien felt like he was on thin ice. What separated him from Bishop should he continue with his rigid demands for his daughter? Yet what assurance did he have that Sam had any real character of his own? He turned around to look out the window and tapped his fingers on his desk, trying to control his anxiety.

"Perhaps, Father," Nathan pushed gently, "he could keep his job, and you could just give him more time to see what he is made of and how he manages on his own. He's not been replaced yet, and you said yourself that he's needed on the farm."

Adrien continued to gaze out the window. It was an unusually nice, warm day for winter—and clear, unlike his mind. Jane and Nathan waited. Adrien grew aware that any hope for Sam's survival hinged on his employment with Coles as well as Adrien's own mercy. He also embraced the reality that he could not prevent his daughter from pursuing the man she loved. He tapped his fingers again. Finally, Jane and Nathan could see their father give a gentle but reluctant agreeable nod. Jane closed her eyes and let out the breath she had been holding, thankful that she would not have to rebel against her father. Nathan glanced at Jane with a smile.

"Should we invite him to supper tonight to bring some degree of comfort to his recent misfortune?" Nathan proposed as he joined his father at the window.

"Don't push it!" Adrien said, turning to give orders to both Nathan and Jane. As he wrote on a piece of paper, he continued, "Take this note to the McGregor Boardinghouse saying that he's expected at the farm tomorrow."

"I don't think that will be necessary," Nathan said as he was still looking out the window.

"And why not?" Adrien demanded, nearly exhausted by the endless discussion.

"Because he's here," Nathan turned to say.

"What!" both Jane and her father said in unison and came to the window to see Sam riding toward the house.

Adrien assumed a firm stance before Jane and looked at her as though she had done something wrong. Jane tried to speak but had no words, and she was only able to shake her head in her defense.

"You stay here!" he ordered Jane. She nodded quickly up and down, assuring her obedience.

Adrien met Sam at the door. When greeting him, Adrien hid any knowledge he had of Sam's troubled situation but was honest with his awareness of his failed departure.

"Mr. Callahan, I have it on good authority that you will not be leaving right away," Adrien said.

"That is correct, sir," Sam said, wondering how he knew already.

"Can I assume, as well, that you will be available to work tomorrow?"

"Of course, sir, if I remain worthy of the position," Sam answered.

"Very well, then. It's settled. Tomorrow it is. Give this notice of reinstatement to Mr. Saunderman." Adrien handed Sam the note and was finished, but Sam wasn't. He remained at the door, looking at Adrien, who looked at Sam curiously and asked, "Was there something else?"

"Actually, the reason I came was to ask your permission to call on Jane, sir." Sam shifted his view to the beautiful figure behind Adrien.

Adrien looked over his own shoulder and did a double-take upon finding Jane staring at Sam. She broke eyes with Sam and looked at her father, who was noticeably irritated. She lowered her head and backed away.

"Call on her?" Adrien asked as he returned his attention to Sam. "What do you mean?"

"I was hoping for a simple walk here on your grounds to take in some of this beautiful day," Sam explained.

Adrien raised one eyebrow, bothered that he could find nothing wrong with that and bothered by Sam's confidence in the midst of so much turmoil. He searched his brain for a way to block Sam's advance, but he was at a loss. In truth, he was giving in to his own compassion for Sam.

"That'll be fine," Adrien said and adjusted his jaw. "Wait here, and I'll send her out momentarily." Again, Sam looked over Adrien's shoulder with an emerging smile. This time Adrien did not turn to look behind himself, sensing that Jane was again at the door with him. "It seems you won't have to wait. Here she is."

As he slowly turned toward Jane to show his disapproval, she squeezed herself between her father and the doorframe, holding on to her hat with one hand and pulling her shawl closed with the other, very eager to join Sam for a stroll.

"Thank you, Father," Jane said, smiling sheepishly. Adrien was not amused.

As they began their walk, Sam extended his bent arm, and she took it, at which point Adrien shut the door and turned to find Nathan leaning on the wall with his arms crossed and holding a patronizing smirk. Adrien ignored Nathan as he took the stairs to his study, except to say, "Nathan, tell Esther we will be having a guest for supper."

Nathan whispered, "Excellent idea, Father."

*****

Jane's head was full of things she wanted to say and ask. She felt she should be cautious for fear of saying something wrong and creating an offense at such a fragile time for Sam. But she also felt that if she ignored his circumstances, she would appear completely insensitive, which would be far worse. So she settled for honesty and spoke gently from her heart.

"Sam, our Father has put it on my conscience to be open with you. I am aware of recent happenings between you and your family. Please don't ask me how. It would break confidences to say. But to pretend I know nothing would be deceitful. The point is, while I am truly very sad about the situation you are in, I am also overjoyed to see you again. Please forgive my selfishness."

Sam thought, *Her father urged her on?* He shook his head upon realizing, *No, not that father.*

Sam answered, "The situation, I believe firmly, could not have been helped and was permitted on a divine level, and I have no regrets. And if the joy of seeing me equates to the sin of selfishness, then we should repent together. Seeing you is all I have thought of, Jane." Jane smiled, obviously relieved by his response.

"Are you comfortable at the boardinghouse?" Jane asked in her longing to be the one to make him comfortable.

"Surprisingly so," Sam answered. "There are no other boarders at present, so I often have the whole house to myself. And my room is…all I need for now." Sam smiled as he withheld its accurate description: private, quiet, safe, a refuge.

And Jane thought, *Yes, for now.*

"What is Rose like?" she asked. She wanted to know more about the one person in his life who spent his days with him. She wasn't jealous of Rose; she was jealous of her time.

Sam became reserved, not from fear of exposing Rose for the wonderful mother she had already become to him but from fear of exposing his deep need for it. He felt vulnerable, so he skirted the truth. "Rose is Rose. She runs her business for one guest the way I suspect she would run it for a full house. I help out when she asks, and she takes it off my rent. It's a good arrangement."

Jane nodded. She was not satisfied with his answer, and she wished she could ask Rose herself. She moved on from topic to topic.

"Elizabeth was in town with her father," Jane said. "They joined us for supper. I know she endures the trip so she can see Nathan. I wish he would commit to an engagement to her."

Sam was a bit thrown upon realizing how little Jane understood about her brother. Should he tell her? Could she handle learning that her brother had a horrible fear of love and that he not only took steps to avoid it, he was also withdrawing, one by one, from all those he loved now, including her? No. What good would come from telling her?

"Not everyone is ready for love and marriage at twenty," Sam simply said.

Jane's thoughts spun. She bit at her thumb to stop herself from asking whom "not everyone" applied to. As they continued their walk through a patch of elm trees, they discussed the pain they both suffered while unable to see each other under Bishop's orders.

"It was absolutely unbearable, Sam. I thought I would never see you again," Jane openly confided. "And carrying the thought that you had left with them, without word…" Jane could not finish her thought.

"I never doubted that we would see each other again. I can't say how I knew, exactly, but I knew. To be sure, being with you now is an answered prayer. I am sorry for any pain I caused. I just needed time to gather my thoughts." Sam and Jane stopped walking and faced each other.

Suddenly, Sam gently maneuvered Jane so that her back was against an elm tree, placing them both out of view of the house. He rested one hand on the tree over her head and slid his other hand under her shawl and onto her slender waist. The look in his eyes exposed his vulnerability to her. Slowly, he leaned in to kiss her lips but diverted to her neck. He knew what he was doing not from experience but from the thousands of times he ran this moment through his mind. He buried himself in her scent. Jane closed her eyes, becoming weak, but not so weak that she did not hear her father's concerns screaming at her in her head.

"Mr. Callahan," she began softly as she looked up at the clear sky through the bare branches above them.

"Mm, hmm?" Sam pressed his rough jaw into the smooth slope between her neck and shoulder as he delivered another kiss. Jane closed her eyes again as her heart began to race.

"Were I my father, I would be asking you what your intentions are with my daughter," Jane staged her question.

Sam continued to caress both sides of her neck gently with his mouth, tasting her soft skin. "Were you your father, I would not be kissing you."

Jane placed her gloved hand on his chest and lightly pushed him back, and she became very serious. "Sam, I have to know. What are your intentions?" Jane had to know not only because her virtue was at risk but also because she had already lost him once, or so she had thought. She did not think she could endure it again. Was it true that he stayed behind for her, costing him everything he had?

He, too, assumed seriousness, looking deeply through her as he wondered how she could not know. He purposely waited to answer, allowing her time to think and letting her see that he was fully in control of his faculties, and this was not just a fleeting moment of passion. He leaned in just enough for her to feel his force against her hand.

Sam answered, "To love you, Jane Pruitt, until the day I die. That is my intention."

Jane examined him and considered his words for a moment; then she adjusted her hand on his chest to a grasp of his coat. She pulled him back to herself and kissed him for the first time, letting loose the passion she had been withholding as she waited for this moment to come.

Chapter 6

Sam went back to work right away. Saunderman was busy tearing down a shed that had run its course, and he said, "Sam, this needs a replacement. Build it today."

By now, Sam had learned that every new task from Saunderman was a test, which was usually met with his inability to pass it until Saunderman or one of the other farmhands showed him how. But not this time. He went to the farm's office, took out a sheet of paper, and drew a few sketches with some measurements. He showed it to Saunderman.

"Something like this?" Sam asked.

Saunderman had difficulty hiding his expression of shock. But shock over what? He knew Sam was book smart. He just didn't know Sam could translate it to everyday life, and he answered, "Yes, something like that." As Sam turned to go, Saunderman said, "Get Danny to help you." Finally, Sam would have a chance to repay Danny by teaching him something.

Sam and Danny stood back and looked at their completed work. Sam opened and closed the door a few times to ensure it was level while Danny walked around the shed making sure all the nails were flush and the seams were tight. Satisfied, Sam smiled, and Danny bit his bottom lip and nodded. They shook hands, which had become a common finishing touch for them. Then the two of them planted themselves in the sun near some trees and took a lunch break.

Sam looked around the farm and saw a few houses that some of the black farm workers lived in. "Can I ask you a question?" he said.

"What?" Danny asked as he rummaged through his sack that was overfilled with food his mother had packed for him.

73

"I thought that when Mr. Coles freed his slaves, he gave each of them some land in Pin Oak," Sam said.

"He offered it, an' mos' of 'em took it, but not all," Danny said.

"Why not?"

"Mmm." Danny thought between bites. "Ownin' land is a lot o' work. Some people don't want it. Some people aren't good at it. So a few of 'em went to St. Louie, an' a few took jobs here on the farm, an' they live here too."

"You don't live here," Sam stated and asked at the same time.

"No. I live in Ridge Prairie. We moved here from Missouri. Lots o' free colored folk do." Danny finished a few bites before continuing. "So how you been doin' with your new home?"

Sam was caught off guard with that question and fumbled around in answering. "Ah, well, you know, I'm settling in." He found himself thinking about what that meant.

"Sam, you talk like I don't know. Everybody knows. Everyone here knows, my parents know, and I know…'bout your father, 'bout Rose, 'bout Jane. God knows too." Danny looked at Sam hard, leaned forward, and said, "I keep tryin' to tell you, you don't gotta hide nothin' here."

After a moment, Sam nodded, accepting of the fact that he was exposed. Sam then went back to looking at the houses across the farm again. "And the people that live there are tenants? They're all free?"

"Uh huh. All the colored folk here are free. Mistah Coles don't have no slaves, no indentured servants, neither. We all get paid, an' good too. Ya know, though, some people, if they been slaves all their lives, they don't know what to do with freedom. It's hard being free."

Suddenly, Sam saw the world spinning around him. He had to close his eyes because he was feeling dizzy. He rubbed his brow and shook his head as scenes from his life flashed before him. One scene after another came of Bishop standing over him dictating his every move, his every thought, his every breath—the beatings he took, and for what? He saw himself in a candlelit closet. Then he saw his mother far in the background as he reached out to her, but she was too far away. He saw Amos wink at him. *Amos*, he thought, *I have to get to Amos*.

He realized for the first time that choosing to stay in Edwardsville was one thing, but it also meant that he was finally free. He was no longer a slave to Bishop's dictatorship and brutality. But Danny was right; it was hard being free. Sam had never done it before, and the very idea nearly paralyzed him. He could only faintly hear Danny calling out to him.

"Sam! Are you all right?" Danny asked again and again.

"Yeah," he was barely able to say as he struggled to come to his feet. "I just feel a little sick." He staggered into the trees and violently threw up.

*****

When the Pruitts arrived for church, Jane sat next to Rose who was sitting next to Sam. Sam had a hard time focusing with Jane nearby. Adrien had a hard time focusing with Sam nearby. After some music, some announcements, and some hymns, Reverend Hunt began his sermon. But it was more like a story.

He said, "A young man entered a church one day seeking to know more about our Lord. He asked the pastor many questions, and it went something like this:

"'There are many scriptures about being a slave to sin,' the young man began.

"'Yes,' said the pastor.

"'Scripture also talks about being a slave to Jesus,' he said to the reverend as he pointed to a passage, and the reverend nodded. 'Then what does Jesus mean when he says that if he has set me free, I will be free indeed?' the young man probed."

Sam quickly looked up at Reverend Hunt; then he looked around the sanctuary. He was certain all eyes would be on him, but they were forward on Reverend Hunt. His chest wanted to cave in as he listened to the reverend...share.

"The pastor answered, 'It means Christ has released you from the grip of this world, and though you are here in this world, you are no longer *of* it. You belong to him," the reverend explained. The young man seemed to struggle with this.

"'So, either way, I am still a slave. Yes?' the young man asked.

"The pastor became cautious yet answered, 'Yes. That is true.' The young man felt like he had reached a dead end and shook his head trying to understand.

"'Then as a slave, I ask again, what does Jesus mean when he says he has set me free?'"

"'What is freedom?' the pastor asked, but the young man could not answer. 'Do you think freedom is being accountable to no one but yourself, that the less you have of God, the freer you become?'

"'I think I do, yes,' said the young man.

"'Then what guides your conscience? You?' The pastor could see the young man making calculations in his head. 'What evidence do you have that you know what is right or wrong? And if you decide something is right today, will it still be right tomorrow or years from now? God, however, never changes. His word is always true, from the beginning to the end. If you are accountable to no one but yourself, doesn't that make you your own god?' The pastor again let the young man think. 'Surely you have seen the likes of those who believe in only themselves…who make themselves gods.'

"'Yes, I have,' the young man confessed.

"'What were these self-made gods like?' the pastor asked.

"'They were…godless,' the young man realized. 'But I have also seen many Christians who can be just as godless.' The young man exposed a problem within the body of Christ that the church has been talking about since its formation.

"'Of course,' said the pastor. 'Did Jesus not expose such people when he confronted the Pharisees? Did the apostles not expose such people when building the church? Churches are full of ungodly people, but God will be their judge. The world is no different now than in Jesus's time. When some claim godliness but clearly walk in accordance with their own will, who is the liar? God? Or the thief who thinks he can use God for his own selfish gain? We cannot let the condition of mankind and of the world sway us from the truth.' Both the young man and the reverend paused here in reflection.

"'Suppose you are your own god,' the pastor continued. 'What can you do about your own life? Can you stop the storms that will come? Can you ensure a painless lifetime? Can you control your own death and what will happen thereafter?'

"'No,' the young man yielded.

"'So if freedom is being your own god, then what is the outcome? If you cannot save yourself from death, then what good is it?' asked the pastor. 'You cannot even save yourself from pain. In fact, our idea of freedom often leads to more pain because it affords mankind the opportunity to destroy itself. We want to do whatever we want, whenever we want, and to whomever we want. What is that but selfishness and what does selfishness produce but pain? And pain can cause people to be drawn deeper into darkness, which is exactly what Satan wants because there we become his prisoners, slaves of darkness rather than light, making ourselves useless to anyone, especially God.

"'In contrast, what is freedom in Christ?' the pastor continued. 'It is release from darkness and sin. It is overcoming the world. It is coming under the shadow of God's hand. It is sanctification into his image where we find our true selves and peace. No matter what our circumstance, be it comfort or torture, there is no greater freedom than being a slave to Jesus Christ. And what must a slave to Christ do? Love God and love others. Now I ask, what is it that causes mankind to resist that so.'

"'I suspect it's my nature.' The young man laughed a little in embarrassment over his discovery. 'Free will, it is a beast,' he said.

"'I must protest,' the reverend said with a soft rebuke. 'Free will is a gift. Free will provides for you a simple choice of choosing which master you will serve. Will you be a slave to Satan or a slave to Jesus Christ? There is no in between. Jesus warns us that if we are not with him, we are against him, and that those not gathered to him, scatter. We must choose a side. We each are responsible for the choice we make, even if we make no choice at all. That is the truth. We can reject the truth, if we so choose, but we cannot reject the consequences. Continue your want to know more, and chase Christ for the truth.'"

Reverend Hunt said, "The reverend finished there, and the young man left with much to consider in his want to know more about God. In Exodus 33:18, Moses says, 'Lord, show me Your glory.'

He said this even after seeing all that God had done for Israel, not out of disappointment or greed, but out of his deep desire to know more and more about the Father, just as this young man in the story was doing. We must all charge ourselves to ask and answer, where am I in my want to know my Lord and to see his glory?"

Reverend Hunt briefly looked at Sam and said, "Let us pray." Sam nodded slightly and lowered his head.

*****

Edward Coles abruptly announced his intention to return East, and his departure was fast approaching. He longed to marry, and with slavery in serious decline in Pennsylvania, living near his roots appealed to him greatly. This decision would eventually impact both Adrien and Sam. Adrien would manage due to his other clients, but Sam had no other prospects, as Sam's employment with Adrien was tied to Coles. Adrien hid the pleasure that this news brought him, thinking surely this would force Sam to return to his family for support, however difficult that might be, and free Jane of her attachment to him.

Adrien discreetly looked at his watch as the last meeting with Coles and his lawyer came to a close.

"Governor, I believe that's everything with the exception of one small remaining parcel in Pin Oak that you have not yet designated," Coles's lawyer said.

"Ah, yes. I want that granted to Samuel Callahan. See that the papers are drawn up for my signature and that they reach him safely. I won't be leaving until tomorrow. That should be plenty of time. Would you agree?" Coles asked, directing his request to both his lawyer and Adrien.

Adrien became alarmed and sat up fully engaged. "Sir? Are you sure? Callahan?"

"Samuel Callahan. Yes, I'm sure. He has satisfied and often exceeded every expectation at Prairieland, has he not?" he asked.

Adrien was caught. He looked back and forth between Coles and the lawyer. "Well, yes. A bit of a rough start, but overall he has, sir." Adrien was compelled to honesty.

"Clearly," Coles continued. "Buck and Robert's assessments all but anoint the young man. It seems proper to ensure he is given a fair start. The parcel is small and affordable, and he has more than earned it, God knows. Most impressive is the way he confronted his father head-on, as he did."

"You know about that, sir?" Adrien was shocked by Coles's awareness to something seemingly so beneath him.

"I know enough. Agreeing to give Samuel a job was for Samuel's benefit, not Bishop's. Bishop Callahan has set himself on a course of ruin. His son, on the other hand, was put to the test and has chosen a radically different course. Frankly, he stands as a model for courage, and he should be credited."

Was Coles somehow comparing Sam with himself? Adrien wondered. "Yes, sir. I will see to it immediately," Adrien said obediently. He found himself ashamed of his resentment of the generosity, and he knew that were it not for his daughter's involvement with Sam, he would share the growing sentiment surrounding him. What would it take for him to give Sam Callahan, at last, a genuine and permanent welcome into his home?

"Governor, before you leave, permit me to express my appreciation for your acceptance of my services. This day is now and will always be remembered as bitter for me as it brings me no joy to see you leave. I pray, sir, that Pennsylvania holds for you abundant joy and blessings." Adrien bowed slightly.

"The pleasure has been mine, Adrien. You have been a superior manager and a true friend, and I trust my decision to consolidate the management of my affairs won't come between us."

"Certainly not, Governor. The decision is a justly prudent one," Adrien spoke sincerely.

As Coles turned to leave with his lawyer, he said, "Gentlemen, I am off to Prairieland to say farewell to some old friends," referring to his former slaves. "May this not be goodbye for us."

After they left, Adrien sat back down in his chair, frustrated by many things, mostly himself.

*****

Saunderman told Sam that Adrien wanted to see him in his office. It was late in the day and Sam was a mess, but Saunderman said it didn't matter and told Sam to go immediately.

When Sam left his meeting with Adrien, he firmly shut the door behind him. He stood on the steps and began to seethe as he contemplated his options, of which he had nearly none. He gritted his teeth, put on his hat, and got on his horse. Adrien was puzzled when he watched out his window at Sam riding away as if being chased by a mob.

Jane arrived at the boardinghouse before Sam to surprise him. She chatted with Rose for a bit; then she took a seat in the parlor and waited somewhat impatiently. She peeked out the window frequently until she finally saw him coming. Then she returned to her seat and made every effort to present herself as poised and contained for his entrance.

Sam saw Jane's carriage at the boardinghouse from a distance and stopped for a moment. He did not expect to see her right now and considered diverting to a tavern. He spun his horse around twice and rode to the boardinghouse.

Jane slowly came to her feet when Sam entered the house. She smiled lovingly and said, "Hello, Sam."

"What are you doing here, Jane?" Sam asked.

"Well, I came to see *you*, of course. What else would I be doing here, silly?" Jane asked, now finding it harder to smile.

"You shouldn't be here," he said, and he turned to walk up the stairs. Jane was mortified. Rose came around the corner and looked at Jane, angry on her behalf. Sam's door slammed closed. Rose nodded her head to the stairs, signaling Jane to go up.

"No. I couldn't possibly," Jane whispered. Her reputation would be ruined were anyone to find out that she and Sam were alone together in his room.

"There is no one else boarding right now. Go!" Rose insisted. "I'll keep watch."

Jane examined the stairs and took a few steps up; then she looked back at Rose, reconsidering her decision.

"Go. It's the first door," Rose insisted.

Jane slowly resumed her climb. When she reached his door, she lifted her hand to knock, but instead, she quickly opened the door, entered, and shut it behind her, giving herself what she thought would be the upper hand. She kept her back to the door. Sam looked over his shoulder and was truly stunned by the risk she was taking, but he acted like he didn't care that she was there.

He had already taken off his shirt, and he was washing himself in the basin. Jane studied his exposure, as this was much more of him than she had ever seen before. She could not take her eyes off him, though she knew she should. Was it the work on the farm that shaped him so fully and firmly, or was that natural for him?

"What do you want?" Sam asked while washing. Jane said nothing. Her head was spinning as she tried to understand his sudden change in temperament. "Are you here to throw me some scraps too? Or did you already do that?" Sam finished at the basin and positioned himself in front of her as he dried off with a towel. Jane held back her tears. "Was it you who convinced your father to give me back my job when my family left? Because it occurred to me later that I never had to ask."

"Sam, it wasn't like that at all," she tried to explain.

"Is that right? Rose keeps dropping my rent for no reason. Your father suddenly wants to hire me full-time because I'm soon out of a job with Mr. Coles, again, who strangely wants to give me a piece of land. I have only ever formally met the man once, so why am I so worthy? What's next for *poor* Sam Callahan? Well, I don't need anyone's pity, Jane." He paused. "Especially not yours," which he hoped she would understand to mean that she could not possibly respect a man that she had to carry.

Sam finished wiping the back of his neck, threw the towel on the dresser, and put his hands on his hips as he stared at her defensively. "I think you should leave." Jane did not move even in straining to hold back her tears. "Now," he insisted. Then he turned his back and walked to his wardrobe to find a clean shirt. He heard the door open; then he heard the door close. Sam stopped in front of his wardrobe, held on to both open doors, and dropped his head.

"I don't pity you, Sam." He turned around quickly to see Jane still there. "You are confusing pity with admiration. Who I pity is your father. And I ache for your mother and brother because I get to be with you, and they don't." Jane walked across the room and stood facing him. A tear finally fell from her eye as she looked at his wet hair and began to comb it carefully with her fingers. "I'm not leaving, Sam. I'll never leave you. Perhaps that scares you more than the idea of having your manhood compromised, which is something I would never do, and you know it." She ran her hand from his hair down his shirtless back as she leaned in and kissed him.

He reached around her with both arms, held on to her tightly, and said softly, "I'm sorry." Then he lifted her up, laid her on his bed, and pressed his lips into hers.

A tap on the door brought them both back to their feet. Jane brushed her hands over her hair and dress to remove any evidence of wrongdoing.

"Jane, your father is coming down the street. I think he spotted your carriage," Rose said on the other side of the door. Jane began to breathe heavily, and she looked around the room in a panic wondering if there was another way out. "Hurry up!" Rose warned.

"One minute, Rose," Sam commanded. He took Jane by the hand and quickly led her to the door. "Go downstairs. Tell your father you came here to dine with me and to celebrate. It's hardly a lie." Jane nodded compliantly. He whispered, "I love you," and he kissed her before he opened the door and forced her out.

Jane ran down the stairs and told Rose she would be helping with supper. Rose understood. Jane had just entered the dining room when her father knocked on the door. They looked at each other and sighed in relief at their timing, and Rose left to welcome Adrien. Jane could hear the inquiry.

"Good afternoon, Rose. Is my daughter here? Her carriage is outside," Adrien asked politely but knowingly.

"She is, indeed, Mr. Pruitt. Please come in." Rose smiled and led him to the dining room where Jane was setting the table.

"Father! What a pleasant surprise. What brings you here?" Jane tried to hide her anxiety.

"I came to ask you the same?" Adrien gave Jane an accusing look, which he followed by raising his eyebrows.

"Well, I'm having supper with Sam, of course. I knew you were sharing big news with him today, and I thought it would be nice to celebrate." Jane set a plate on the table, and she held her hands together at her waistline. She waited for her father to give some sign of his acceptance to her honest explanation, but her nervousness returned, and she became short of breath. "Won't you…stay and join us…Father?" Jane remained very still.

Without blinking or moving his head, Adrien shifted his eyes to Rose and back to Jane. "Might I have a word with you, Jane? Privately?" Then he gestured to the parlor off the main entrance.

"Certainly, Father." Jane answered, apprehensively. She walked past her father on the way to the parlor, and Adrien followed, loosely closing the double doors behind him.

"My dear," Adrien began, and he meant business. He adjusted his stance to his other foot, placed one hand on his hip, and whispered forcefully as he leaned forward and pointed outside, "Your carriage sits in front of the place where the man who is courting you sleeps. Where is your sense of decency? Where is his! Does he even know you are here? I certainly hope not!" Jane could not look her father in the eye.

"Father, I, I just thought…," Jane stuttered.

"I beg to differ. Had you thought, you would not be here now. It's probably already making the headlines. What of your reputation?" Adrien looked over her head and across the room, thinking, and then he looked at her again. "What of *my* reputation? When I think of your mother…"

"I see now that you are right, Father," Jane said, genuinely and fully yielding. Her admission of her error caused her nervousness to vanish. "It was rash of me, and I don't know what I was thinking. Would it be best to leave now? Perhaps, I should walk out with you?"

Adrien unbuttoned his coat in need of more air and pulled it open as he put both hands now on his hips, shaking his head, still thinking. Finally, he said, "I'm disappointed." Tears began to drop from Jane's eyes, but she made no sound. She quietly wiped them away. "*Twice* disappointed," Adrien said as he raised up two fingers. "I met with *your* Sam today to offer him full employment with me and to share the good news of Governor Coles's gift to him on the heels of his termination, and he just *sat* there. He never said a word. I handed him the papers to his new property, and he took them and simply left." Adrien threw his arms in the air, disgusted. He walked to the window. "Some days, Jane, I truly want to support your interest in him. I had moments, fleeting ones mind you, of thinking this property could lead to a prosperous future for the two of you."

"And other days, Father?" Jane probed softly.

"I just want you to be happy, Jane. It might sound simple to you, but it can be very hard to come by in life," Adrien said, still facing the window, reviewing the near and distant landscape of his memories.

Sam had been on the middle of the staircase listening to most of the discussion. He leaned his head back against the stairway wall, closed his eyes tightly, and gritted his teeth, angry with himself that he allowed things to reach this condition. He made his way down the rest of the stairs, and upon spotting both Jane and her father in the parlor, he pretended to be surprised.

"Mr. Pruitt, Jane?" Sam made a gesture over his casual appearance. "Forgive me. I was not expecting visitors," which was true.

"Hello Sam, again. And goodbye. Jane made an inappropriate stop, and I am here to see her home. I trust you understand," Adrien stated.

"Of course. I confess, sir, we sometimes lack judgment. I beg your forgiveness," Sam stated to share in Jane's guilt.

"Well, I suggest you both *gain* judgment. And fast! Or I shall intervene most unpleasantly!" Adrien was not going to miss another opportunity to establish a territorial line with his daughter. "Jane." Adrien signaled her to leave before him.

Jane turned to Sam and said, "Good evening." She glanced at Rose, who held the door for her, and opened her eyes wider to punish Rose for promoting bad advice, though Jane was also thankful. Where would she and Sam be now had it not been for those few dangerous and forbidden moments in his room?

"Mr. Pruitt, may I speak with you for a moment before you leave, sir?" Sam asked.

Adrien was very spent and told Sam, "Be quick."

"I also want to apologize for my conduct at your office today. I have been given a lot lately. I submitted myself to my pride, and I am ashamed. I hope it is not too late to express my gratitude."

Damn, Adrien thought, *if this boy does not reach new heights that far exceed his lowest low.* Instead he answered, while putting on his gloves and looking out the door, "Mr. Callahan, few if any men make it out of life without sending or receiving some kind of serious breach. It's how they respond to it that exposes what defines them." Adrien looked directly at Sam. "Apology accepted." And he walked out.

While Mr. Pruitt and Jane were talking in the parlor, Rose had prepared a basket of breads and jams. She caught Adrien off guard when she followed him out and offered it to him. He received the basket cautiously, not because he didn't want to, but because it was the first time any such gesture had been made toward him of this kind, and it left him reaching for what to say.

"Thank you, Rose," was all he could get out. Sam watched from the door while Jane watched from her carriage, and both were mindful to conceal their surprise. Rose walked back to her house seemingly a little taller, and she was grateful for the chance to finally express her appreciation of Adrien's regard for her that day at church.

*****

Sam did not have supper that night. He went back to his room and lay on his bed with one hand under his head and the other across his body while staring at the ceiling. He thought about what had taken place in his room with Jane: her words, her promise, her touch. "Admire," she had said, and he smiled. Admire? He dropped his smile, certain that Adrien did not share her view. Yet did he rightly recall Jane's father tell them both to exercise better judgment? If so, could that mean that he was blessing their mutual affection? Sam strained to remember what he heard Adrien say about a courtship and wanting to support their relationship and the land becoming prosperous toward their future. Yes, Adrien had conceded that he understood their relationship would be long term. Sam tapped his fingers in his chest.

Sam's mind continued to race for the next hour or so. His eyes danced around in the dark while thinking thoughts he tried to ignore, but they persisted. "Fine!" he said, facing the truth. He lied to Adrien. It wasn't his pride he submitted to. It was something much deeper, much heavier. Such generosity from Mr. Coles and Adrien came with a burden he couldn't quite name. It worried him. He whispered, "For unto whomsoever much is given, of him shall be much required: and to whom men have committed much, of him they will ask the more." He winced with resentment over the gift. Why would they place such a burden on him? Rather, why did it seem like such a burden?

And then there was Jane. Why did he tell her to leave? Why did he try to force her out of his life? Why did her promise that she would never leave him also feel like such a burden? Sam's breathing became rapid as he realized that Jane was right, and he confessed, "Fear, that's why." Not pride, but fear. The same fear he had carried all of his life that he would fail at everything he touched. That was his thorn and now he knew it. And so did Satan.

Adrien's words screamed in his mind, *Few, if any, men make it out of life without sending or receiving some kind of serious breach. It's how they respond to it that exposes what defines them.*

What defines me? Sam wondered for the first time in his life. Was it his father? It couldn't be. Could it? If not, then what? He kept examining himself. What breach had he committed? For some time, he believed his breach was being born to Bishop Callahan. He squinted his eyes and rejected the notion. He had no control over that. *What do I control?* Sam wondered more. "My response," he said aloud. In fact, that was the only thing he could control, he concluded. Adrien said that his response would expose what defined him. But his response to what? What was his breach? What was Adrien so afraid of? He closed his eyes tightly, and then he opened them again, trying to see through the darkness, longing to understand. He prayed, "Tell me, Father." Then a realization began slowly to sink in. Sam sat up in bed and gazed blankly as his mind became more and more focused.

I no longer have a father, Sam remembered telling Reverend Hunt.

Yes, you do, Sam remembered the reverend telling him. *How will you respond?*

Sam's mind reached again for understanding. With a little more clarity, he began to realize that there had been no breach. And whether or not there would be a breach hinged on one thing: a choice. To whom would he be a slave?

So it is true—my father does define me, he realized. The question was, which one? Bishop? That would be the ultimate breach. That was what Adrien feared most, and that was what failure looked like to Sam.

"No," Sam said aloud and shook his head slowly to keep pace with his emerging awareness. "No," he declared and concluded. After a few minutes, he lay back down, closed his eyes, thanked his Father in heaven, and sank into a deep and restful sleep.

Chapter 7

Buck Saunderman and Sam were finished with their last day of work. Sam shook a few hands knowing he would see his friends again, but it was different for Saunderman. As Sam was mounting his horse to leave, he saw Saunderman encircled by the farm workers, and he waited patiently. After a few minutes, Saunderman rode up beside him.

"This is goodbye, Sam. I'm moving out," Saunderman said.

"Where will you go?" Sam asked. Saunderman looked west and squinted to endure the setting sun.

"The mountains," he said. Sam looked west briefly; he was finally able to understand this transient man, and he nodded. Saunderman pulled his hat down. "Would you do something for me?" he asked.

"Anything," Sam said, eagerly. A chance to do something for Saunderman was like finding an unexpected priceless gem in a deep, dark cave.

"Tell Rose I said goodbye." And that was just as unexpected. Sam found himself swimming in questions that he knew better than to ask. In character, Saunderman cut the moment short and extended his hand. Sam shook it, still dazed, and Saunderman affirmed, "You're ready," and he turned to leave.

On those words, Sam realized that Saunderman stayed because of him, to teach him as much as he could before answering his own call in life. "Saunderman!" Sam called out. Saunderman turned his horse around. "Thanks...for everything. I mean it," Sam said.

Saunderman nodded, and he rode away. "It's Mr. Saunderman to you, Callahan," said his distant voice. Sam laughed, but it faded quickly as he watched a major source of stability ride out of his life.

*****

Rose did not ordinarily join guests at the supper table, but it had become normal for her and Sam to eat together and talk. Sam ate quietly but stared at Rose throughout his meal. Rose tried to ignore it, but when she finished eating, she stared back at Sam as if to make it a game. Sam smiled and broke away.

"Ha!" she said. "I win." Sam resumed his stare. "All right. Are you going to tell me what's on your mind?"

Sam squinted as he searched for the perfect delivery. "Mr. Saunderman left today. He's headed for the mountains." Sam watched for her response.

"Well, it was only a matter of time. Buck has been headed for the mountains for years," Rose said as she abruptly picked up the plates and went into the kitchen. Sam noticed her use of Saunderman's first name and followed her.

"He very specifically asked me to tell you goodbye," Sam said. Rose set the plates down and gazed as she recalled something from the past, something like a choice.

"Well, I would think he could have done something that simple himself," Rose said with a forced smile.

"Rose—"

"Let it be, Sam," Rose said firmly. And though he didn't want to, he let it be.

*****

Nathan had been away visiting Elizabeth in Quincy. He asked Sam to join him for a drink. Sam stepped up to the bar at the tavern and reached into his pocket for money, but Nathan beat him to it.

"You can owe me," Nathan said.

"I don't want to owe you. I can pay for my own beer," Sam said.

"Well, I do want you to owe me. It keeps you on the hook for a future seat with me in a tavern somewhere!" Nathan insisted. Sam wasn't sure what that meant, but he brushed it off as part of Nathan's drama.

They sat and drank and talked and laughed for a solid hour before there was a lapse. Sam set his beer down and stared at Nathan, who had seemingly entered into a trance. "I deeply admire my father," Nathan said. "Deeply." Then he turned his attention back to Sam.

"As do I. *Your* father, I mean," Sam said in earnest.

"We don't always see eye to eye, but I would never intentionally disappoint him," Nathan said.

Sam sat up. "I can't imagine you ever being a disappointment to your father," he said and wondered where Nathan was going with his point.

Nathan relieved the seriousness with a smile. "What's next, Sam? Will you work for my father?" Nathan resumed his normal demeanor as he drank his beer and was a bit surprised when Sam nodded no. "Do you have a plan?"

"As a matter of fact, I do," Sam said, calm and relaxed.

Nathan leaned forward for details, but Sam offered none. Nathan smiled in his defeat, and then he stood up from his seat, threw back the last of his beer, and prepared to depart. "Well, I have a plan too! Come by for supper tomorrow. I'll be announcing it then." Nathan made a face to Sam suggesting it was quite a secret.

Sam leaned back in his chair and delivered a smirk. "An announcement, you say? Have you been holding something back from your old friend?" Sam asked in reference to the growing expectation for Nathan to marry Elizabeth.

"Don't worry." Nathan laughed. "It will all be clear tomorrow night. You can come, I assume." Nathan was glowing.

"I wouldn't miss it," Sam said. As he watched Nathan leave, he placed his hand on his breast pocket and felt his plan coming closer too.

*****

The next night, Sam was greeted at the door by Esther, who was excited about Nathan's news.

"Mistah Sam, please come help me. I can't get Miss Jane out the kitchen. She been in there all day thinkin' she's helpin'." Esther looked up at Sam, shaking her head. Jane was an excellent cook and everyone knew it. She planned the extensive menu for the evening of celebration, and she thought it nothing short of cruel to leave its preparation to Esther alone.

"I'll do my best, Esther." Sam laughed.

Sam entered the kitchen but remained in the doorway. He saw Pierre polishing the silverware for each place setting. Pierre looked up at Sam, and Sam lifted his chin as a greeting. Pierre tilted his head toward Jane, and he shook his head, thinking this was no place for the lady of the house. But he also knew Jane would never ask him nor Esther to do anything she would not be willing to do herself. She was typically by their sides during their workdays sharing in the chores.

Jane was in her day dress and apron, and she was so feverishly at work that she did not know Sam was there. Sam looked at Esther and shook his head to mean no as he waved his hands back and forth. As he let the kitchen door close, he saw Esther put her hands on her tiny hips and look at him as if betrayed.

Jane stepped back and looked at the beautiful outcome of her and Esther's effort, which was ready to be presented. She made two fists of joy and hugged Esther. Esther suspected that the meal was more about impressing Sam than celebrating Nathan's news, and she was right.

"Miss Jane, please go get cleaned up. I'll take it from here," Esther insisted. Jane agreed and retreated quickly to prepare herself for supper.

It was not long before Jane entered the room where Adrien, Nathan, and Sam were standing and sharing conversation. Sam was stunned by her transformation from what he had seen in the kitchen just moments before. *How did she do it?* he wondered. He could smell her perfume as she passed close by him to take her seat at the table. He secretly inhaled her lingering scent, and he was certain she did that on purpose. Everyone sat down, including Esther and Pierre.

Conversation bounced back and forth during supper for quite a while until Adrien took over and said, "All right, Nathan, we have waited long enough. Please satisfy our curiosity and make your announcement."

Nathan was still smiling from the previous discussion and wiped his mouth with his napkin as he made the transition to his news. "You're right, Father. I have instilled enough anticipation, and I should get on with it." He sat up tall in his chair as all eyes were on him. He looked at his father, who sat at the other end of the long table, and announced with pride, "Father, I plan to volunteer."

All at once, everyone became silent and still. Adrien looked at Jane and Sam but realized they knew nothing of this, as they had dropped their smiles to expressions of confusion.

"Volunteer?" Adrien asked after a brief pause as he tried to hide his shock. "Volunteer for what?" But he knew exactly what Nathan meant. He was stalling so he could think. The engagement announcement faded quickly from everyone's mind. Pierre and Esther shared looks of concern.

"For the militia under General Atkinson. I intend to help squash the Indian rebellion," Nathan said.

"What Indian rebellion?" Adrien asked dismissively and continued to eat. The scene reminded Sam of his last family supper.

"Well, Black Hawk and his band of warriors have returned to Illinois to resettle—"

"*Chief* Black Hawk, you mean—a title of respect that he earned at the age of twenty-one, which came quickly to him as one who became a brave at the tender age of fifteen. If that does not suit you, you may refer to him as *General* Black Hawk, a title he earned from the British in the War of 1812. Let your first lesson, in or out of the militia, be a healthy sense of respect for the perceived enemy."

"The perception, Father, is real. *Chief* Black Hawk is directly violating the treaty. Are you not aware?" Nathan asked him, surprised.

Sam was searching his memory for any hint Nathan might have given in previous discussions; he did not see this coming, but his conversation with Nathan in the tavern now made sense.

"The disputed treaty," Adrien asked in near protest, "justly disputed for nearly thirty years now? Is that the violated treaty you speak of?"

"They signed the treaty. They ceded their lands. What is there to dispute?" Nathan lifted his chin, somewhat arrogantly.

"Son, it is you that are not aware. The 1804 Treaty of St. Louis was drafted with deceit by men who knowingly dealt with tribal members who had no authority to deal. Then they got the tribal members drunk and shamefully tricked them into selling away the tribe's lands for pennies on the dollar, thus leading to the forced removal of the remaining Sauk nation rather than conducting a coherent and fair business arrangement. Furthermore, Chief Black Hawk pleaded relentlessly with every ear that would listen, including former Governor Coles, that his men never agreed to a treaty and no payment was ever made. Even Governor Coles aches for Chief Black Hawk and his people, but as *former* governor, he has no power to influence a fair resolve. And those that do have the power to influence, simply won't!

"This flawed treaty, Nathan, has been an ugly point of contention for Illinois and its native tribes since. Chief Black Hawk's people have been literally beaten off their ancestral lands, and now he is moving back with his warriors and with his tribe's women and children, many of whom are starving. And that calls for military action? Wouldn't a fair renegotiation of the treaty suffice?" Adrien was educating his son, but it was Sam that was benefitting, watching, and listening closely as if he were a pupil in a school.

"Sir, they have formed alliances with other tribes. They are making trouble and mean to continue, and the very safety of our countrymen is threatened. Skirmishes have already occurred, and our neighbors fear for their lives. Some of them have already been killed, and some have already left. Governor Reynolds is forming the state's militia to fight, once again, the very nuisance you fought in the War of 1812!"

"Don't try to justify your ambition by somehow bonding it to me. I fought the British, not the Indians. And make no mistake, Nathan, the army will, quite easily, move Chief Black Hawk back across the river without any help from you. Put your thoughts on college where they belong. You'll be leaving in a few short months."

"Father, I must protest. As citizens, we must do something," Nathan was beginning to plead.

"It is what this nation has done, Nathan, that is precisely the problem!" Adrien struggled to contain himself. "Son, what is the purpose of an Indian treaty?"

Nathan begrudgingly obliged his father with a quick well-stated definition. "To arrive at an agreement between the United States government and Indians within territories where we have settled or want to settle for the mutual interest and security of all. What is your *point*, Father?"

"If *this* government really intended to honor and uphold Indian treaties, then why does President Jackson have a policy called 'Indian Removal'? How did President Jackson arrive, so arrogantly, at opposing a Supreme Court decision to protect Cherokee sovereignty in Georgia? He and a small group of opportunists cared not one bit about the law, about humanity, and certainly not about well-crafted treaties. President Madison's policy was to protect the Indians from losing their territory to expanding settlement. In contrast, under Jackson's authority, all Indians east of the Mississippi will be forced from their homes and to foreign lands west of the Mississippi, making void all treaties previously signed, even though all the Indians have upheld their end. *This* government does not care about the mutual interests built in these treaties; it cares only about its own interests, which is the often tireless and ruthless acquisition of other people's land!"

"But removal, Father, is exercised when treaties are broken." Nathan's relief that he could produce an answer was brief.

"Ha, indeed!" Adrien roared, in disgust. "Which the government has seen to most effectively. How do you think it will manage to rid all the land east of the Mississippi of Indians? It's called strategy, my son. Promises have been made, will be made, and will be broken, but not by the Indians who see treaties as their only hope of survival—rather, by authorities who fail to enforce them. Once the Indians are provoked by encroaching settlers, they rebel. And why should anyone be surprised? The real sadness is found in the twist: the government then justifies military action in response to conditions the government created. I predict, with confidence, that the worst is yet to come!"

"Nevertheless, Father, I am compelled to defend the nation of which I am a citizen! And I am simply seeking your blessing," Nathan said, refusing to yield.

Adrien remained still for a moment. He looked at the others in the room and adjusted his jaw. They all waited for his decision. Then Adrien stated plainly, "Well, you won't find it."

"Is nothing worth fighting for, Father?" Nathan reached on principle.

"There are many things worth fighting for, son. And yes, some include battles with Indians, some with foreign countries, some even with neighbors. But none which are connected to the evil of engaging in war begun on false pretenses, which is exactly what prompted this war." Adrien was reaching for Nathan's young mind.

"Am I to understand that you are opposed to dedicating your service to our country?"

"Watch your step, Nathan! I dedicate service to my country every day in subsequent response to my dedication to God, who guides my conscience and to whom my citizenship belongs first."

"Well," Nathan said with an exhale as he prepared to state what he thought was obvious, "the very God we serve has blessed the people of this nation with great abundance. Is service to one not the same as service to both?" Nathan leaned forward with his palm stretched out and raised in support of his logic, waiting for his father's answer. Adrien became limp in his chair, and after a moment, he turned his head away. Nathan looked at Sam as though he were the victor, but Sam knew better.

Adrien was now fifty-five. He was born at the onset of the Revolutionary War and was raised on the nation's enlightenment ideals, only the best of which seemed to be losing ground on the expanding nation. The Enlightenment gave root to reasoning and fine-sounding arguments that were so often used to propel selfish motives of the people, the states, and the nation. These motives produced sins that Adrien knew would eventually come with a price, as all sin does.

He believed firmly in natural law, which convicts humans of right and wrong regardless of their understanding of God. This further explained his friendship with Edward Coles as well as his advocacy of freedom and equality for all. In his mind, man's humanity was revealed only through the extension of God's commands and love. In contrast, man's inhumanity was evident throughout history and was a result of greed, often found in various forms of property ownership such as slaves and land and natural resources and wants upon wants, all of which were linked to money. Using God as a source to justify greed is a deadly sin.

Adrien arrived at a pivotal point in understanding that his son had departed from his upbringing. He wondered where he had failed. Was it when his wife died? Or was it he who departed from his children, unable to rear them as he had done prior to her death? Did he think they could naturally find their way through a world geared toward devouring people as when an animal eats its young? As he now watched his son put his entire future at risk, he found himself filled with remorse, and he was sorry to his wife for his shortsightedness. And the worst of his realizations was that now he was too late.

Sam was becoming anxious over his want to know Adrien's mind. *Slow down*, he thought, *I need more time to think about what you just said.* And what would Nathan do? Was he beyond his father's reach? How could he be? Did he not know what he had in this man, his father, especially having been witness to the likes of Bishop Callahan?

Jane looked at Sam. She felt him studying the exchange, and she observed his mental battle. It was written all over his face. She held her focus on him until his eyes landed on hers at which time her thoughts revealed, *I know.*

"Please repeat your question, Nathan," Adrien said, rubbing his eyes.

"Sir?" Nathan was confused. He was sure he had articulated his point with perfection.

"Please. Your question, repeat it. I want to make sure you heard yourself."

Nathan paused. He looked around the room wondering if he was the only one tiring of Adrien Pruitt. "I said"—he lowered his head, opened his eyes fully, and raised his eyebrows, feeling quite badgered—"the very God we serve has blessed the people of this nation with great abundance. Is service to one not the same as service to both?"

Adrien waited, hoping that his son would finally grasp the ongoing flaw in his thinking, but it did not happen. So he said, "What people, exactly? I ask because I doubt very seriously that the Indians feel blessed with great abundance as they are forcibly moved year after year to new soil. I doubt very seriously that the slaves feel blessed with great abundance as they work the fields. And what about the Mexicans? Are they not all people of this nation? Please spare me the proposition that we can justify inhumane and unfair treatment toward various peoples based on their blocked citizenship to this nation. And please spare me the proposition that all American labor and expansion is a gift from God. As the government motivates its citizens to embrace some kind of destiny to occupy and govern the entire stretch of land, coast to coast, you should be reminded, somewhat fearfully, Nathan, that we reap what we sow. I am stunned by how little you know of God's nature, especially with the parenting and tutoring you have had. There is no sign that you have thought this through, yet you present what thoughts you have so freely." Nathan was feeling the full effect of being no match for his father. Adrien continued with escalated frustration. "The blessings, Nathan, to which you refer are not the result of divine design but the result of man's self-assigned dominion over others. One fist is larger than the other, which has been the case since the fall of man—a reflection of man's nature, to be sure, but certainly not a reflection of God or man operating within God's will!"

Pierre raised his hand to fully cover his mouth, in awe.

"Father! How am I to look my countrymen in the eye if I do nothing to defend them in their hour of suffering?" Nathan took his final stand, though knowing fully that he had already been defeated.

Adrien came to his feet with force, still holding his glass of wine. "Please clear my confusion! It's not an Indian rebellion or your loyalty to the country or the safety of your countrymen that drives your passion for war. It's your personal honor you mean to defend. Perhaps if we give you more time you will have several new reasons. Do you really even know why you are volunteering?"

Nathan just stared. Yes, he knew why he was volunteering. He knew, and that was all that mattered.

Pruitt then yelled, "You will be able to look them in the eye, Nathan, based on two principles...," but when he thrust his wine glass forward to emphasize his point, his glass suddenly burst under the pressure of his grip, and wine and glass slivers sprayed his place setting. He winced in pain when he opened his hand to find a large piece of glass protruding from his palm from which blood dripped on the white tablecloth. Jane and Esther ran to his aid. Sam backed his seat up to rise but remained seated, certain that Adrien was not finished, and he did not want to interrupt the momentum further. "Damn," Adrien said, "look at this mess. I am terribly sorry, Esther. This discussion has caused me to lose my temper."

"That's all right, Mistah Pruitt. I can clean this up," Esther said, placing her hand on his back and under his forearm. Adrien's hand shook as he pulled the glass piece from his palm.

"Father, come to the kitchen and let me mend this," Jane said as she covered his hand with a napkin and pushed him gently. Sam panicked internally. What were the two principles? He had to know. Nathan, though, was relieved.

Adrien pulled away from Jane. "Just a minute!" he barked. "I want to answer Nathan's question." Now Sam was relieved, and Nathan was disappointed to have to endure any more. "What was it you said? How will you be able to look your countrymen in the eye if you do not engage in this war? Something like that, was it? First, that you guarded your honor by refusing to lunge into a war that is the consequence of and rooted entirely in greed. Second, you will be able to look your countrymen in the eye because you will be *alive* to do so!" Adrien held the napkin over his hand to catch the dripping blood and left the room with Jane, Esther, and Pierre.

Nathan continued to look ahead as if his father were still sitting in front of him. "Not if Black Hawk has anything to say about it," he said. Then he left the table.

Sam sat alone at the table and reflected on yet another dismantled family dinner. He placed his hand on his breast pocket, reached inside, and pulled out a ring, which he had intended to give this night to Jane.

In the kitchen, Esther and Pierre were still with Jane cleaning and wrapping Adrien's hand when Sam joined them.

"Father, surely he will reconsider, having not gained your blessing," Jane said.

"Sam, it's late," Adrien said, ignoring what even Jane knew was wishful thinking. Sam took that to mean that the evening was over, and he should probably return to his home, but he was surprised when Adrien said, "Please stay the night. Use the guest room." Adrien knew he was sending Sam a much stronger message; he was allowing Sam to navigate within the boundaries he set around Jane just days before. Sam knew it too.

Sam looked at Jane, who stood up from helping her father while displaying an expression of hope that he would agree. Her eagerness made him very aware that he was in the midst of another test.

"Thank you, sir. That will ease my burden tonight." Or so he hoped.

Later that night, Jane knocked on Nathan's door. There was no answer. "Nathan, let me in." She knocked again and called to him.

"Not now, Jane," she heard him growl.

Sam's room was across the hall, and he heard Jane at Nathan's door. He reached for his door to open it, but withdrew, knowing it would lead to another disaster. And he stepped back.

Jane knew she has been sufficiently loud to draw Sam's attention. She faced his door wondering briefly why he had not explored the noise. She stepped back and walked to her room.

Sam could not sleep. Sam knew that some things were indeed worth fighting for. He was already experienced in that. But what did he know about following his own conscience? How and when did Adrien come to understand such things about himself so comfortably?

Sam threw his covers back and sat on the edge of the bed, resting his head in his hands. Surely, Nathan was thinking some of the same thoughts and was grinding his mind to understand what his father was saying. But no, he wasn't. Sam heard Nathan leave his room, which was soon followed with the sound of his horse.

Adrien sat quietly in the dark in mental conversation with God, with his wife, and with Nathan as a child as if to torture himself by wondering what words he had left out of his many talks with his son. His presence went completely unnoticed by Nathan, who descended the stairs and walked on near tiptoe to the door that he so quietly closed between sense and madness.

Soon thereafter, Adrien was somewhat surprised to see Sam also descend the stairs, walk to the fireplace mantel, and place a letter conspicuously for Jane's eyes.

"You too, Sam?" Adrien asked, impassively. Sam turned abruptly in the direction of the voice and saw Adrien's silhouette sitting at the dining table, where hours before, blood was spilled.

"Mr. Pruitt, I just heard Nathan leave. He's going to volunteer."

"You can't stop him, Sam," Adrien affirmed.

"No." Sam agreed. Adrien squinted his eyes. Sam came to the table and sat down.

Adrien lit a lamp. "You mean to be his guardian, don't you?" Sam was quiet. "It's foolishness, Sam." Sam was still quiet. "What if you don't return, or worse, if I may be so candid, what if you come back maimed? What then?"

"I feel called, sir. I don't know how to explain it except to say that I would not be able to live with myself if something happened to him, and I did nothing. He's a brother to me. I cannot abandon him."

"Even though he wants you to?" Adrien asked, which he knew was true, he just couldn't put his finger on why.

Sam thought for a moment, once again needing time to process Adrien's words when there was no time to spare. If Nathan got too far ahead of him, he would miss his chance to ensure they would be assigned together. All he could think to say was, "I will return, Mr. Pruitt. With Nathan." And he left.

"We shall see, Mr. Callahan," Adrien whispered.

Jane heard a door close. She opened her eyes and got up to look out the window, but it was dark and foggy.

Adrien could hear Jane knock on Nathan's door, then Sam's. He rubbed his fingers over his eyes, bracing himself for her coming grief. She was in a white nightgown, and her long dark curls covered her back and blew gently behind her as she raced down the stairs. Her bare feet made no sound when she came around the corner and found her father looking at her, clearly depleted. Her eyes were wide and fearful. She blinked once and swallowed, afraid to ask any questions.

"He left a note for you on the fireplace," Adrien said. He watched her open it, read it, then drop it on the floor before she fell at his feet and cried in his lap.

*****

Sam caught up to Nathan and rode ahead of him to block the dark narrow path. Nathan's horse came to an abrupt halt. "Why are you doing this, Nathan?" Sam yelled.

Nathan spun his horse around. "You heard my reasons, Sam. You know why I am doing this. Now move out of my way!"

"You're afraid. Why don't you face it? You saw what happened to your father, and you can't face the possibility of it happening to you. Better to throw it away than risk any suffering that comes with it."

"Shut up, Sam! You would have to have something to lose to understand! It was easy for you to lose what you had."

"You're right, Nathan, it was easy to lose *nothing*." Sam spoke falsely, but what he said next was the solid truth. "What's hard is losing *something*, and the very idea of it scares you to death! Only a coward would run from the love of his family and friends and a beautiful woman because he is too afraid of the pain it will bring when it's gone!"

"Coward? Is that what you're calling me as I leave for war?" Nathan defended himself and breezed past Sam's point.

"You're not leaving for war! You're running for your life! This is the ultimate retreat! Choosing the militia as your hiding place only makes it ironic, not brave!"

Nathan backed his horse up a distance, and dug in his heels, intent on ramming Sam out of the way. But instead, it brought them both to the ground. Nathan wanted to make sure Sam stayed out of his way, once and for all. Before Sam even made it to his feet, Nathan slugged him and back down he went. Sam came up on his hands and knees and spit blood from his mouth.

"Get up!" Nathan yelled.

When Sam came to a stand, he didn't even try to block the next blow. Down he went again. Nathan walked around him just waiting for him to stand. Sam was a little slower getting up for a third time, but once stable, he stood before Nathan, ready for more. Nathan slugged him in the gut, and he threw another swing across his face, breaking the skin on his cheekbone. Sam went down hard again, coughing. He lay there for a moment, forced to acknowledge Nathan's powerful rage; then he worked his way back to his feet. Blood ran from his nose, mouth, and cheek. Between heavy breaths, he spit again and waited.

Nathan began to realize that he was dealing with a man who was used to taking beatings. After a moment, he lowered his fists in defeat and bent over with his hands on his knees to support himself. Sam continued to wait, trying to remain stable on his feet.

Finally, Nathan told the truth. "There was blood everywhere," he said factually. "She screamed in agony for over an hour. The baby never even showed. We lost them both, and there was nothing we could do. Father shook her over and over again, calling out her name even long after she was gone. The hole it left in our lives was devastating." Nathan came up off his knees. "I can't go through anything like that again. That's why I have to let my father and sister go. And Elizabeth. And you. And even God, who was *clearly* busy that day. You're damn right it scares me to death. And watching Jane wear herself out crying and praying day after day, night after night over the thought of losing you brought it all back. Nothing is worth that. Nothing," Nathan finished.

Sam wiped the blood off his mouth with his sleeve. Nathan's horrific description of that awful day pierced his mind, and he grieved silently for his friend. But he said, "You're wrong, Nathan. It's all worth it. Even knowing now how it would end, your father would go through it all again."

"Well, not me," Nathan said coldly, and he mounted his horse.

"If you go, I'm going with you."

"Suit yourself," Nathan said. Then he abruptly rode off.

Chapter 8

Nathan enlisted into the Fourth Regiment of Mounted Volunteers, a rifle company, for no reason other than it was not a draw for men from Madison County, making the distance from his home and family more secure. Sam simply followed Nathan's lead. They didn't even know what that meant other than being surrounded by highly charged volunteers who were eager to kill Indians, some of whom joked that Sam looked as though he had already been in battle.

Sam rubbed his tired eyes and rotated his sore jaw, and he felt the cut on his cheek, knowing it would leave a scar. Another scar. Then he became distracted by an excited gathering, and he moved in to see what was happening.

"Cast your votes, men! Will it be Abraham Lincoln or William Kirkpatrick?" one of the volunteers announced as he walked through the crowd handing out torn pieces of paper and pencils.

"What's going on?" Sam asked another volunteer.

"Votin' to see who the comp'ny cappin'll be," he answered. Sam watched but did nothing with his ballot. "Ainchya gonna vote?" the volunteer asked Sam.

Sam shook his head and said, "I don't know them."

"What? What county you from?"

"Madison," Sam answered.

"How'd you end up in this comp'ny?" Sam shrugged his shoulders and realized that was a good question. In fact, how did he end up there at all?

The volunteer took Sam's paper and pencil out of his hand and filled it in. Then he moved through the crowd to submit the votes. Sam never knew whose name he wrote. After a while, there was a roar in the crowd, and Abraham Lincoln won by a landslide. Sam watched on. He had never seen someone surrounded by so much support, yet his new captain seemed humbled by it rather than prideful. Sam almost smiled, and it was that day that he decided to embrace his experience in the militia.

*****

Sam kept to himself and kept quiet except when it came time for drills, which was all his company did for the first two weeks. Several men left before the first phase of drills was complete. He was tempted to leave, as well. Just like on the farm, he recognized how little he knew about his surroundings, so he did what Saunderman told him to do: he paid attention. "Just do as you're told and get home alive," he counselled himself.

Nathan, though, showed no signs of wanting to go home. He was home. He bonded well with the other men and maintained a withdrawn position from Sam, which was difficult for Sam to endure. He had hoped that he could shield Nathan and eventually return him to his family, but Adrien was right; Nathan didn't want Sam to shield him.

Captain Lincoln watched and participated in the drills. He observed each man's response to the drill commands and the demands of militia life. He listened to their conversations, their songs, and even their silence. When initial training was complete, he and his two officers, First Lieutenant Thompson and Second Lieutenant Brannan, inspected his men. He paused on Sam's face, which had not quite healed. "What is your name?" he asked.

"Private Callahan, sir. Samuel."

Lincoln nodded and continued his inspection. When he was finished, he released all of the men, except one. "Private Callahan, a word, please," and he led Sam to his tent. Lincoln positioned two chairs facing each other, and they both sat down. "What led to your wounds?" Lincoln asked, and he watched Sam think.

"A disagreement, sir." Sam watched Lincoln think.

"Was the disagreement with a man in my company?" Sam's eyes looked away. "I saw no other man with the marks of a disagreement."

Sam said, "With respect, sir, I prefer not to say."

"Hmm. I find myself concluding that you are either not a good fighter, or you let your opponent win. In either case, you present an integrity and a discretion that I want to keep close by. I am assigning you to be my personal aide." Sam was surprised. "But I won't require you to accept. You need to know that you won't sleep much. You'll take care of my needs, great and small. And you must be in a state of readiness around the clock and conduct yourself with the integrity and discretion that you seem to possess. Please take a moment to consider the offer before you make your decision."

And Sam did take a moment. Then he said, "I accept, sir."

"Pitch your tent next to Lieutenant Thompson," Lincoln said.

*****

A soldier tore his tent apart looking for his pocket watch. Another soldier searched for his shoes. And another soldier could not find any of his money. Each of them looked at the other soldiers suspiciously. The air was thick with anger.

Sam waited outside of his captain's tent to secure the privacy needed therein for a meeting between Lincoln and his officers. Although they kept their voices down, Sam could hear the discussion.

Brannan said, "We have received orders, sir, to increase security immediately."

Thompson said, "Two other camps are having the same problem. It could pass as lost or missing items were the problem not so widespread."

"One thing is certain, Captain, there is a thief among us," Brannan said.

"Perhaps even more than one," Lincoln added.

Thompson said, "This kind of thing will destroy trust and morale rapidly. All order will be lost before the first battle is even fought!"

"Order is paramount," Lincoln agreed calmly. "I want each man to know he is instrumental to the solution of stopping this madness by following the order of security and protecting the camp and company overall. Gentlemen, you advise the corporals and sergeants—quietly, though. Leave the privates to me."

As the officers left, Sam was summoned inside. Lincoln sat at his table, thinking, and he tapped his knuckles on the table so gently that they made no sound. Sam remained at attention. Knowing Sam had heard every word, he continued the discussion where it was left with the officers. "Sam, I don't think mustering the men and announcing the security order is best. Let's be less overt. Can you effectively give word from tent to tent that all men are to secure their belongings tightly and keep a sharp eye for suspicious movement? If the culprit is somehow unaware that we are expecting him, we might just catch him."

"Of course, sir," Sam answered, but inside, he dreaded it, knowing he would have to face Nathan, who made it clear that he did not want to face Sam.

The next day, Sam walked from tent to tent and quietly delivered the orders to which each man nodded with understanding. Nathan sat before a wooden box he was using as a table while he meticulously cleaned his rifle. He was so engrossed in his work that he did not see Sam approach. Sam stood by the fire and waited, during which time another soldier came out of his tent.

"Callahan! What brings you to the low country?" Nathan's tentmate jabbed in fun, and Sam forced himself to smile. Nathan looked up, saw Sam, and immediately looked back down at his rifle's parts.

Sam walked to Nathan, knelt down, and signaled the other soldier to join him. He said, "There's a thief making his way through all the camps." Nathan stopped cleaning his rifle and listened, almost as if he longed for such a moment. "We are all on orders to secure our personals as fully as possible. Be discreet. Look out for each other and for the tents around you. Watch for suspicious behavior and report it immediately to me or any superior. Let's get this guy."

"Damn right," the other soldier said. Nathan looked firmly at Sam for the first time since their fight, and his nod of agreement was like a breakthrough.

Sam came to his feet hoping for something more, anything more, but Nathan said nothing. Sam licked his lips and said, "All right then. Enjoy the rest of your evening. We'll be riding out first thing." And he left disappointed.

Sam returned to Lincoln's tent to finish packing his commander's belongings for the morning's departure. He looked inside the tent and found Lincoln sitting with his officers again. Before Sam could withdraw, Lincoln waved him inside. Sam continued with his duties while the officers talked.

Brannan spoke as if there had been no interruption, "So you're saying that Governor Reynolds is giving commands directly to Major Stillman without consulting General Atkinson at all?"

Thompson answered, "General Atkinson is en route now with his men and some regulars from St. Louis. He doesn't know that the governor is giving orders. His orders to Stillman were to secure the frontier without waiting on him to arrive."

Brannan continued, "I understand that the governor is a general and making a presence on the field, but it begs the question: who is in charge?"

Thompson answered, "We're still under General Whiteside and his brigade, but there is no indication that he has taken over command of Major Stillman or his forces."

"This is preposterous!" Brannan barked. "Major Stillman has almost no experience, and now he has received conflicting orders, which is worse than no orders at all! He might as well be orphaned!" Sam whipped a look at the lieutenant. Then he remembered his station and resumed packing. "It must be observed that any one of us could be in Stillman's shoes right now. I hope the governor will also take responsibility for the consequences!" The lieutenant looked at Lincoln and rebuked himself. "Pardon me, sir. I apologize."

"So," Lincoln summarized, "Major Stillman is being sent by the governor to persuade Chief Black Hawk to surrender. Could it work?"

The officers looked at each other, and Brannan began to say, "Well, I suppose it could—"

"No," Thompson interrupted. "It won't work because Chief Black Hawk thinks he has the support of the British. He won't withdraw as long as he thinks that."

"Does he have British support?" Lincoln asked.

Thompson was torn. "I seriously doubt that he does, but I am not convinced yet that he doesn't. Sources say that the British will not engage, but that might be just what they want us to think."

"Well, what now?" Brannan asked.

Lincoln answered, "The general's orders are to protect the frontier, so we are to continue to advance and meet up with Major Stillman."

As Lincoln's officers left the tent, Thompson looked over his shoulder at Sam to send him a visual message that his presence made him privileged and obligated to silence.

Lincoln sat quietly at his table, and Sam finished his tasks. He gently asked, "Will there be anything else, sir?"

Lincoln stood and answered, "I wish I knew how to answer that, Sam."

*****

Sam lay down in his cot. It was hot for May, and his tent was like an oven that held on to the day's heat. Beads of sweat surfaced on his forehead that seemed to originate from his brain, which raced. He thought of Jane. She never left his mind, but the world she lived in was so far away that it was hard for him to remember what it was like. He lit a candle and began to write her a letter, but his pencil froze. He couldn't figure out what to say, and he rubbed his face repeatedly like he was trying to bring something to the surface. Then he forced himself to just start writing.

Later that night, there was an outburst within the camp. There had been another robbery. A fight was about to break out with two men ready to pummel each other. The lieutenants, the sergeants, and Sam were nearing the chaos when Nathan diffused it, saying, "Maybe that's what he wants, this thief among us! Whoever he is, he will not come between us. Who's with me?" The two men looked at each other with everyone looking at them, and they lowered their fists.

Brannan said, "All right, men, break it up. Back to your tents. We have an early start tomorrow, so get some rest."

Thompson said, "Nice work, Private Pruitt."

Nathan scanned the group of dispersing men and met eyes with one who remained. It was Sam. "Words of wisdom, Nathan," he said. "*I* am with you."

Nathan started to speak but changed his mind and walked away.

The next morning, the heat hinted that the trip would be brutal, even on horseback. The men were sweating within minutes, but their journey was interrupted causing them to stop, and for a long time, they wondered why.

Whiteside's aide rode from the front of the line to the back to deliver the situation and orders to each commander of the long line of troops. He saluted Lincoln. "Yesterday, Chief Black Hawk lost hope for British support. With no weapons or provisions coming from the Brits, he sent three men to negotiate his return across the river, and it's said that they even carried a white flag. But Indian scouts were spotted nearby, and it caused a panic. There's talk that Major Stillman's men were drunk, that Black Hawk planned a skirmish, or that there was just some kind of misunderstanding. Whatever that case, Major Stillman's men fired upon the three messengers, killing one. It led to a battle last night. Many of the major's men lie dead, most of them in the field up ahead, all scalped and badly mutilated."

"Major Stillman and the rest of his men?" Lincoln asked.

"In fear, they disserted their camp along with all of their possessions and provisions. Major Stillman is reorganizing his men. Over fifty have gone missing. You are to move your company forward, sir. A burial party is being formed."

By the time Lincoln reached the field where Stillman's men were killed, their bodies were already baking in the hot sun. Walking across the gruesome field, Sam stayed close to Lincoln, his officers, and two of his sergeants who carried blankets. Lincoln knelt beside one man whose head had been split open with a hatchet and then scalped. He covered him with a blanket. Others had missing hands, feet, eyes, tongues, and one man's intestines were ripped out of him.

Nearby, Whiteside marked a spot in the field for the digging of a common grave. Lincoln volunteered his company for the detail. Nathan dug while Sam helped the corporals wrap the bodies in blankets. Sam had never lifted a dead body before, and it traumatized him more than the mutilations themselves. At one point, Sam was helping a corporal who lost his grip and dropped the body, causing the blanket to come loose. He raised his hands, backed up, and walked away, leaving Sam to figure it out.

"Hey! Where are you going?" Sam hollered but received no response. He looked as his fallen comrade, whose eyes and tongue had been cut out. He knelt beside him and gently wrapped him again in his blanket. He flagged down another soldier, and they moved the body to the burial site. Then he did it again and again, leaving behind pools and trails of blood.

There was a whistle beyond the field where two privates were waving their hands. Thompson said, "Sergeant Armstrong, go see what that's about. Take Private Callahan with you."

Sam and the sergeant rode their horses to the alarmed privates where they had discovered another body. The dead young private had run a good distance from the pursuing braves but fell under their force. He was laid to rest beside his commander, who left behind a wife and eight children. In all, twelve American men and three Sauk braves died in the first battle of the Black Hawk War.

Sam felt a heavy finality with each shovel of dirt that was thrown over the bodies. The demoralized army was silent during the brief ceremony that involved only a rifle salute. When it was over, Sam went to find his horse, and he saw a stranger rummaging through his saddlebags. He snuck up on him and put his pistol to the back of his head and cocked it. "Don't move," he said. Then he hollered for the first person he saw, "Lieutenant Thompson!"

When the lieutenant began walking over, he heard Sam say, "I'll take that," as he ripped some of his belongings out of the man's hand and put them back in his saddlebag. "Get on the ground." The man was forced all the way down with the help of an aggressive push from Sam's foot. Then Sam kept his foot and pistol on him until the lieutenant arrived.

"What's going on, Private Callahan?"

"I think we have our thief, sir," Sam said.

The lieutenant quickly pulled a kerchief out of his pocket, and as he tied the man's hands, he said, "General Whiteside and most of the commanders are already headed out to make camp. We'll bring him with us and let Captain Lincoln decide what to do with him."

When they raised him to his feet, the lieutenant was surprised by his youthful appearance. "How old are you?" he asked.

Sam noticed a long red birthmark that ran from his ear down his neck and beneath his shirt line. "The lieutenant asked you a question," Sam said, and he shoved him, but the young man did not answer. They put him on Sam's horse, and Sam rode with him, following the lieutenant.

When they arrived at camp, tents were going up, and Lincoln was already settled. As the lieutenant escorted Sam and the prisoner into the camp, the men became curious and followed them, Nathan included.

"Who ya got there, Sam? Is that the thief?" a man asked.

"It is, isn't it?" another man said.

"Get the captain! Callahan caught the thief!" said another man.

Excitement rose in the camp until Lincoln arrived, which settled everyone down. Sam and the lieutenant helped the man out of his saddle.

"Who do we have here, Sam?" Lincoln asked.

"He won't say, sir," Sam answered.

"My name is Francis Sterns, sir," the man said.

Lincoln raised his brows at Sam. "Bring him to my tent," Lincoln said. Thompson joined him.

The men gathered around Sam and cheered him on, but he politely withdrew to go set up his tent. Before long, he saw Sterns being escorted out of Lincoln's tent by two sergeants.

Thompson walked over to Sam and said, "He's just a kid. Sixteen is all. He said his father disappeared, and he has been stealing to help take care of his family. He didn't mean any harm, he said." The lieutenant rolled his eyes somewhat and rolled his shoulders as he looked up at the dark sky.

"What's going to happen to him?" Sam asked.

"Hard to say. The captain is having him bound to a tree under the watch and guard of two privates for two hours at a time. He'll face General Whiteside tomorrow. It doesn't look good."

Sam was noticeably weighed down. He tried to transition. "Can I help you set up your quarters? I'm almost finished here."

Thompson stared at Sam for a moment. Then he said, "It was a tough day, Sam, for all of us. If we don't all have nightmares tonight, then we're probably dead, too, and don't know it. Don't let it shame you. As for Sterns, you did a good thing there. Everyone is relieved to know it's over. You're not responsible for how it ends." Sam nodded. The lieutenant pulled a flask out of his breast pocket and removed the lid. "Do you want a drink? Might help you rest."

Sam shook his head. "No, thank you."

The lieutenant took a drink and said, "See you in the morning."

Sam finished with his tent and washed with lots of soap. It was late, but he didn't want to close his eyes. He set up his table and chair outside and lit a lantern so he could read the fine print in his Bible.

Nathan appeared, surprising Sam. "You were right, Sam. I ran. I was scared. I'm still scared, I confess," Nathan said.

"You used me," Sam said. "I was to be your replacement for Jane and your father. You promoted me to both of them from the beginning. You had it planned all along."

"No. Not from the beginning. Promoting you came naturally, not with ill intent. But over time, it was the only answer I could find. My friendship with you was drawing me back in to closeness with my father and Jane. You became the distraction I needed to break away, or so I thought. Oddly enough, you also became the distraction that brought me back."

"What do you mean? Have you changed your mind?" Sam asked.

"Not exactly. Mended it, perhaps. My mother's death ruined me. But your brutal honesty the night I left helped me face my foolishness. I am sorry for my outburst. You were just…in the way. But your being here has been a constant reminder of how confused I've been. I hated you for coming, but had you *not* come, I may have never corrected my thinking. I thank you, truly. And best of all, I'm able to pray again."

Sam adjusted himself in his seat. "So does this mean you're coming home?"

"No," Nathan assured.

Sam felt defeated. "I don't understand. You just said you corrected your thinking. Why continue to distance yourself?"

"I'm not anymore. I'm here aren't I, making amends? I've written to Elizabeth, begging for her forgiveness. I'm going to write father and Jane to express my regret for the way I left and make sure they know I love and miss them. But I like it here. I like the military, and I think I have found my place in the world, and I'm staying as long as they will allow. Maybe even make West Point my pick." He smiled. Sam ached in both relief and sadness, and Nathan's intuitive nature saw it. "If I see things clearly, Sam, you and I will be family soon. This is a new beginning," Nathan said. Then he looked over his shoulder to the sound of his name being called. "I have to go. It's my turn for watch. You're a hero, you know, for catching that thief." He turned to leave and after a few steps, he turned back around. While walking backward and pointing to Sam he said, "You still owe me a beer!" And they both laughed. Sam held his smile as he watched Nathan run to his post.

*****

Dawn was coming, and a soldier kicked the feet of his sleeping tentmate to stir him awake. "Wake up! We were supposed to be on watch hours ago."

The soldier sprang to his feet, alarmed. "Why didn't Pruitt wake us?" They dressed, grabbed their rifles, and ran to their post to relieve Nathan and the other soldier. When they arrived, they stopped cold in their tracks and stared. One soldier fired two shots in the air to alert the camp. Three more soldiers ran to join them, one of whom threw up.

Sam stood over Nathan who still gripped his rifle even though he rested in a puddle of his own blood from having his throat cut. The second guard's midsection was sliced open from his belly to his heart. His eyes were still open and seemed to express his pain. And the prisoner was gone.

Sam suddenly understood the soldier who dropped the corpse, backed away, and left the scene. *I can't take this*, Sam's mind said over and over and over. His body trembled.

Of all things to shake Sam from his daze, he heard someone say, "Indians did this."

He shook his head, squinted, and said, "What?"

Others repeated the accusation with excited hatred, and Thompson intervened just as Lincoln and Brannan arrived. He said, "Shut your mouths! If Indians had done this, these men would be scalped, as would the prisoner, who is now gone, and as would all of us! Not another word about Indians attacking our guards and releasing a prisoner! Is that understood? No such talk will interfere with an investigation." The lieutenant was furious, and he immediately began to reestablish order. "Sergeant, form a party to honor these men with some decent respect. When you're finished, meet me in my tent with details for my report."

"Yes, sir," the sergeant said and began choosing men to move the bodies. Thompson engaged Lincoln and Brannan privately to the side.

"Don't touch him," Sam said softly, but no one heard him. "Don't touch him," Sam said again louder, gaining some attention. Then he pulled the men away from Nathan and yelled, "I said don't touch him!" Everyone's eyes were fixed on Sam. "We have to send him home. Please. Just let me send him home." The sergeant looked at Lincoln, who gave a nod of approval.

Chapter 9

"Finally, a letter," Jane said to her father, Esther, and Pierre. She smiled.

"Well," Adrien said, "open it." She hesitated as they all stared at her. "Just share what you can. You can leave out the romance." And she blushed.

She read, "May 13, 1832. Over a week ago."

> Dear Jane,
>
> I've been sitting here trying to write, but it's hard to know what to say. I'm consumed with missing you, and I want to be home with you now, which helps me understand why men desert. But I also understand, now, the call of duty and an unspoken comradery that binds men together for war. Forgive me for staying.

She paused, and Adrien introspected.

> I am an aide to the commander, which fills every minute of every day, leaving little time to dwell—a blessing, surely.

She gasped a little when she read ahead silently. "He saw Nathan. He says,"

> I was able to see Nathan today, briefly. He is what every soldier should aspire to be. He drills with excellence, as though he had been born just for this. Men flock to him, knowing that if you must have someone beside you in battle, you would want it to be him. Please share that with your father.

Jane, Pierre, and Esther all smiled at Adrien, who simply nodded. Jane said, "He goes on to say,"

> I find myself in a peculiar state of mind, as I have no particular grievance with Black Hawk. An occasional hope that this will all end free of incident for both sides is later met with another day of marching and riding on, which is teaching me to purge all expectations, lest I fall into despair. Though still, I pray. I ask that you do the same.
>
> Time is a luxury here. I cannot write as often as I like. In the lapse of correspondence, know that...

She paused again, smiled, and continued,

> my day always begins and ends with thoughts of you and prayers for you. I keep focused on the day that I will see you again, which gives me endurance.
>
> Until next time, all my love,
> Sam

Her eyes read over the letter again. Esther rubbed her back, and everyone moved on with the day. The letter revived Jane, and she went about her household chores humming, while Esther and Pierre went about theirs.

*****

Esther batted the dust out of a rug that she hung over the front porch railing. The sun was setting, and it was hard for her to make out the wagon approaching the house. She stood all the way up and placed her hand over her eyes to shade the sun. Then she took several steps back. "No," she whispered.

Jane was in the kitchen ironing linen she had just taken off the line. Esther walked in and looked sorrowfully at her. "There's a wagon comin'," she said.

Jane stared at Esther's frightened expression. She stopped all movement to the point of scorching the tablecloth under her hot cast-iron. When she saw smoke rising, she lifted the iron quickly and put it back on the stove. She moved to the hallway by the stairs and hollered for her father with a calm voice intent on rejecting the painful reality soon to arrive on her doorstep.

Just as Adrien came down the stairs, he saw through the open front door the wagon coming to a stop near the porch steps; it was carrying a casket, and a horse was tied to the rear. He waited a moment, glanced at Jane and Esther, and then stepped outside, shutting the door behind him.

Jane and Esther waited in silence. Jane tried not to think, tried not to picture who was dead, knowing that neither outcome would bring her any relief. The door slowly opened, and the wagon continued to town with the casket to arrange for the burial, leaving the horse behind.

"Our Nathan is gone," Adrien simply stated. "Here, a letter for you from Sam." Adrien handed it to Jane without looking at her and slowly walked back upstairs.

Esther began to cry deeply. "Only God knows why," she said several times through her wails and made her way to Jane's arms. Jane held on to Esther, but she did not cry.

"It's getting late," she said to Esther with kindness but free of emotion. "Why don't we leave the rest for later. I think Pierre is still chopping wood. I'll let him know." Esther tried to wipe her tears, but she couldn't keep up with them.

When Jane was finally alone, she looked at the letter, ripped it open, and read.

May 16, 1832

My dearest Jane,
There are no words… With the sadness of a broken heart, please forgive me.

Love,
Sam

She walked back into the kitchen, set the letter on the table, and continued with her ironing. One item after another underwent the aggressive press of her iron just as one thought after another underwent the aggressive press of her anger. She remembered that last supper and how Nathan spoiled the evening for everyone. She was furious with him for leaving and was certain that Sam would be with her now had Nathan not so selfishly snuck off to war. Why wouldn't he listen to the wisdom of their father? How could his loyalties be so confused? She concluded that she would blame him forever for the suffering his decision would bring their family. She was sickened that he put Sam in a position to have to write such a painful letter that would now be a memory of grief planted in their relationship.

She pushed the iron back and forth. She looked over at the letter on the table and thought about Sam's choice of words, "There are no words…" He was right because she would never again have a chance to say any words to Nathan. She could never scream at him for dying; she would never again be able to speak to him about how she missed their mother, about how thankful she was for their father, about how she loved Sam, and how she loved him. And she hated him for taking that from her. She stopped ironing, picked up the letter, and ripped it just below "There are no words" because it reflected perfectly the way she felt. Then she burned the rest of the letter in the stove and condemned Nathan for Sam's sadness. She watched it disappear and asked bitterly, "Why did you have to go, Sam?"

The general's letter of condolence was written as well as any such letter could be. Adrien read it and pondered, "Died bravely during this Indian engagement." He was briefly conflicted as a flame of anger tried to rise toward Black Hawk's band, which he suppressed. Nathan made his choice, and this war did not make him a victim. Or did it? Adrien read the letter again and asked, "'Died bravely during this Indian engagement?'" But he was not scalped, he observed. His anger was beginning to rise again but not at Black Hawk. What wasn't the army telling him? He suppressed another rising conflict. What did it matter how he died? Adrien closed his eyes. Swimming in blame was dark and pointless. Nothing would bring his son back.

"Oh God! Not my son," Adrien said as he wrestled with his grief.

Adrien was no stranger to war. He had written such letters himself during the War of 1812. He recalled that his wife was pregnant with Nathan when he left for the conflicts in Upper Canada under the leadership of Lieutenant Colonel Winfield Scott, and he confessed to himself that he was not unlike Nathan on that day: eager to serve, eager to defend, and thirsty for blood, right up until he saw it. But it was not his blood. Because of his age and status, he was put in command where he led others into battle, and sometimes unsuccessfully. And then he wrote painfully sad letters to mothers. Among the hardest of his letters were the ones he wrote to the mother of his own newborn son where he tried to explain that the brutal fight was absolutely necessary for the future of their young country, which was at very real risk of falling back into the hands of the British. *That*, he thought, *was worth fighting for.*

By the turn of the nineteenth century, immigrants had been flooding into Indian territory surrounding the Great Lakes, and no different than in the original colonies, tribal land would be lost to these new occupants. Most of the Indians in the territory had grown bitter from dishonest dealings with Americans, including Black Hawk, so they sided with the British during the War of 1812 in order to preserve their future. But soon they would learn that it was hopeless, and their loyalty to the British would prove costly as it prolonged the war, contributing to American casualties, the wounds and losses of which were still fresh in American minds that were now engaged in the Black Hawk War.

"Consequences," Adrien said. Numerous and sometimes bad or broken treaties drove Indian support to the British, America's first and current enemy, which then further drove American forces to rise up fiercely against the Indians, as with the present Black Hawk rebellion. "We live in a world of consequences, and ideals ignite them," Adrien whispered. It was often difficult to discern sound ideals from twisted ones. Was Nathan blinded by it all? It disturbed Adrien that he knew so little about his son's true motives.

*****

The war against Black Hawk continued, but some of the militiamen were being released. Colonel Atkinson's handling of the war frustrated President Jackson, so General Winfield Scott was called to action with federal soldiers. Sam's unit was mustered out on May 27, 1832. The very next day, his commander, Captain Lincoln, reenlisted as a private when the troops were reorganized under federal service. Sam's cause was different, though, and now gone. So he went home.

As Sam prepared to leave, he said farewell to his commander. "You were surrounded with corporals and sergeants. You never needed me as your aide," Sam stated.

"No," Lincoln confessed.

"Why did you do it?" Sam asked.

"Because you needed to be an aide. You didn't bond with the other men. You didn't follow drills with drinking or gambling or wrestling. You quietly retreated alone somewhere and often read your Bible. You didn't come here for the conflict with Black Hawk. You came for a different conflict," Lincoln said.

Sam looked down and said, "And I still lost."

Lincoln asked, "Did you?" Sam looked up at him, curiously. "Time will tell."

"Well nonetheless, it's been an honor," Sam said, trying to smile.

"It certainly has, Sam. I hope our paths cross again."

*****

The ride to Edwardsville was painful, slow, and long for Sam while he blamed himself for Nathan's death. He snuck into the boardinghouse unnoticed and made his way to his room. He searched scripture seeking relief, and he prayed, "Father, search me and tell me the truth," which drove him to deep grief and tears. But he pulled himself together, cleaned himself up, and changed his clothes. He quietly retrieved his buried treasure and hung his satchel across his body. He stood at his door for a moment to build his courage before leaving to face the Pruitts.

Esther answered the knock at the door and could hardly move when she saw Sam. "Oh, Mistah Sam! Thank God, you' safe! We been so worried! Git yourse'f in here!" Esther's greeting eased Sam's nerves. Pierre came to the entryway and was just as happy to see him.

"Sam, Miss Jane and Mistah Pruitt will be so pleased to know you are back." Pierre shook Sam's hand.

"It's very nice to be back and hard at the same time," Sam confessed.

"These are hard times," Pierre confirmed. "Jane and her father are in town at supper with the mayor. He called on them to try to ease their sorrow. They didn't really want to go but felt they should. They'll be home soon. Let's sit in the kitchen. Can I fix you something to eat?"

Sam sat down, heavily. "No, thank you, Pierre. How is Danny? I thought of him often while I was away," Sam asked.

"He's fine," Esther said, and she tapped Sam's forearm as if to thank him for asking. "He'll be so glad to know you' home. He been worryin' 'bout you. He wish he could o' volunteered, too, but... you know..." Esther shook her head to convey that she knew blacks could not join the militia.

"It's better that he didn't volunteer," Sam said.

"What was it like, Mistah Sam? The war?" Esther asked. Before Sam could answer, Pierre scolded her with a disapproving look.

"That's all right, Pierre. I don't mind. There's not much to tell. For me, it was short and boring. Lots of advancing, no fighting for us. Others, though, saw the brutal side of war and did not fare so well, especially those we buried." Esther and Pierre watched Sam stare for a moment as his memories stirred. He was pulled from his thoughts by some noise at the front of the house.

"Sam? Sam? Where are you?" Jane's voice yelled from the entry-way. She saw his horse as the carriage pulled up, which had hardly come to a stop before her feet hit the ground. She was taking off her shawl as he came out of the kitchen. She dropped it on the stairs. Then she rushed to him and threw herself into his embrace. Meanwhile, Pierre met Adrien outside, and Esther stayed in the kitchen to give Sam and Jane some privacy.

"Sam is back," Pierre said joyfully.

"Yes, I know. Some good news, for a change," Adrien said, though somewhat somberly.

"Let me take care of the carriage," Pierre insisted.

"Thank you, Pierre. It was a trying night. Sam's company will prove to be uplifting," Adrien said wishfully. His entrance interrupted Sam and Jane's intimate moment.

"Jane, I need some time with your father, please," Sam said.

Jane nodded with some resistance, and she released him and stepped aside. Avoiding an emotional greeting, Adrien gestured toward the upstairs study, and then he led them to his balcony and waited, seeing clearly that Sam had something to say.

"I failed," Sam began. He forced his bloodshot eyes to look at Adrien when he said, "I am terribly sorry."

"Nonsense! It was never in your hands, Sam. Make peace with that." Adrien was firm. As he looked out at the stars, he asked, "Was it Indians?"

"Some say it was." Sam spoke carefully.

"But you don't believe it." Adrien looked at him.

"No. But I can't explain it either. And neither could the army. There was a thief that kept robbing the camps. When we buried Stillman's men, I caught him and brought him into camp. He wasn't a soldier. He was a sixteen-year-old trying to feed his family. He was bound and guarded, then gone in the middle of the night, leaving us with two dead men. No one knows what happened. He hardly looked like a killer and he had no weapons."

Adrien was frustrated. "So the army blamed the Indians. Why? To further rally the men?"

Sam said, "It wasn't the army that blamed the Indians. It was some of the men claiming to have seen various things. No one believed them, either."

Adrien handed the letter of condolence to Sam, saying, "That explains the choice of words."

Sam scanned the letter and struggled to stay focused. "I do know that he was not in battle when he died," Sam said.

"Wasn't he?" Adrien huffed, looking at Sam. "Life *is* battle, Sam. On a battlefield we all are born, and on a battlefield we all die. It all comes down to how we fight and on which side of the battlefield we fall." He paused, thinking. Then he added, "I've been reflecting recently on my life, wondering how my Savior will judge me. It can be difficult sometimes to see the battle lines, and I can remember well the times I lost sight of them. There is only one way to see them, and that is by listening to the Shepherd's voice. Then and only then, they are clear, and when you are faced with a decision, however difficult, you will know what to do and do it without guilt."

Sam quietly studied Adrien while he spoke, and he hung on every word.

Adrien went back to looking at the night sky, angry with himself for not preparing his son for life's battles. "Is there anything else you can tell me? I had hoped for a letter, but nothing came."

"Nathan and I hardly saw each other, but I can tell you that he intended to write to you and Jane to say that he was sorry for how he left and that he loved you both, deeply."

Adrien felt blessed. He would have never known Nathan's state had Sam not followed him, and this revelation somehow softened the blow that the death of his son brought. "You'll make sure Jane knows this?" Sam gave a confirming nod.

"Mr. Pruitt, Nathan was a very good soldier. Unlike me, it came naturally for him, and his passion for it helped him develop his skills quickly. He was happy where he was."

Adrien took it all in and tried to picture his son as a soldier. He lost himself for a few minutes, reflecting on his own military experience, placing himself within Nathan's experience as best he could. He struggled between thoughts.

"We must turn this corner quickly, Sam. Extended grief is… poisonous." Adrien was referring to the years he lost grieving over his wife's death and how his inability to move on eroded his level of functioning. She would have never wanted that for him, and he aimed to prevent that for Sam and Jane. Sam was contemplating Adrien's point as the conversation took another abrupt turn. "What are your intentions with my daughter?" Caught off guard, Sam laughed lightly. "You find that amusing?" Adrien asked.

"I was just remembering," Sam began as he looked across the yard, smiling, "that Jane asked me that same question. It was right over there in that patch of elms that first time I came to call on her." Sam pointed to a tree in the moonlit distance, which steered Adrien's attention that way.

"What did you tell her?" Adrien asked, still looking at the trees.

"I told her that I'll love her till the day I die." He looked at Jane's father knowing he had finally asked for Jane's hand.

Adrien swallowed. "Did you mean it?"

"Yes," Sam said, nodding.

"There's no mistaking her love for you. I suspect you know by now I want to give you my permission to marry Jane, but how can I under the circumstances? I must be sure that you can provide for her security. You are not yet in a sufficient position to marry and start a family. But in time, when you land on your feet…" Adrien assured with a soft smile.

"What of your blessing, have I not earned it?" Sam was respectful but uncommonly blunt.

Adrien retraced his steps. What had he said, or failed to say, that would leave Sam wondering? "Blessing? My boy," Adrien began but then stopped and smiled. Sam was no boy. "You had my blessing that day at Rose's house. Didn't you realize? The fact remains, and I take no pleasure in saying, that you have hit rock bottom," Adrien said.

Sam removed his satchel. Adrien looked on curiously as he lifted the flap, pulled out a thick stack of bills, and set it on the desk.

Adrien's mouth dropped. But it was when Sam dumped the contents out on the desk that Adrien said, "Good God, man! Where did you get this?" he asked as his fingers swept across a mound of jewels glittering before him.

"Let's just say it's my inheritance," Sam said when he handed Adrien the embroidered kerchief.

Adrien held the kerchief up and looked at the letters on it. Sam said, "I've not touched this since the night I left home."

"Why now? Why not tell me of this before I withheld my permission?"

"I'm well aware of the apprehension you've had with me. I would feel the same if I were you. So your approval carries more weight than your permission," Sam confessed. "I wanted to know if you understood that Jane will be cared for far more than economically. That I'm the right man for your daughter. Your blessing gives me that assurance." Sam stood confidently man to man with Adrien.

"What now?" Adrien handed the reins to Sam.

"I need your help with getting top dollar for these pieces. I'm hoping for five or six thousand dollars," Sam said.

Adrien picked up a diamond necklace and examined it. He said, "More, I should think. Much more. St. Louis is close and should render a fair deal. I have business there anyway. We can make the trip together." As he looked at the light reflecting off the gems, he became determined to tighten all loose ends on this night. "I owe you an apology, Sam."

"For what?" Sam honestly did not know.

"I never meant for you to work on the farm. When your father met with me about his plan to have you work for Mr. Coles, I knew why. I found it horrifying that a father would use his son in such fashion. So I told him that the only option for you was a spot on the farm, and though true, I was certain that he would reject it. When he agreed, I saw just how dark his soul was."

You have no idea how dark Bishop's soul can be, Sam thought.

Adrien continued, "My intent was to stop him and spare you, fearful of what it would mean for you if you failed. I told myself that I was stuck, but that's not the whole truth. Rather than intercede, I did nothing at all, especially after learning of your interest in Jane."

Sam looked away, and Adrien braced himself for backlash, but Sam only asked, "Mr. Pruitt, did Mr. Saunderman know about this?"

"No. This is the first I've spoken of it. Why?" Adrien asked. Sam did not answer. "Sam, if you're worried that Mr. Saunderman thought to go easy on you, you are mistaken. Clear your head of that thought. I left you entirely in his hands and to your own ability to succeed or fail. Coddling is good for no man, even if he is the son of Bishop Callahan. To my relief, you worked out, and beautifully, I should add. It seems God arranged it all, using it to strengthen you and to humble me. Nonetheless, I confess that my motive was as impure as it was negligent, brought on by my resentment of Bishop's motive and my guardianship of Jane. I knowingly left you in the middle. It was a delicate situation that could have ended horribly, and I am truly sorry that I had any part in putting you at risk."

Sam didn't need an apology, but he understood Adrien's need to deliver one. He nodded agreeably, returned his fortune to his satchel, and looked at Adrien, waiting.

"Go," Adrien said as he tipped his head toward the door. "We've kept Jane waiting long enough." He was referring to much more than their discussion. Sam nodded and turned to go.

"Mr. Pruitt," Sam said before leaving the room. "Nathan's decision was not in your hands, either." Adrien looked at Sam and nodded but with resistance.

Jane was pacing the floor wondering what could be taking so long. Finally, Sam entered, walked straight to her, and kissed her forcefully. She was concerned that her father would see, but Sam wasn't, and the time he gave to his passion made that clear.

"We need to talk, Jane." Sam took charge, which was welcomed by Jane. "Let's go outside." Sam led Jane to the porch, and as he paused to find the right words, she studied his face. He was different. She gently touched the scar on his cheek, and he looked down.

"Nathan's death is…," he started to say, but Jane put her fingers on his lips and shook her head.

"No," she said. Then she turned away. "I can't find it within me to forgive him, Sam. And I suspect Elizabeth can't, as well. I have reached out to her, but she will not respond."

"Jane, will you let me tell you about him? That he missed you and loved you. That he was brave and committed. That what happened was not his fault," Sam said. She continued to shake her head. He put his hand on her shoulder and turned her back around, but she kept her head down, resisting his attempt to explain. "Nathan did what he thought he had to do. I didn't agree, but I did respect him for that. Jane, look at me." Sam lowered his face toward hers, and she looked up. "Nathan was right where he wanted to be when he died."

For the first time, she cried over the loss of her brother. Sam held her and let her take as long as she needed, comforting her to the degree possible. Jane was still wiping her eyes when she stepped down from the porch and started walking toward the tree where they first kissed.

"I just don't want to hurt anymore, Sam. I'm so tired of hurting," she confided. She stopped at the tree and faced him. "Please tell me you won't leave again," Jane asked.

"I can't promise that, Jane. And I certainly can't promise that you will never hurt again. What I can promise is that I will love you, always."

Adrien looked out his study window, and he could see by the moonlight Sam on one knee holding Jane's hand. Sam came back to his feet and kissed her. Adrien closed his eyes and made a point to remember his wife with peace.

Chapter 10

Sam came down the stairs full of energy. Rose was stunned and thrilled to see him, and before she knew it, Sam lifted her up in a hug and swung her around.

"Good morning, Rose!" he said as he put her back down. Rose was pleasantly flattered as she used the back of her hand to wipe her forehead.

"When did you get back?" Rose asked excitedly.

"Last night." Sam paused. "I was at the Pruitts' until very late," he said, which created an immediate somber mood over both of them.

"Are you hungry?" Rose asked.

"For Rose's cooking? Very hungry!" Sam opened the door to the dining room, and to his amazement, it was nearly full of tenants. He looked back at Rose, who welcomed the season of profit, and he smiled.

Sam took a seat and joined in the light conversation. Among the many guests was a man named Arthur Gunderson. He was single, young but nearly bald, and although thin, he looked round, especially with his round-framed glasses. His voice was a little squeaky, which might explain why he cowered a bit when talking. But he was one to follow the rules even if he did not agree, and that was what helped him secure the position of the new County Clerk. He looked up briefly at Sam, smiled, and returned to eating his meal.

Besides the two gentlemen passing through, there was the Mueller family, who traveled all the way from New York to live closer to family already settled in Illinois.

Conversation was underway with great concern over General Scott's battalion, which was slow in crossing Illinois to join forces against Black Hawk. Many of his men had contracted the cholera and were stuck in Dearborn, suffering daily losses. To Sam's relief, he had no time to respond before a hand reached across the table to make introductions.

"Charles Mueller. This is my wife, Julia and my daughter, Hannah." Charles Mueller was a tall and hefty man, and he was gentle unless provoked. Both women greeted Sam with a smile, but Hannah held hers for an uncomfortable period of time.

Hannah was excessive in appearance and eager in conduct. She had blond hair and brown eyes that she batted unnecessarily. Sam turned his attention elsewhere but could still feel her staring at him.

"Sam Callahan," Sam answered back. "Pleased to meet you. What brings you to Edwardsville?"

"Family, mostly. Their experience here has been an inspiration for us, and after that long stretch of travel, we are glad to be here," Charles said.

"And you, Mr. Callahan?" Hannah asked in a surprisingly inviting tone. "What brings you to Edwardsville?"

Rose was walking around the table replacing some of the empty platters with freshly filled ones. She looked at Sam and discreetly widened her eyes to tease him. Sam had to work to hide a response.

"I live here, Miss Mueller. My family returned East recently, and I am staying here until my fiancée and I are married," Sam said, knowing he had just lowered a hammer on Hannah, but this was also the first time he spoke of his engagement to Jane with anyone, and he found himself warmed by the reality of it. The guests all extended their congratulations, even Mr. Gunderson, but Hannah became sour and asked to be excused. This was not the way Sam wanted to tell Rose, and he looked for her approval. Rose then understood Sam's greeting to her just moments before, and her eyes began to water in joy. Sam was glowing.

*****

Adrien told Jane he wanted her to go into town with him to take care of some business. Jane asked no questions as it was a common trip, but when he stopped in front of the dress store and signaled her to go in, she was stunned.

"Father, no. It's too much. I have a dress that's very becoming for such an occasion," Jane said, which was not entirely true. But what she knew of the budget constraints prompted her to resist wanting to indulge.

"Nonsense. My daughter is getting married, and she will have a new dress," Adrien insisted, and Jane smiled as he opened the door for her. She entered but he did not.

"You're not staying, Father?" Jane asked, disappointed.

"No. I want to be surprised," he said. Jane turned her attention to the various options before her. Adrien looked at the shopkeeper and said, "Andrew, send the bill to my office. Spare no cost. She will need the necessary accessories…gloves, hats, and such, and see that she is fitted for two dresses—one for travel." Jane spun around to look at her father and became nearly paralyzed in excitement as she watched him leave. Andrew and his wife approached Jane, eager to serve her.

*****

Sam wiped his eyes and stood up from Nathan's fresh gravesite. Nathan was placed beside his mother in the family plot of the town's cemetery. His headstone was simple; it revealed that he was loved and told when he died but not how, which reminded Sam of the obscurity behind the loss of his friend.

"What happened to you, Nathan?" Sam whispered. He mounted his horse and slowly rode away from the cemetery toward his next stop.

Pin Oak Township was a blend of whites and blacks. What started off with a few freed black families from Coles's inheritance had become a colony of approximately three hundred free blacks nestled in with white neighbors, not all of whom appreciated the situation. Overall, though, it was quiet.

As Sam rode his horse from corner to corner of his ten-acre parcel, he recalled vividly all the things Saunderman had taught him. Were it not for his time on the farm and all the transient foreman had forced on him, Sam would have no idea what to do with this gift from Edward Coles. His thanks to Saunderman upon parting ways was genuine, but it hardly seemed sufficient now. He wished for that moment back so he could deliver an itemized list acknowledging how Saunderman made him ready for this day, even knowing that Saunderman already knew and neither needed nor wanted recognition of his part.

Sam made note of his bordering neighbors, all of whom were black. Then he rode to the center of his land and imagined a house with the land divided in four sections around it, which would be constructed for the best use of natural light and heat. He plotted out sections for the barn, the stables, the corral, the gardens, the corn, and the fruit trees. He could see it all clearly. As he was riding out, he saw one of his neighbors and stopped to say hello.

"So you're the one Mr. Coles gifted this parcel to. I was wondering when you were going to show up," Joseph Pope said without reservation. He had already heard agreeable things about Sam and was relieved that his new white neighbor would not be a problem for him. Sam got down from his horse and shared Joseph's hidden sentiment as they greeted each other.

"It will be a while before we move here, but you will see us coming and going to build the house and tame the land," Sam said.

"Well neighbor, let us know if we can be of any help," Joseph said, and Sam immediately acted on the invitation by asking Joseph if he had a few minutes to talk business.

*****

As Jane stepped out of the dress shop, she found herself accidentally in the path of two other young women who were walking through town together.

"Jane Pruitt," Talia Green said condescendingly while she noticed the store. "Dress shopping, finally?"

"Browsing," Jane answered, deliberately short and with intent to end the conversation having revealed nothing.

These women grew up with Jane in Edwardsville and represented a side of town far less amicable toward those who bonded with Edward Coles. Coles might have freed his slaves, but most did not, and his opposition to the norm caused deep resentment among many.

There was no mistaking Jane's curt answer. Talia looked disapprovingly into Jane's eyes, and Jane did not flinch. Then Talia closed her eyes and lifted her head as she turned to walk away with her friend. Jane watched their slow steps lead them down the walk as Talia leaned over to her friend and whispered something in her ear. Jane withdrew her attention from them as she heard her father call her name from across the street. Jane walked to him.

"No dresses?" he asked curiously. Jane put her arm in his, and they began walking together.

"On the contrary, Father"—Jane looked at him as though he were crazy—"there are two beautiful dresses undergoing alterations as we speak. And Andrew is adjusting the hats with beautifully coordinated ribbons. Everything will be ready in a few days. I did use good judgment, but they were still expensive," Jane warned with concern.

"Well, that is troubling," Adrien said, and he scratched his chin. Jane became even more concerned. "This is not the time to use good judgment," her father said, smiling.

Jane closed her eyes and exhaled in relief. Then she opened her eyes in surprise upon hearing her father laugh because she was not used to it.

*****

The first person Sam saw as he rode onto Prairieland was Robert Crawford, who also spotted him and walked up to say hello.

"Sam! What brings you out here?" Crawford asked. Crawford was genuinely kind, and those who knew him did not mistake it for bring weak. His firmness and confidence were magnified by his deep voice, and his leadership on the farm and in the church seemed to come naturally for him.

"I was hoping to talk to Danny. Do you mind?" Sam asked as he got down from his horse.

"Not at all. He's in the stable," Crawford said as he walked with Sam.

"How have things been here on Prairieland?" Sam asked. He had not been back since he and Saunderman left together.

"'Bout the same," Crawford said. "Still tryin' to make a profit. Prairieland has never done much better than break even. The fire in '24 was hard to overcome. Los' hundreds o' apple and peach trees and nearly all the buildings. Took a long time to recover. I wanna send good news to Mr. Coles, but we jus' cain't seem to git ahead." Crawford thought he was sharing common knowledge, but it was all new information for Sam, who had no idea the farm struggled. "But we mus' thank the good Lord, Sam, for all he do and know it's by his grace that we stand here today."

"Amen," Sam said, in full agreement having just returned from the war completely unharmed.

"Sam"—Crawford stopped walking and looked at him—"I was ridin' by your parcel the other day. I stopped and asked our Lord to bless your land and whatever you decide to do with it." Crawford put his hand on Sam's shoulder, wished him well, and left him at the stable. Sam watched him walk away and felt changed somehow by the brief discussion.

"Sam?" a voice came from behind.

Sam turned around to find Danny standing there. He wasn't sure if Danny was angry or happy to see him. They had become close friends, but there were still many things Sam did not know. He did not know that he provided Danny with a view of how the world should be, yet would not come to be in his lifetime. He did not know that he exposed Danny to a place of safety, a place without judgment and prejudice, a place that would be hard, if not impossible, to find again were something to happen to Sam. He did not know that Danny panicked when he left for war and that he suffered from his understanding of God's meaning of brotherly love. And what Danny did not know was that the same was true for Sam. When Sam smiled, though, so did Danny. As he walked up to shake Sam's hand, he said softly, "Mama said you was back."

Sam stared briefly at Danny's open palm. He shook his head, hugged him, and said, "I got back yesterday."

"Come here. I wanna show you something," Danny said, displaying more ease. He led Sam into a stable where a mare was close to giving birth. Sam was captured by the moment and quickly recounted the numbers of foals he and Danny helped bring into the world. "She should deliver tonight. You wanna help out?"

"Yes, I do," Sam said firmly.

Danny asked hesitantly, "You been by to see Nathan?"

"Yes, just this morning, in fact."

Danny took a deep breath and gave himself a moment to think about Nathan and what visiting his grave must have been like for Sam. "I'm real sorry."

"Me too." Sam nodded.

"Mama, she loved Nathan like he was her own. She cries all the time. Uncle Bobby came by a couple times, and he prayed for her, but there ain't no comforting her. Never seen nothin' like it." Sam covered his eyes with his hand. "I'm sorry. I shouldn't a said nothin'."

"That's not it. I think we all feel the same way. It just makes what I'm about to say seem wrong," Sam said.

"What?" Danny asked. Sam looked away, letting anything he could see serve to distract him from continuing. "What? Tell me." Danny pushed.

"Last night, I asked Jane to marry me," Sam said, shaking his head.

"Well, it's about time! Wha'd she say? She said yes, didn't she?" Danny asked eagerly. Sam was still a little apprehensive.

"Mr. Pruitt said we needed to move on quickly, so"—Sam looked around—"I did."

"What did she say?" Danny asked again, but Sam still did not answer. "Sam?"

"We should be mourning now, Danny. Not celebrating."

"We are mourning. But Mistah Pruitt is right, Sam. If you die, would you want us all cryin' day afta' day, night afta' night. Being happy 'bout something don't mean we forget Nathan. He's still with us. He'll always be with us." Sam tried to agree. "Now come on. Tell me what she said."

"Yes. She said yes," Sam said, managing to smile.

*****

Jane could still see in her mind the snarl from the woman outside the dress store. She only ever had a few close friends, and one by one, they moved away, leaving her to fend for herself among the cats that remained. She would rather be alone than with those girls who befriended her when she was around but belittled her when she wasn't. And she was alone a lot until the Callahans came.

"Father, I need to make a couple of stops, if you please."

Jane observed that the graves of her mother and brother had been groomed and brightened with fresh flowers. She thought of Sam. She stared at them for a long time while her father waited patiently in the carriage.

Finally, she confided aloud, "I never prepared myself for a life without the two of you," while staring down at their graves. Tears filled her eyes. "Especially for this part of my life." She began to weep. "I have been so angry, and I think that I hold on to that as a way of remaining close to you or as a way of blocking the pain, I'm not really sure. It's just so unfair. Maybe I am afraid of the guilt I will feel if too much time passes without thinking of you. And perhaps being angry keeps my memory of you fresh." Adrien watched Jane nearly break down. He began to step down from the carriage, but she seemed to pull herself together. "You have moved on. And I must do the same, knowing that our mutual love remains unchanged as we wait to be joined in eternity." She dotted her eyes and cheeks with her handkerchief and returned to the carriage. Her father welcomed her back and held her close, until they continued to Jane's next stop.

Rose opened the door and had to contain herself upon seeing Jane and Adrien. "Sam is not here right now," Rose said as she led them to the sitting room. Rose noticed that Adrien's expression revealed that he did not know why they were there.

"Well, then my timing is perfect," Jane said. "Rose, Sam and I are getting married."

"I know," Rose said joyfully. "Sam announced it this morning at breakfast to all the guests. I am so happy for you both." Jane was a little surprised, yet flattered, by this news.

"Well, it will be a small, intimate wedding at our home, and I want you to come. I should have written a formal invitation, but we were in town, and I just wanted to ask now." Rose was clearly honored. Before she could answer, Jane continued, "I don't know if you'll agree, but I ask that you give some thought to a request."

"Of course. What is it?" Rose asked.

"Well, you see…" Jane had a hard time continuing.

"Jane, what is this about?" Adrien asked.

Jane cleared her throat. "Rose, I think of us as friends. I even confide in you as a daughter would her mother. Would you please step in for my mother?" Jane struggled to finish. Rose moved to sit closer to Jane.

"Yes," Rose said. "It would be an honor." As Jane hugged Rose, Rose looked at Adrien, who appeared both uneasy and warmed.

*****

Reverend Hunt gave Sam and Jane a question to consider, and he called them in before their wedding day to discuss their answer.

"Please sit down," the reverend said, and he pulled a chair up to join them. "I asked you each to think about one thing: what is it you fear most? Now I ask, what have you concluded?"

Sam took a breath and answered, "Failure."

The reverend nodded and turned his attention to Jane.

"Injustice," Jane answered.

The reverend said, "As with the apostle Paul, we all have a thorn in our flesh. We don't know what his was, exactly, but God left it there. Perhaps it was to remind him of his constant need to depend only on the Lord, and Paul seemed to grow to appreciate God's purpose in his pain. Now you are more aware of yourselves and each other. You need not only be aware. You must also beware, as these fears are thorns that can puncture and pierce the joy of your walk with the Lord and the joy of your union. They must be examined in order to recognize their traits and then surrendered to the Lord, perhaps only once in your life, or perhaps once a day throughout your life. That's between you and God and an appropriate portion of his grace and your own willingness to be obedient. Gird your loins with the truth, always, and your marriage will belong to God. And what can rise against that which belongs to the Lord? Nothing. No power on earth or in heaven can stand against the Lord."

Sam and Jane looked at each other with understanding and commitment, and Reverend Hunt led them in prayer.

*****

Reverend Hunt mingled among the guests and family, who included the Pruitts, the Hays family, Rose, Sam, and a musician from the church. It was a flawless Saturday morning in early June, and the ceremony would begin at ten o'clock. A breakfast of eggs and various breads was already prepared and staying warm on the stove. Esther made a dark fruitcake with white frosting, which would be served after breakfast. She rushed about, ensuring everything was in its place. Then she joined Rose and Jane in the readying room.

Sam spent the night in the Pruitts' guest room and was busy getting dressed when Danny showed up. Danny helped straighten and polish Sam's presentation, and his last touch was to help Sam put on his coat. He adjusted the shoulders and straightened the tails. Then he ran a brush over Sam's entire outfit. The coat was royal blue with gold buttons, and the tails dropped to the back of Sam's knees. His trousers were white and tucked into his black boots. It was a little too quiet and serious for Danny.

"Well, Sam Callahan, now you' ready for your weddin' day. Are you ready for your weddin' night, or do you need some tutorin' on that?" Danny asked and held a straight face as long as he could. Sam was a little shocked until Danny broke a smile and began to laugh.

"Oh, and who's going to tutor me? You?" Sam jabbed back. They were laughing so loud that they could be heard throughout the house.

Esther, Rose, and Jane looked around at the sound of distant laughter. Rose went back to work and tucked the last little flower into Jane's hair. She stood back to look at her, and she sighed.

Rose said as she turned Jane toward the mirror, "Jane, what a beautiful bride you are."

"Yes, indeed," Esther said.

When Jane focused on herself in the mirror, she did not drop her head. Rather, she raised it.

Her dress was dark blue with black pinstripes. The broad shoulders and bell skirt made her slender waist disappear. The sleeves flared at her wrists and were trimmed with beautiful gold ribbon, which matched the ribbon on the hem of the skirt. She did not wear a hat for the ceremony, only a piece of blue lace that hung over the back of her hair, which was pinned in a high bun, less the select ringlets that fell on their own accord. It was completely unplanned that her dress would match Sam's attire.

Sam and Danny joined the others who were patiently waiting for the ceremony to begin. Sam looked around at the decor for the ceremony as he listened to the musician quietly play hymns on the piano. He was impressed by all the flowers and ribbon that lifted the room to a heavenly feel, appropriate for setting apart this day of ultimate commitment between himself and Jane. The morning sun was beaming perfectly into the multiwindowed room without glare or offense.

Rose and Esther left Jane's readying room and joined the others. Reverend Hunt gently announced that it was time and asked everyone to take their places. Adrien stood at Jane's door waiting for her ceremonial entrance.

Jane rose to her feet from prayer. It was not a prayer of concern or petition but one of thanksgiving and joy. Her union with Sam was a heavenly arrangement that would be able to withstand the trials and tribulations that life would surely bring. She did not give a final glance in the mirror as all of her preparations for this day were complete, and she was ready.

When she opened the door, her father faced her with a smile that quickly fell to astonishment. He had to tell himself to close his parted lips. She was not the same. His daughter was a woman now, and in only a few short minutes, she would belong to someone else. He controlled his watering eyes by resuming his smile and nodded approvingly at her. He raised his bent arm to lead her to her new life.

While Sam waited, he, too, thanked God and knew that with Jane, the future was clear. She was strong, and that made him stronger. What he lacked, she possessed. He remembered that prideful day that he opposed her when he thought she was trying to carry him, and now it comforted him to know that she could if she had to. Everything he had been through since arriving in Illinois seemed to have divinely moved him to arrive at this point. When she entered the room, things seemed to move in slow motion, yet before Sam knew it, Adrien gave her hand to him, and they turned to face Reverend Hunt.

The reverend looked deliberately at Sam and Jane, and then he began, "Friends, we come together today in the presence of God to witness the marriage of Sam and Jane. Let us surround them with prayer and share in their joy. Scripture tells us that the union between a man and a woman is symbolic of the union between Christ Jesus and the Church. It is a holy and sacred covenant. And, above all, it reflects the faithfulness of God's love.

"Let us pray. Almighty and ever-blessed God, whose presence is the happiness of every condition and whose favor hallows every relation. We beseech you to be present and favorable unto these your servants that they may be truly joined in the honorable estate of marriage, in the covenant with you, our God. As you have brought them together by your providence, sanctify them by your Spirit, giving them a new frame of heart fit for their new estate. Enrich them with all grace, whereby they may enjoy the comforts, undergo the cares, endure the trials, and perform the duties of life together, under your guidance and protection, through Jesus Christ, we pray. Amen."

The pianist played very softly between major parts of the ceremony during which Reverend Hunt led Sam and Jane in their declaration and in their vows to each other. Then Sam held the ring he chose for her many months ago. It was a gold band with an inscription inside that pledged his love as of 1832.

"Repeat after me," Reverend Hunt told Sam. "With this ring, I thee wed, with my body, I thee worship, and with all my worldly goods, I thee endow. In the name of the Father, and of the Son, and of the Holy Ghost. Amen."

Sam slipped the ring onto Jane's finger and held her hand until he had her complete attention. He looked deep into her eyes. Then he kissed her.

Upon completion of Reverend Hunt's closing prayer, the pianist played a jovial tune, and everyone stepped toward Sam and Jane in celebration.

After breakfast and cake, Adrien made his way out with the guests. He was packed.

"Father, where are you going?" Jane asked.

Adrien looked around his home before answering. "Jane, it is customary for the bride and groom to be alone after their ceremony. The house is yours. I believe there is an empty room at the McGregor boardinghouse. I'll be staying there tonight, and I will see you in church tomorrow. And then"—Adrien stopped abruptly and looked at Sam—"have you told her?" Sam shook his head no. "Well, that's all you need to know for now." Adrien kissed Jane on the cheek and whispered, "You are beautiful, Mrs. Callahan." That was the first time Jane had been addressed by her new title, and it made her blush. Then he left. Finally, she and Sam were alone.

"Sam, what did my father mean when he asked if you had told me yet?" Sam took her hand and led her to the sofa. He reclined on some pillows, and she reclined on him, resting her head on his chest with his arm around her.

"Jane, you've never asked me how we will get by, what I will do for a living. I have often wondered why."

"Because I trust you, Sam. You would not lead me astray. I know you have a plan. I am simply waiting for you to reveal it," Jane said, fully sure of her answer.

"I am going to breed, train, and trade horses," Sam said. He looked down at her and she looked up. He could plan to breed pigs for all she cared, and her smile expressed it.

"How can I help?" she asked. Sam closed his eyes in relief.

"Well, you can't help until after we celebrate our new life together. We are leaving in two days for St. Louis. We will take a steamboat down and a wagon back." Jane sat up with a look of thrill. She had not been out of Illinois since her childhood years. "I should warn you, I have some business to take care of, but as little as possible, I promise. Your father will join us there to help with that and take care of some business of his own, but otherwise, it will be just the two of us."

"I like business, Sam. Managing everything in this home is business. My father fully leaves it to me, and I do it well. You would be wise to make use of what I know."

"I am counting on that," Sam assured. Jane did not expect that answer, which made her aware of how much she still did not know about the man she loved. "I am asking you to be with me on every endeavor," Sam said with a smile. He stood and then helped her up, as well. "Which room is ours tonight? I think we should change and go for a ride. There's more to discuss."

Jane led Sam to her room, which required them to pass Nathan's room. Sam stopped at Nathan's door. Jane waited, wondering if he would enter, but instead, he entered the guest room across the hall to retrieve his belongings. Then he continued behind Jane. She opened a door, stepped inside, and invited Sam in.

"This is *your* room," Sam stated as he stepped inside and looked around with intent to learn more about his wife. She stood still and watched him as he examined her space, which made her feel a little uncomfortable. Jane was practical but stylish. Her room was feminine but not overly so; it was mature, functional, and well-kept. Sam released his bag, took his coat off, and laid it on her lounge chair.

As he walked from corner to corner of her large room, he took in details of her private space. He ran his hand across her vanity and touched her brush and then her perfume. He looked in her mirror and imagined her preparing herself, perhaps for a day with him. He took special note of one doll that was neatly positioned alone on a shelf, and he suspected a connection to her mother. He walked by the bed without obvious observation, but he observed it completely. He looked out her window, and then he pulled the drapes closed. One of the doors to her wardrobe was loose; he opened it, looked at her neatly arranged clothes, and ran his hand down the sleeve of one of his favorite dresses. He leaned in and closed his eyes as he pressed the fabric to his face and smelled it. He shut the door. He walked to her dressing divider and before peeking behind it, he looked at her, confirming that this was where she dressed and undressed. He looked within to find a chair, a small table, and several decorative hooks hanging on the wall. Still looking behind the divider, he reached his hand out for her.

Jane became nervous, but she stepped forward and took his hand. He gently drew her toward himself behind the divider where there was little room for two. He reached over her head and removed the piece of lace, the tiny flowers, and the pins holding her hair up. He let her hair fall into his hands. Her heart was beating so hard that he could almost hear it. He moved her to the chair where she sat as he removed her shoes. Her wide eyes watched him as he continued to undress her by slowly reaching his hand under her dress where he untied the ribbons holding up her stockings. Then he slid her stockings off as he softly ran his hands from each of her thighs down to her feet. He brought her back to a stand and, piece by piece, he undressed her until she stood bare before him. She waited, breathing heavily, still watching him.

Sam raised his hands to his tie and began loosening it, but Jane took over. She pulled his tie from around his neck and dropped it. She slowly unbuttoned his trousers to untuck his shirt. Then she unbuttoned his shirt and cuffs while his eyes were locked on hers. She removed his shirt and hung it on a hook.

Sam bent down to remove his boots, but on his first tug, he lost his balance and tipped over into Jane's dressing divider, taking it down to the floor with him and breaking it. Jane gasped and covered her mouth as Sam tossed the divider's pieces to the side. She knelt beside him, and her hair draped her body. Together, they exploded into laughter. Sam grabbed her and pulled her to the floor and into his arms. He lifted his head and foot at the same time to look at his partially removed boot and began laughing again.

"Maybe I should have taken Danny up on his offer." Sam laughed, somewhat hiding his eyes behind his hand. Jane looked at him curiously. "Never mind," he said. As he came to his feet, he reached for her hand. When Jane rose, Sam embraced her and said, "Let's just stick to the ride for now?"

*****

Sam drove Jane in her carriage to his land. He drove the carriage right to the middle of the undeveloped property through the tall grass. He helped her down and began describing his plans for a house. Jane was mesmerized by his animated descriptions of their future home.

"Tell me, Jane, what do you want for your home?" Jane walked a bit, looking around as she tried to imagine what Sam was seeing: horses, a garden and barn, and their children. Sam watched her think.

"There is one thing, I must confess," Jane said.

"Name it. And don't hold back."

"A new dressing divider." Jane laughed.

"Jane, I'm serious. Whatever you've dreamed of, whatever you've longed for, I'll make it happen." Sam probed. She looked blankly at him; then she walked a little more. Sam became a bit nervous. Had he overlooked her desires? Would this not suit her? "Jane, what is it?" She faced him.

"Don't be foolish, Sam. I love that you want to dote over me, but surely you know me better than that. I am not one of many wants. I have what I want. I have my Lord, and he has blessed me with you. My hope is simply to live a peaceful, quiet, long, godly life here with you, or wherever life takes us."

Sam took her arm under his, and they walked together against the resistance of the tall grass in the fierce heat of the sun. He should have felt relieved, but he didn't. He wondered if she knew just how difficult her wants would be to fulfill. Diamonds and gold would be easier demands, easier to guarantee than luxuries like peace, quiet, long, and godly.

"I'll do my best to give you what you want," Sam promised.

They spent hours discussing the layout of the property and house. Jane knew what she needed to make the house functional and comfortable. Sam took notes. They talked about fruit trees and vegetable gardens, where to place the barn for easy access to milk and eggs on bitter, cold mornings, and furnishings that Sam wanted to make for her.

Sam explained his horse trading and breeding plan and how he had already arranged with their neighbor, Joseph, to rent his fields for grazing the horses as Sam's property was considerably smaller. He asked Jane to include that in their budget. Jane talked about their children as though they had already come, and Sam listened in amazement. On the ride back, Jane wondered how her father was doing.

*****

Adrien had been surrounded by Rose's house guests all day. There seemed to be no escape except retreating to Sam's room, but he yielded instead to ongoing conversation when he realized just how unsocial he had become over the last few years. He found himself enjoying, to his surprise, a lengthy conversation with Charles Mueller about life back East and what the future might hold for the frontier. They agreed on little but relished their debate that became so loud that Rose had to shush them. Charles eventually asked what Adrien was doing there, and upon sharing the news of his daughter's wedding, a new wave of roaring came. Charles told Adrien he had met the young man who married Jane and was rather impressed. Then he told Adrien to stay put while he disappeared for several minutes.

Charles returned with two bottles of brandy as well as the other boarders whom Charles insisted join him and Adrien in a toast. Even Julia and Hannah joined in where, in other houses, they would have remained in the lady's sitting room, separated from the men. Many cigars and glasses of brandy and hours later, Adrien was near needing assistance getting up the stairs to his room.

*****

Back in Jane's room, Sam was undressing at Jane's vanity when she came up behind him and appeared in the mirror. In the reflection, he saw shadows dancing on her skin from the glow of the lamp until he blew it out.

Chapter 11

J ane left the bedroom door open upon going downstairs to make
breakfast. Sam woke to the soft sound of her beautiful humming
and singing. He had never woken so comfortably and peacefully
before, and he let the experience envelop him. He heard Jane coming, and he closed his eyes, pretending to be asleep so he could make
the moment last a little longer.

Jane entered the bedroom with breakfast and quietly stared at
Sam for a moment. She set the tray of food down on her dresser,
moved to the edge of the bed, and watched him sleep as she ran
her fingers through his hair. He gave himself away when he began
to smile, and when he rolled over on his back, she fell into his arms
laughing.

At the boardinghouse, Adrien struggled to get out of bed. He
was certain he aged twenty years overnight as he was well out of
practice with excessive drinking and now feeling deep regret. Cold
water on his face seemed to bring a little life and color back to him.
He entered the dining room to find a table full of used place settings,
picked on food, and various half-filled glasses but no guests. Rose
entered from the kitchen upon hearing him.

"Good morning, Mr. Pruitt," Rose said, seemingly loud. "How
are you this fine day?"

"I confess, Rose, not well. How is it that you are so chipper? I
do recall you holding a glass or two last night."

"Serving a glass or two, Mr. Pruitt. I never touch the stuff,"
Rose confided.

"Ah, where was your wisdom when I needed it most?"

"If you don't mind my saying so, last night was just what you needed. I reserved my wisdom for this morning. Here, drink this." Rose handed him a warm drink, and he did not even ask what it was before he began sipping on it.

Adrien looked around at the empty table. "Where is everyone?" he asked.

"They have all moved out," Rose said.

Moved out? Adrien wondered. How did he miss that?

Rose continued, "The Muellers have family here, the two horsemen rode out together, and Mr. Gunderson found a place to buy. There is still plenty of time before church, and you should eat." Adrien resisted. Rose insisted. About halfway through his drink, Adrien was sitting up a little straighter, and his head was feeling better.

"Is it my imagination, or is this curing my ailing condition?" he asked of his warm drink. Rose just smiled. "I mean it. I feel much better. What's in this?" But Rose only continued to smile. "Hmm, a secret concoction. Well, you should be a druggist. You could make a fortune on this," Adrien said as he found himself able to eat. "Rose, may I escort you to church, knowing that doing so comes with the risk of talk?"

"I would be honored, Mr. Pruitt," Rose responded, obviously flattered.

"Adrien, please." He urged the use of his familiar name.

Adrien and Rose met Sam and Jane at the church, and they all entered together. Sam and Jane were in their wedding attire, as was customary. Upon taking their seats, Talia Green looked back and across the church at them. She stared.

"The Pruitts have adopted that Callahan boy," she whispered to her husband, Vincent, who by now had learned to ignore her. "How sweet," she said with a disgusted tone.

The music began, and everyone stood to sing the hymn. After the first song, Reverend Hunt seated the congregation, and he made a few announcements to include the most recent deaths, births, and weddings. Upon announcing the wedding of Sam and Jane, Talia whipped another look at them, then she faced forward again as her mind began to rage over Jane's lie at the dress shop. But that was not what really bothered her.

Talia was blonde, blue eyed, and pretty until she exposed her darker side. She was married to one of the wealthiest men in the county who fell in love with her and committed himself to her before knowing what he was getting into, much to his parents' disappointment. His wealth gave her endless direct access to everything her heart desired except one thing: other people's joy. Destroying that took more than Vincent's money. This would be the last day the Greens would attend Reverend Hunt's church. She would force them to move to a different and larger church, one that would better hide the evil within her that was intent on getting out.

At the end of service, many congregation members congratulated Sam and Jane on the church lawn. Talia could hardly wait to shake Sam's hand.

"Mr. Callahan, is it?" Talia gripped his hand, and Jane ground her teeth. "Mrs. Green. Congratulations on your choice, though other eligible women of Edwardsville hardly stood a competitive chance. You were only rarely seen since arriving here over two years ago. Time will tell if you chose wisely."

Sam was stunned, but Jane anticipated Talia's sting. Just as Talia was about to release Sam's hand, he tightened his grip. "Mrs. Green, is it? There was never any competition. Be sure to spread the word. You strike me as being proficient at that." Talia did not appreciate Sam's piercing reciprocation, and she jerked her hand out of his as she turned to leave. Vincent's expression to Sam was one of helpless horror. Then he looked away in shame.

Jane was profoundly moved by Sam's quick and well-stated response. Sam immediately found himself shaking another church member's hand as he watched the Greens get into a dispute near their carriage. Adrien and Rose caught up with Sam and Jane when they were finally free of the crowd.

"Jane, who was that woman?" Sam asked. Adrien and Rose waited curiously, having missed Talia's infliction.

Jane was still rerunning through her mind Sam's defense of her and his management of the town's witch. "Talia Green," she finally answered. Upon mention of her name, Adrien looked away in disgust. "She's one of Madison County's proslavery advocates. Though really, she could care less about slavery. She just uses it to satisfy her thirst for injuring others."

"So you've met Talia Green," Adrien said. "Her parents were among Edward Coles's top enemies because of his abolitionist viewpoint and over the issue of free statehood," he explained. "And when that eluded them, they joined others in viciously attacking him financially for, they said, illegally freeing his slaves. He won in court, and though it would have cost him twenty thousand dollars had he lost, he paid in other ways. The ordeal wore him down considerably. Even though he has moved to Pennsylvania, his former slaves are still here and hated by many. And now you live among them."

"What has this to do with Jane?" Sam asked.

"Guilt by association, no doubt. The Pruitts have long been condemned by many in this county because of our ties with Governor Coles and our antislavery position. And I am afraid, Sam, you're a part of that now. Be warned, Talia is intent on being our enemy. She prides herself on being offended whenever she can, which prompts her to make people pay, something she has done rather well since her childhood."

As Sam contemplated how to navigate through the crowds of Talias in the world, Jane felt herself becoming sick over the thought of misleading him.

"But let's not sour the occasion with the likes of Talia Green," Adrien continued. "She is just a pawn in this dark world, and were it not her, it would be someone or something else fulfilling the role of persecution. We have better things to do. Sam, St. Louis, tomorrow. I'll meet you at the hotel." Adrien walked to his carriage and opened the passenger door. "Your chariot, madam." Rose smiled and climbed in.

Things were quiet in the carriage as Sam and Jane rode home. Finally, they both spoke at the same time. Sam began to laugh, but Jane broke down in tears. Sam pulled over.

"Jane! Why are you crying? What did I do?" Sam was reaching for her, but she resisted. "Jane, this will not do. Tell me what's wrong."

"Sam," she cried, "as God is my witness, I didn't mean to deceive you. Please forgive me." Sam had no idea what she was talking about.

"Deceive me how?" Sam asked, unconvinced of her error.

"It never occurred to me to tell you about these troubled relationships. I had buried them long ago, but now they are resurfacing. I just didn't know that would happen." Sam looked around trying to find the words to console her over something that didn't matter to him.

"Jane, I am not worried about Talia Green. Nor do I think you deceived me by not educating me on Edwardsville's darker history. I asked your father what this had to do with you to know better how to protect you, or rather, us. There are people out there that mean to meddle and cause harm. Talia is one of many that we will encounter." Jane started to calm down. She wiped her tears as Sam put his arm around her, and she kept her head down toward his chest. "It breaks my heart to see you so upset. Please don't pull away from me. You scared me half to death."

"I'm sorry. You've been so quiet that I thought the worst, that you might see me differently now," Jane said, still upset.

"I do see you differently now. I didn't think it was possible to love you more, but I do." Jane pulled on his lapel to bring him even closer to her. "I was quiet because I was trying to determine if I should get your thoughts on what is going on between your father and Rose." Jane sat up and looked shocked. Then she softly hit him in the arm. Sam raised his arm to protect himself, not sure if she was going to hit him again.

"Sam Callahan! You weren't even thinking about what my father just told you of the enemies we've brought into your life?" Jane barked. "And I was out of my mind worried that you thought you had made a mistake marrying me." Sam was confused. He moved his lips to speak, but nothing would come out. Jane crossed her arms and looked ahead. Sam had no idea what just happened or what to do next. He tried and tried to hold it in, but he lost control and started laughing very hard. Jane glared at him, but Sam kept laughing, and she broke down and started laughing too.

"In the last twenty-four hours, Jane, we have gotten married, we have made a disaster of your bedroom, we have planned the next ten years of our lives, we have *made love*, we have faced enemies, and we have had our first and, hopefully, only fight," Sam said, shaking his head. "You know what I think?" Sam looked at her with eyebrows up. "I think we should go home and make up." And he flinched to act like he thought she was going to hit him again. She tilted her head in shame, and Sam leaned toward her and waited for her to meet him for a kiss, which she did. Then he got back on the road.

"I haven't seen father this happy in years," Jane simply said.

Chapter 12

Adrien stopped by his office before leaving for St. Louis. He sat back in his chair, thinking. Then he removed his ledger from his safe and opened it to a section labeled Reserves, which contained pages and pages of deposits made over the years to account for his retirement and for each of his children. Nathan's account would have paid for his college. Jane's account would provide for several years of security in or out of a marriage. His retirement account had twenty-five thousand dollars, Nathan and Jane's accounts each had over five thousand dollars, and Jane had no knowledge of any of them.

He held his pen over his ledger for some time before he made a note to withdraw all of Jane's money, and he moved Nathan's money to a charity account. Then he put his ledger back in his safe and stopped at the bank before departing for St. Louis.

Sam looked out the window of the carriage on the way to Alton, Illinois, where he and Jane would begin their trip to St. Louis. The road had some very rough spots, which occasionally threw Jane and Sam back and forth. Sam thought about which worried him more: the likelihood of a wagon's broken wheel or the likelihood of a horse's broken leg. The horse's leg would be far worse, he easily concluded. The horse would have to be shot. *How thoughtless was man with live-stock*, Sam thought. Travel between Alton and Edwardsville was common enough to justify constructing and maintaining a decent road.

He held Jane's hand while making mental calculations again on what his mother's jewelry might bring in. He used the worst-case figure of six thousand dollars, based on Adrien's initial assessment, from which to subtract the cost of the hotel, dining, entertainment, some shopping, and the purchase of four good saddle horses: three mares and one stud. What would that leave for his property and house? He heard Jane's voice in his head saying that she knew he had a plan, that she trusted him. She was comfortable depending on him, and he knew he had to deliver. He nodded to himself, confidently.

"Sam?" Jane startled Sam out of his thoughts. "You're a million miles away."

"I'm sorry, Jane. I'm just enjoying the scenery," Sam said. Jane kept looking at him.

"Didn't you even hear me?" she asked.

Sam sat up, more attentive. "Did you say something?" he asked. Jane had been talking about the exciting things they would see in St. Louis, and he missed it all. She became aware that he was in deep thought, but she could not tell if he was worrying.

"Yes, I said thank you for taking me away," Jane said with a soft smile, and Sam squeezed her hand. Just then the carriage came to a stop.

"We're here," he said. Then he stepped down from the carriage without looking and found himself in inches of mud from the wet and heavily traveled upon conditions of Alton's port. Disgusted and irritated, he told Jane to wait. "Driver, pull up to that dry spot over there," Sam hollered at the driver for his oversight. He walked through mud beside the carriage until it came to a stop at the designated spot. As he stomped the mud off his boots, he scowled at the driver.

He then helped Jane down with confidence that the new dress her father bought her for travel would not be ruined. Together, they turned their attention to an enormous and beautiful steamboat, and the driver helped with their bags all the way to the boat ramp where he then handed them off to a black steward. As Jane boarded, she had to focus on dulling her excitement to appear composed as she and Sam traveled in first class on this short five-hour ride down the Mississippi River.

As the boat began downriver, Jane observed the banks of Alton to the east and the banks of Missouri to the west. Alton had become a desirable landing point for runaway slaves from Missouri. The clash between pro- and antislavery ideals created a bittersweet environment for the growing port town of Alton, as slaves risked their lives crossing the river in hopes of finding freedom. Some would arrive in the safe hands of abolitionists, while others would arrive in the hands of Illinois's own proslavery activists or the slave catchers from Missouri, both of whom profited on the merciless return of fugitive slaves to their Missouri masters. And still others did not make it at all, having fallen victim to the unforgiving current of the mighty Mississippi. Jane closed her eyes to try to block the images from her mind, for now.

Sam escorted Jane around the upper decks of the steamboat, and the breeze off the river cooled the hot, humid air of this cloudless summer day. Lunchtime came quickly, and Sam and Jane experienced fine dining at a beautifully arranged table with a small vase of flowers and decorative dishes. They sat by an open window and spent the rest of the journey there as Sam shared some of the details about business he had to do in St. Louis. Their discussion was interrupted by a pleasant visit from the boat's captain who stopped at their table to congratulate them on their recent union. He warned them to keep a sharp eye while in St. Louis.

Jane stared across the table at Sam. His expression probed for her thoughts, and she began to answer, "I often wonder," but she stopped and lowered her eyes. Sam placed his hand on hers. "I want to know you, Sam, completely. I'm awed by how you became the man you are, having come from where you came. Give me at least a glimpse of how you did it." Sam did not move or speak. "I ask not only as your wife but as someone who simply wants to understand."

Sam's lips parted, his thoughts raced, and his eyes wandered off briefly. "I don't know how to explain it, Jane. I want to understand it too. There seems to be no explanation other than God's grace. He pulled me out. It wasn't anything I did. It was entirely him. And the hardest thing for me to understand is why. I am not the only one to have been raised by a Bishop Callahan, nor was my lot as bad as so many others—others who deserve grace far more than I do. Why me and not them? I have to make peace with God's providence and trust his purpose, but, frankly, it scares me. What does he want of me? I am…nothing."

Jane smiled slightly. "Well, there it is. That explains it." Sam narrowed his brows in confusion. "Sam, we all are nothing, apart from him. You surrendered to him, and with him, all things are possible because you are willing." Sam squeezed her hand, and she looked out the open window for a while, taking in her new and clear view of the world while Sam was still trying to focus it. Finally, she said, "Your thoughtfulness at Nathan's and my mother's graves meant a great deal to me."

Sam hesitated. "What do you mean?"

"That day you cleared their grave sites and placed fresh flowers on them. I know it was you."

He hesitated again. "Jane, that wasn't me. I thought it was you."

*****

St. Louis ran the length of a mile and a half on the banks of the Mississippi River, which was lined with the city's wharfs and buildings. Most of the streets were dirt or mud, and achieving a civilized standard for the disposal of waste, any and all kinds, had yet to occur in St. Louis, as was the norm for many cities in America. Those most bothered by the mess in the streets and stench in the air were visiting Europeans who had long enjoyed paved and cobbled roads and widespread sanitation customs. They grumbled over what they saw as subhuman conditions, but that did not sway them from coming to and oftentimes beyond the frontier's edge.

St. Louis was the main supply source for anyone heading west or returning from the west with trade goods. In 1832, the city was busting at the seams from tripling in size since the previous decade. Trappers, fur traders, mountain men, Indians, settlers, and squatters were mixed with opportunists, the law and the lawless, preachers and their colliding denominations, slaves, and free blacks; all were subject to the rapid changes associated with unplanned city growth, unpredictable rises and drops in commerce, cultural shifts, moral stressors, and immoral pursuits.

Upon arriving, Sam and Jane met Adrien at the National Hotel, one of the nicest hotels in St. Louis, and even though it was new, room accommodations were modest. But hotel events, such as magic shows, balls, and lectures along with hotel guests and curious crowds, were numerous and made for a lively atmosphere. And there was no shortage of good food nearby upon which they could indulge. Entertainment was widely ranged between pure and raunchy that Sam had to be careful what he chose so as not to offend his modest wife. Jane was constantly shifting between expressions of excitement and disgust. This city, as did many cities in their early stages of settlement and development, had something for everyone.

Diverse crowds and entertainment were not all St. Louis had. It also had disease. The faraway epidemic of cholera in Europe had abruptly taken thousands of lives, creating a state of panic across the Atlantic Ocean. It made it all the way to St. Louis by way of European travel to New Orleans, then up the Mississippi River on steamboats. Or did it travel across Canada and move south to the Mississippi Valley? Perhaps it came directly from the east and moved west. The only reason it mattered was that victimized communities wanted someone to blame. By the summer of 1832, St. Louis was experiencing the early signs of its own panic. And so was Jane.

Jane sat in a hotel parlor reading a pamphlet and waiting for Sam and her father when a commotion broke out. Less than two hours prior, Jane was sitting in the hotel's restaurant having supper with her husband and father within view of a man who was noticeably becoming ill. He left the restaurant repeatedly to address his discomfort. Jane observed that, on the third departure, he did not return. Now she was seeing the same man being carried through the parlor and out of the hotel by two friends because he was unable to walk on his own. As he passed through the evening crowd, Jane could see that he was a ghastly blue shade and his eyes were open, but it was hard to tell because they had become terribly sunken. Whispers rose as people were able to see that this poor man had soiled his pants.

"The cholera. He has the cholera," Jane heard, and increasingly in volume. People began to leave the hotel so quickly that they bumped into Jane and nearly pushed her over. Sam and Adrien came out of the restaurant after paying the bill and saw the last of the crowd leaving.

"What was that all about?" Sam asked, clearly concerned. Adrien was still watching the crowd rush away as he waited on Jane's response. All Jane could offer was fear in her eyes as she covered her mouth with her hand.

*****

The few full days of leisure in the shadow of quiet concerns of the growing numbers of cholera cases prompted Adrien, Sam, and Jane to move on to business. Breakfast was hearty, but Adrien ate lightly as was his norm. He wiped his mouth and waited patiently for Sam and Jane to finish. Sam sat back in his chair giving a signal to Adrien that he was ready. Sam stood up and secured his satchel across his chest and under his coat. Then Adrien led the way.

Adrien had three jewelers picked out with intent that the highest bidder would buy Sam's inheritance. Along the way, Sam stopped at a furniture shop where he arranged a meeting for Jane and the shop owner.

"You intend to leave me here? By myself? While you go about business with my father?" Jane asked with a very disgruntled voice. "I'll do no such thing." The shop owner bowed slightly and backed away to allow for their privacy. Adrien backed away, too, leaving Sam on his own to face Jane's opposition. "Did you not tell me on our wedding day that you want me with you on every endeavor? Do you mean now to withdraw your promise?"

Sam gently took Jane by the arm and moved to a spot with even more privacy. "Jane, it's not that I don't *want* you with me. This particular endeavor is of a risky nature, and one I am not comfortable having you share."

Jane had her rebuttal ready, but she saw honesty and even agony in Sam. She changed directions. "Sam," she whispered gently, "don't push me away either. It breaks my heart." Sam recognized that he was being quoted. Her big blue eyes waited for him to look at her and concede, which he did but with reluctance.

"We'll be back," Sam told the shop owner, and Jane took Sam's arm.

Adrien paused on Sam's decision, but he then led them to the first jeweler. He spoke to the jeweler privately, who could not afford a deal. The second jeweler was unexpectedly away on business. Adrien's determination became noticeably heightened and was equal to Sam's frustration, while Jane didn't understand the pursuit.

The third jeweler was very interested in what Sam had to show him, and he escorted them all to a private room in the back of the shop. Jane was puzzled until Sam produced the jewels. Her mouth parted and her eyebrows shot up. Adrien whispered in her ear how Sam came to own this collection. The jeweler showed no expression, which told Adrien a great deal. The jeweler spread out the display so he could see each piece clearly and then sat on the edge of his tall stool, crossed his arms, and rubbed his jaw. He looked at Sam. He looked at Adrien. Then he did it all again, only this time, he examined them with a jeweler's loupe.

"Do you know what you could get for this back East?" the jeweler asked.

"I know what you could get for this back East," Adrien stated with confidence.

"Well"—the jeweler laughed—"you won't get that here," he said in a very stressed tone. He wanted this collection, badly.

"You regularly travel to, say, New York, Philadelphia, even Boston, do you not?" Adrien asked. "How could you acquire your vast inventory if you didn't? Jewelry makers are rare in these parts. You could profit well on this collection on one of your routine trips." The jeweler confessed nothing. "Come on! Make an offer," Adrien pushed. The jeweler hesitated but could not resist engaging on the idea. He rose again and ran his hand over the jewels.

"I couldn't offer more than five thousand dollars," he said. Sam grieved internally. That was even less than what he thought would be the lowest offer. But he left all communication to Adrien.

"Bah! Nonsense! Five thousand dollars? Are you mad?" Adrien was genuinely disgusted. "We won't take less than twelve. There are other jewelers here who will laugh when they've heard you've passed on this," Adrien said, and he was right, on a normal day. Sam was a little shocked by Adrien's figure, but he remained hopeful. "Come, Sam. Put them away. We'll move on to a serious business offer." Sam began to retrieve the items, but the jeweler stepped forward again.

"I can't do twelve. Ten, maybe, at the most," the jeweler said. Sam stopped storing the jewels and waited.

"There is easily twenty thousand dollars in jewelry here. You can do twelve, or you can say good day." Adrien waited while the jeweler stared down at the jewels. There grew an uncomfortable lapse of time. "Good day, then!" Adrien concluded sternly, and Sam resumed picking them up.

"Twelve! Very well, then. Twelve. I need to go to the bank. I don't keep that kind of money here. Meet me back here in an hour," the jeweler said. Adrien looked at him like he was crazy. "Gentlemen, I have to go to the bank!"

"No doubt, but we'll wait right here. Now that what we are carrying has been made known, it's hardly wise to roam the streets."

The jeweler agreed and took every minute of the hour he said he needed. Once back, the jeweler wrote out a receipt while watching Sam out of the corner of his eye as Sam took the bulk of bills and wrapped them in a large cloth. Adrien had Jane review the receipt for accuracy, and she demanded each jewelry item be listed, which was very time-consuming. When Jane was satisfied, Sam placed his satchel over his shoulder, put on his coat, and nodded to Adrien, who asked the jeweler where they might find a good restaurant to celebrate the deal, one with fish or beef or even both.

Sam, Jane, and Adrien left the jeweler and returned to the furniture store so Jane could choose a few items she wanted for her new home. After a while of discussing options, Jane made her selection, which Sam agreed to pick up before leaving town. As they exited the shop, two men intercepted them, and each discreetly held knives to Jane and Adrien. They forced them all down an alleyway and shoved Sam forward to a comfortable distance.

"Take it easy!" Sam said. "What's this about?"

"Oh, I think you know what this is about," one man said with a smile. He was filthy and had rotting teeth. "I'll take that bag." Sam hesitated. "Now!" the man yelled, causing Sam to jolt. "Or I cut her wide open!" He jabbed the knife closer to Jane's side. Jane was terrified.

"Give it to him, Sam!" Adrien said, forcefully. "It's not worth it!"

"All right! All right!" Sam said, showing his hands. Sam took his coat off.

"Nice and easy, now. I don't want no tricks," the robber said. Sam slid the satchel over his head and tossed it to the thief that was holding Jane, causing him to release her. The two robbers laughed and ran away with the bag. Jane ran into Sam's arms. All three of them were shaken up, and Sam examined Jane to make sure she was not hurt.

"The next time I say no, listen to me!" Sam said. She threw her arms around him, and she was sorry, so sorry. "I just thank God you're all right." Then he gave a look of relief to Adrien.

"Come. Let's get back to the hotel," Adrien said. He remained on one side of Jane, and Sam remained on the other, mindful of everyone around them as they walked near double-time to the hotel.

"What can we do? Should we tell the police?" Jane asked nearly sobbing.

"There's nothing we can do," Adrien said. "It's done. I knew that jeweler was up to something by the way he was watching you, Sam." Sam didn't say anything.

Back at the hotel, Sam spent a few minutes at the front desk talking to the clerk and retrieving the room key. Once in the room, Jane threw herself into a pillow on the bed, traumatized over what had happened.

"Twelve thousand dollars. I can't believe it! And my satchel. I'm going to miss that. I've had that since my school days," Sam said, disappointed and shaking his head.

A knock came to the door from a young man who delivered a bottle of champagne on ice. Jane looked up, confused. Sam popped open the bottle of champagne and let it run over onto the floor. Adrien smiled slightly as he held each glass while Sam poured. Sam handed them out and proposed a toast, and Jane looked on as though the two had lost their minds.

"To Adrien Pruitt!" Sam raised his glass.

Adrien protested, "Not at all. The raised glass goes to you," he said to Sam, "and to Jane, of course."

"Yes, to Jane. She was brilliant, wasn't she?" Sam asked. They both conceded and bowed.

Jane was angry, but she yielded in agreement. "Yes, thank God for our lives."

Sam reached into the side of his boot, pulled out a stack of bills, and tossed it on the bed in front of Jane. Then he drank.

"What? But how? I saw you put the money in your satchel?" Jane said.

Adrien explained, "You saw him put a bundle in the satchel. The money went elsewhere. Sam's boots, his pants, his coat, my coat." Adrien reached into his breast pocket and pulled out another stack of bills. "While you were distracting the jeweler, Sam and I were protecting his inheritance," Adrien said as though it were every-day business. "Trust no one when dealing with that kind of money."

"I still can't get over the twelve thousand dollars," Sam said in amazement. "How did you know the value of the jewelry?"

"I didn't know. But the jeweler did. It was written all over his face," Adrien said between sips of champagne. Then he laughed quietly, pleased by the experience.

"And those thieves? Were they from the jeweler?" Jane asked.

"You can be sure of that," Adrien said. "And you can bet they are not celebrating right now having stolen nothing but a brick. They'll still be looking for us."

"We knew it could get rough, Jane," Sam said. "That's why I didn't want you to come." Jane nodded in understanding.

"But you're coming actually saved the day," Adrien said. "Until you pulled the jeweler's attention off Sam, I didn't know how we were going to get out of there securely. Brilliant of you, Jane, to demand he make a list on the receipt. That gave us more than enough time to hide the money." Jane smiled, and Sam gave her a kiss. Adrien added, "But we still have business ahead, so we'll have to keep our heads down. I propose that tonight you dine here at the hotel. And tomorrow we should wear our most casual clothes."

"We will all dine here at the hotel, Father. Together," Jane insisted. Then she held up her glass of champagne and finally joined in the toast.

*****

The next day, Sam went searching for a wagon, and Jane joined him. Adrien had business to complete and said he would meet up with them for lunch.

Adrien met his business associate in a tavern, paid him rather quickly, and left. Thereafter, he sat across the street from the furniture shop sipping on coffee, watching. He knew the two thieves would be back in search of Sam, and it wasn't long before he was proven right. They went into the shop and soon came back out. Then they stood on the street corner looking around. Adrien ran across the street and entered the shop to ask the shop keeper what the two men wanted. The shopkeeper said they asked about Sam, but he did not tell them anything. Adrien thanked the man and went back outside. The thieves were still on the corner.

Adrien summoned two policemen and explained that he and his family had been robbed by the two men the day before. He also said that he was certain they were hired by the jeweler. The police were hesitant to respond because it would be hard to prove, but Adrien convinced them to see if the men would eventually find their way to the jeweler. If so, they would know. The policemen agreed to commit some time to waiting but grew impatient knowing St. Louis could use their attention elsewhere. Finally, though, the thieves were on the move, which took them all straight to the jeweler.

The policemen entered the jewelry shop with Adrien, and the two thieves were in a heated discussion with the jeweler. One of the thieves was carrying Sam's satchel. When the policemen approached them, they all became quiet.

"Pardon me. This man says he sold you some jewelry, then you hired these two men to rob him of your payment to him." One policeman did all the talking.

"I don't know what you're talking about," the jeweler said. "I paid him for his jewels, and that's all. And I don't know who these men are. They came in asking questions."

"Then why is this man carrying my son-in-law's satchel?" Adrien asked. "Look, his name is stamped inside. He stole it off him while he had a knife in my daughter's side threatening to cut her open. And now it is a coincidence that he is here with you? I think not." The thieves began to panic.

"Now hold on! He said he would pay us a hundred dollars to steal the satchel and bring it to him," the thief said of the jeweler. The jeweler grew angry.

"Shut up, you idiot!" the jeweler said.

"Then you admit it," Adrien said. "You did rob us." The other thief began to run, and Adrien threw his arm out like a tree branch, causing the thief to fall backward to the floor with force. The second policeman pressed his foot on his chest to hold him there.

"There's no evidence of a robbery. If they robbed him, then where is the money?" the jeweler yelled but glared suspiciously at the thieves.

"I told you! There was no money in the satchel! Only a brick. If we had stolen the money for ourselves, why would we have come back?" the thief asked. The jeweler reached for the thief's throat but was stopped by the first policeman.

"That's true," Adrien said. "We did not put the money in the satchel, but that is hardly the point. The point is that this jeweler is crooked, and his criminal activity needs to be exposed and put to a stop. These men, on his order, robbed us and threatened to kill us."

"All right, that's it," the policeman said. "You two are going to jail," he said to the thieves, and he handed Adrien the satchel. "And you," he said to the jeweler, "give him back his jewels."

"What?" the jeweler asked in protest.

"Yes, what?" Adrien echoed. He was confused by the order.

"Give him back his jewels!" the policeman said.

"Then I want my money back!" the jeweler yelled.

Adrien answered, "The deal was not mine, and I don't have the money. I simply want justice."

"Look, this is how it's going to go. These two are going to jail. And you," the policeman said to the jeweler, "will join them in prison while you wait for your trial, which will end with you losing not only your case but all this"—he waved at the shop—"and the best you can hope for is visits from your wife. Or you can end this now, forget the money, and give him back his jewels. A small price to pay for your mischief." He turned to Adrien and asked, "Will that satisfy you?"

"Well, I don't know. Who's to say he won't do it again or hasn't done it before? Innocent people are at risk because of him."

"Wait! Please wait!" a voice from the back of the shop cried. The jeweler's wife came running to the front of the shop. "Please, it's all there." She placed Sam's jewels on a counter to show that she was telling the truth. "I thought we ran an honest business. I swear, it won't happen again. Please take them and go." She put the jewels back in the satchel and shoved Adrien toward the door. As Adrien was leaving, he heard the wife call the jeweler a stupid fool.

Adrien stood in the street completely stunned as he held up the satchel and looked at it. The policemen walked by with the thieves.

"I don't want to see your face again, either," the first policeman said to Adrien. "Consider this the end of your jewelry business in St. Louis." Adrien gave a confirming nod.

Adrien heard the second policeman say to one of the thieves, "What kind of sick bastards threaten to cut a man's daughter open right in front of him?"

"I wasn't going to hurt her," the thief said in his defense.

"Well, it's too late for that now," the policeman said while pushing the thief forward.

*****

Sam stepped into a wainwright shop called Bender's Wagons. He looked around and saw two black men doing some work in the back.

"Can I help you?" the older man asked.

"Good morning. I'm looking for Mr. Bender," Sam said. "Is he here?"

The older black man looked at the younger worker and said, "Out." The younger man lowered his head and left abruptly. Then the older man said, "I'm Bender."

George Bender was one of St. Louis's few elite free black men. He bought his freedom some twenty-five years ago and had been working on the banks of the Mississippi River ever since, building wagons. He was highly skilled and educated well enough that the whites left him alone. He had occasional problems with competitors who resented his prosperous business, but he had become a model citizen in town to both blacks and whites such that they came to his defense if anyone messed with him. Even the law protected Bender. But with so many transient people, Bender never really knew what kind of mindset would come in his shop, and he stayed on guard.

Jane smiled and looked around. Sam was a bit surprised that Bender was the owner but only because Missouri was a slave state. "Excellent," he said in earnest. "Have you time to make a sale?" Bender laughed a little.

"Time? Yes, sir, I suppose if I want to stay in business, I better have time." Bender took Sam out back to his yard and showed him various farm wagons and Conestogas. "I build and repair these farm wagons, but I don't build Conestogas. I only repair and resell those. And unless you're moving an army's worth of supplies, you don't need a Conestoga. I also sell covers to drape your belongings, if you want." Sam walked around the different farm wagons, two of which were new and the rest were used.

"I'll take one of these new ones and some covers. I'll trust you to choose which one, if you don't mind," Sam said.

"Not at all," Bender said. "They're all the same, so it doesn't matter much. Where y'all headed?"

"We're from Illinois," Sam said.

"Ya don't say. I have kin there. They live in Madison County, Prairie something."

"Ridge Prairie?" Sam asked.

"Yeah, that's it," Bender said. Sam and Jane looked at each other in disbelief.

"It's an awfully small world we live in," Jane said. "What's the name? Maybe we know them."

"Hays," Bender said. Sam and Jane could not break their stare. "Did I say something wrong?"

*****

Adrien waited at the restaurant for Sam and Jane before ordering any food. Finally, the two showed up and apologized for being late.

"Father, you won't believe what just happened!" Jane said. She explained the whole story about meeting kin to Pierre and Esther Hays, and Adrien maintained a straight face as he listened. Jane was deflated by his lack of response. "Father, you hardly seem surprised. Really, what are the odds?"

"Odds?" Adrien asked. Then he looked up and squinted, adding, "I've got you beat."

"What do you mean you've got me beat?" Jane asked, somewhat offended. Adrien removed the satchel from his lap and handed it to Sam.

"You found my satchel? Where?" Sam smiled. As he took the bag, he could tell by the weight that something was in it. He and Jane looked inside, and Sam pulled to the surface a handful of the jewels he had just sold. They both looked at Adrien, utterly speechless.

"I've got you beat," Adrien confirmed.

Chapter 13

Sam, Jane, and Adrien took a carriage to the outskirts of town to talk to a horse breeder. Bill Garvin was his name, and he had a very good reputation for being honest and fair. Ordinarily, he would not be interested in helping his competition, but Bill was winding down. He wasn't old, but he felt like it. He was very thin and had a hallow look to himself, but time had not taken away his genuine good nature, and doing business with Sam boosted his spirit.

Bill had several dozens of various saddle and stock horses. After a long conversation with Bill, Sam spent some time examining his choices. Jane and her father quietly watched. The fillies and mares that were up for sale were all corralled together. The stallions were in the stable.

Sam kept a distance at first, but after a while, he sat on the fence and waited. He used no food and made no sounds to entice any of the horses. He just watched and closely studied the details of each horse. Quite some time passed, and it was hot, causing Adrien and Jane to grow a little impatient. They were about to start walking around, but finally, a horse began to walk toward Sam. It was a bay mare with a lot of mane, and she was about fourteen and a half hands with very bright eyes. She nosed right up to Sam, which restored Adrien and Jane's interest. Sam slowly climbed down from the fence, placing himself inside the corral so he could get a closer look at her. Soon, a second mare walked to him. He looked her over and admired that her shiny, dun coat emphasized her strength. She held her head and tail high and was even more friendly than the first horse. He had his first two mares chosen.

He walked to the gate and unlatched it. "Jane, come here," Sam called softly. Jane looked around as if there were more than one Jane to call. He waved to her to come. She both complied and resisted. He opened the gate enough for her to enter. Then he latched it again. He kept her close to the gate and remained beside her.

"What are we doing?" Jane whispered nervously. Jane was only somewhat experienced with horses but, even then, typically with only one at a time. She was now inside a corral with ten.

"Sharing every endeavor," Sam said. "You can choose your horse. Better, though, to let her choose you. Try to be calm. Breathe easy."

The horses were stirred a little by Sam and Jane's presence. As they moved around the corral and passed Jane, she pressed her back against the fence. Adrien watched in fascination. One palomino horse stared at Jane from across the corral. Eventually, she started to walk in Jane's direction but stopped and became disinterested. Jane took it somewhat personally, and she turned to Sam and whispered that his method could take hours. When she looked back among the horses again, she was face to face with the palomino, which became Sam's third mare. All three mares were young, ensuring years of foaling for Sam.

Sam and Jane exited the corral, and Jane found the experience to be rather thrilling. Although Sam had picked out his three mares, he remained at the corral and kept watching. He rubbed his jaw while he studied one mare in particular that had an unusually independent streak. She was unsocial and withdrawn. Bill joined Sam at the corral.

"Well, what do you think?" the breeder asked.

Sam pointed out his choices. Then he said, "I'm curious, though, about that tall chestnut one. She's a bit skittish."

"I'm not surprised you didn't pick her, but I would have said something if you did. She carried to term with her first foal, but it came stillborn. We took the foal away immediately. Might have been a mistake. She's been a little ill-tempered since. We've had to keep her separated from the other mares, and we only just rejoined her with them," Bill explained.

Sam looked concerned as he watched the chestnut mare among other mares. He confirmed in his mind that it was, in fact, a mistake not to give her some time with her stillborn foal.

Bill explained, "There were no problems with the delivery. The stillborn foal was a surprise to all of us. Very tragic. She is young, strong, and ready, though. She's not even six yet. She was saddle trained by four, but it's been a while since she's been ridden."

Sam watched the mare a while longer. "How has she responded to a stallion?" he asked.

"We haven't tried yet," the breeder answered.

"Rope her," Sam said.

"You sure? I won't take responsibility if she becomes a problem for you."

"I'm sure," Sam said.

Then the breeder took Sam to the stable, and they walked among the stallions. The stud he chose was over fifteen hands and all dark brown except for the white dagger-shaped mark running between his eyes and down to his nose. He was beautiful, and he seemed to know it. Sam also bought two draft horses that he needed to pull his new Bender wagon and Jane's furniture back to Illinois. They would also help clear his land.

Bill cut Sam no special deal except to come down slightly for taking a chance on the skittish mare. When Sam went to settle with Bill, Adrien laid down enough money to pay it all.

"What's this?" Sam asked Adrien. Jane's expression had the same question.

"Payment," he said.

"If you're investing, it's a risk," Sam warned Adrien.

"I doubt that," Bill stated before Adrien had a chance to. "Look around," the breeder said of his large and comfortable ranch. "I started all this with one mare. I didn't even have a stud. I had to hire one out. Took every penny I had and even that was not enough. I had to get a loan. But I knew I was right, so I wasn't worried. There's always a demand for horses. Any fool can make a living at selling them. But a wise man will make can make good living at it."

Jane intervened and said, "Father, your investment is too generous. You cannot afford this."

"Perhaps not. But you can," he said. Jane was confused. "I'm not investing. And this is not a gift. It's your money, dear—money that I have been saving for you since you were born. This is less than half. The rest was deposited in an account for you." Both Jane and Sam were shocked. "Between your inheritance and Sam's, your years of mediocrity are over."

Bill watched the young woman humble herself before her father with expressed, soft, and genuine appreciation as she hugged him and said, "I've not spent a single moment of my life in mediocrity. Thank you, Father."

Bill resumed business. "You'd be wise to hire out your stud. And make 'em pay," he said of breeders wanting to use Sam's stallion. "You're young, but you seem to have an eye for what you are doing and the heart for it too. Once folks know what you have here, they'll come for miles to do business."

"Do you still have that mare?" Jane asked.

"Yes, I do." Bill smiled. "Eleven foals later, I still have her, but she's done breeding. Autumn's Hope is her name. Come meet her." Bill escorted Jane back to the stable to show off his first and favorite mare. Jane was captivated by the memories he shared.

"Mr. Garvin, is there a Mrs. Garvin?" Jane inquired gently.

"Yes, there is. She's right over there." Bill pointed to a fenced plot across his land. "And she has been there for nearly ten years now."

"I'm sorry." Jane lowered her voice.

"Well, young lady, she and I had a good run together. Losing her was hard, but I'm thankful for the years we had."

"And all these? Are they your children?" Jane asked of his horses as she admired Autumn's Hope.

Bill smiled. "I guess you could say that. May and I never had any children of our own. We were both overcome with love for every horse we ever owned."

Sam had a little fear of his occupational choice before taking the trip to St. Louis, but meeting Bill increased his confidence. When he arrived the next morning for his horses, he spent a good hour or so just warming up to his chestnut mare with intent to ride her home, but she resisted fiercely. He walked her, nurtured her, fed her, rubbed her, and even named her. But when it came time to put a saddle on her, she won the battle.

"Shhh, Crimson, shhh," Sam said to her over and over as he rubbed her neck, combed her mane with his fingers, and fed her slices of an apple. "We have to go home, and I need you to take me. You're going to be all right. I'm going to take good care of you," he told her in a soft voice. Bill watched with Jane and Adrien, and any reservations he had about Sam becoming a breeder fled.

Bill walked over and held the reins as Sam made another attempt at the saddle. Crimson moved but not in time, and the saddle was on. Sam slowly tightened the saddle belt around Crimson and looked at Bill, knowing that was the easy part. Bill handed the reins to Sam and told him to be ready because the degree of Crimson's resistance was yet to be known. Bill held onto the harness as Sam began to mount. Sam intended to walk Crimson immediately once he was in the saddle, but Crimson pulled her harness out of Bill's hands and reared to a near full stand. Sam leaned his body forward as far as he could, hanging on to the saddle horn with one hand and putting his arm around her neck to balance his weight, which prevented him from being thrown. When Crimson landed, Sam immediately moved her forward and rode her around in several circles until she calmed down. Sam leaned forward again to whisper in her ear as he patted her neck. Bill was impressed.

The brief time spent with Bill seemed much longer; Sam and Jane felt very close to him as though they had known him for years.

*****

The trip back to Edwardsville was long and slow, but no one seemed to mind. Once ferried across the Missouri River, the scenery was new for Sam and Jane, and Adrien observed some mild improvements to the roads, though Jane's furniture still bounced around considerably. Sam rode Crimson and tied his stallion to his saddle horn to better acquaint the two. His other three mares were tied to the rear of the wagon that Adrien drove. Jane sat beside her father and winced every time they collided with a major dip in the road. She would reach for her covered and secured furniture with her hand as if to comfort a wounded child.

Sam took advantage of the time on the road to plan. After about a mile, he opened a new discussion with Adrien about his plan to hire help in the construction of his house, barn, and stable to expedite their completion. He discussed the layout and schedule with Adrien at length. Winter would be on them with force before he knew it, and Sam wanted to be settled before the first frost. He was comforted by Adrien's insights and blessing.

And what of his horses? Crimson already rode like she had been with Sam for years. If all went well, she would breed first, and the others would follow, except for the bay mare. Sam had other plans for her.

Sam also found himself with time to think about things he had not had time to consider recently. For what seemed like several miles, he wondered about Amos. His younger brother was sixteen now. As Sam tried to imagine what Amos might be like, he remembered what he was like himself at sixteen. Several descriptions came to his mind, but one summed it all up: defeated. Why hadn't Amos answered any of Sam's letters? Did Amos even receive them? Sam was now married, and he suddenly had land to clear, a house to build, and a business to manage. He also wanted to go to Washington to get his brother, and that pressure weighed heavily on him. Was it from knowing the journey would create a burden on him and Jane? Or was it from knowing he would have to face Bishop to get to Amos? Both, Sam concluded. *One more year*, he thought. Amos would be seventeen or so. Then Bishop wouldn't have a say. After nearly eight hours of travel, the Pruitt home was a welcomed sight.

*****

The next morning, Pierre and Esther came for their first day of work since the wedding. Adrien left for his office, purposely ignoring the condition of his home. Pierre saw Jane's dressing divider laying out with the trash to be burned and wondered what happened to it. Sam showed up and dropped another load on the low pile. Pierre watched Sam light a fire to the collection of garbage and quickly walk away without explanation. Pierre raised his eyebrows and shook his head.

Esther found Jane's room in a mess before Jane had a chance to divert her attention away.

"Esther, I'll clean in here. Surely there are needs elsewhere," Jane said, and she blushed from embarrassment.

"Mrs. Callahan! There are needs everywhere! What happened? This ain't no way to start your marriage!" Esther said with her hands on her hips. Then she turned to walk down the stairs and said under her breath, "I never seen this house in such a mess."

"Pierre!" Sam came back. Pierre became interested, hoping Sam would share the story behind the burning evidence. "Can you and Esther come for supper tomorrow night? And bring Danny?" Pierre was noticeably disappointed but accepted the supper invitation.

"Do we have to cook?" Pierre barked as Sam walked away. Pierre shook his head and stirred the fire.

Danny had not been to the Pruitts' often. The wedding was the first time in years. He dressed up for the supper invitation and preferred to stay that way in spite of everyone else's casual attire. Much of dinner revolved around descriptions of the trip to St. Louis and the handing out of several gifts. Adrien drank his wine and enjoyed watching the Hays's reactions to Jane's picks for them. Then Sam asked them to come to the barn to see his new investment.

Sam introduced his acquisitions. "This is Silhouette, this is Crimson, this is Sunny, and this is my stallion, Simon."

"What about this one?" Danny asked of the bay, two stalls over.

"Well, I think the owner should name his own horse," Sam stated. Danny shrugged his shoulders, waiting for Sam to give a name. "So go ahead," said Sam. Danny's eyes slowly showed signs of understanding that Sam was giving him the horse. Neither Jane nor Adrien had any idea this was Sam's intent when he bought four mares instead of three. Danny could hardly move. "What? You don't want her?" Sam asked in jest.

Danny moved his eyes from Sam to the horse and walked to her. He slowly raised his hand to pet her neck, and he looked her all over. Everyone quietly watched Danny meet his new friend, except

Adrien; he watched Sam. After a few minutes, Sam joined Danny while the others talked amongst themselves.

"Why'd you do this, Sam?" Danny whispered.

"Remember all that time together on the farm? I wouldn't be here now, Danny, were it not for you," said Sam. He leaned his back against the stall and talked to Danny as Danny faced his horse. "And I am not going forward without you. If you're willing to help me, together, we might be able to make something of this. And I'll make it worth your while if anything comes of it." Sam looked around at the horses. "I should tell you now, though, it's going to be a slow start at first and a lot of work, and I plan to bring Amos in as soon as I can." He looked at Danny again. "Danny? Are you listening to me?" Danny finally broke his trance from the horse. "Are you in?"

"Yeah," Danny confirmed and smiled. "Yeah, I'm in."

"Sam?" Jane called. "Wasn't there something significant about this wagon?" She smiled. She could hardly wait to tell the Hays family about meeting one of their family members in St. Louis.

Sam retold the story about his wagon purchase from a man named George Bender. He was dramatic when he shared the details, such that it reminded Jane of Nathan. He finished with saying, "I think he has some sons."

"Mama! That's your name," Danny said. "Do you know 'im?" Both Pierre and Esther became quiet. Esther tightened her lips and walked back to the house, leaving everyone, except Pierre, confused. They waited for an explanation.

"George is Esther's brother, and they were slaves with the same master," Pierre began with sadness in his voice. "George bought his freedom and never looked back. Esther got her freedom a few years later only because when her master died, he freed all his slaves. But she could still be a slave today, and George wouldn't care. It's been so long Esther didn't even know he was alive. Don't know why he even bothered to mention he had kin. And last I knew, he didn't have no sons." Pierre looked apologetically to Danny. Then the two went to join Esther at the house. Danny was hardly affected by this news. Sam, though, all but disappeared in thoughts of Amos.

Chapter 14

Adrien stared at the letter given to him by the postmaster for a while before placing it unopened in his breast pocket. Now was not the time. After a full day of business and dinner alone in town, Adrien went home and sat privately in his dark study for nearly an hour. Finally, he lit a lamp, pulled the letter from within his breast pocket and opened it.

> Dear Adrien,
>
> I received word about your son and bear with you the burden of brokenheartedness. I cannot claim to understand the Lord's ways in these matters, nor do I cling to my own understanding, for God's purpose exceeds human knowledge, and the magnitude of such a loss is unfathomable, well beyond the reach of any man's mind. The pain that must have come when such a bright light was extinguished is a fearsome thought, and were I able to lift it from you and carry it myself, I would. Please come to Philadelphia and permit your heart and mind a period of reprieve from your grief. Your guest room is already prepared.
>
> Your very sincere and devoted friend,
> Edward Coles

Adrien read it again and let the depth of it drive him to tears, though only briefly. Then he pulled out a sheet of paper, dipped his pen in ink, and began drafting a response of appreciation with a promise to make the much-needed trip in autumn.

*****

"Black Hawk Is Finished!" the newspaper's headline read.

> One bad Indian treaty; lots of white settlement on ceded Indian land.
> One Chief's pursuit for justice; boundless empathy from powerless generals, former politicians, and friends.
> Black Hawk's misplaced trust in native allies and British loyalties; pleadings and warnings from General Atkinson not to cross the river into Illinois.
> Indian skirmishes leaving a trail of blood through white settlements; sloppy retaliation from the poorly trained State militia.
> Mixed and confusing messages of surrender from Black Hawk's braves when British help did not come; deep rooted fear of this mighty foe led to deadly outcome.
> Gruesome and vicious Indian mutilation tactics; merciless military response to all Sauk including women and children.
> More mutilation; more annihilation.
> Blood; blood.
> Defeat.

The Battle of Big Axe brought an end to the four-month war, the only war to be fought in Illinois. Hundreds of Sauk died on the east side of the Mississippi River. Nearly one hundred more died upon defenselessly crossing the river and facing the Sioux nation who aligned with the army as a known enemy to the Sauk. Black Hawk, his lower chiefs, and his braves were now prisoners, handed over to the US government by the Winnebagos, with whom he had sought refuge.

Adrien folded the newspaper, let his memories run through him, and then he stored it in his desk. Sam did much the same, except he tossed the paper in the fireplace, trying to let it go.

"Up for a short trip?" Adrien asked Sam upon visiting him.

"To where?" Sam asked.

"To catch a glimpse of Black Hawk. He and his braves are being held at Fort Crawford under the authority of Colonel Zack Taylor. They're being transferred to Jefferson Barracks by steamboat. The public hopes to see him near Galena, but I know a better spot. And I want to introduce you to an old friend," Adrien answered, and he pointed them to Fort Armstrong on Rock Island.

Prior to settlement, Rock Island had been home to many Indians and, in more recent years, primarily the Sauk. Black Hawk was born, raised, and trained to brave and chief status in this area. This was his home, which was lost in tragic treaty dealings.

In 1816, Rock Island became home to Fort Armstrong, which was a strategic stronghold in and adjacent to Indian territory. It was named for a general from the Revolutionary War and former Secretary of War, John Armstrong. The purpose of the fort was to support the removal of Indians that were east of the Mississippi River.

General Winfield Scott asked the messenger, "Visitors? Who are they?"

"Mr. Adrien Pruitt and Mr. Samuel Callahan. The commander will allow it, if you wish, sir," the young officer advised.

"Pruitt?" Scott asked. The officer confirmed. "The risk they accept has me curious. I'll see them."

The tall, lean Adrien Pruitt met his even taller friend, Winfield Scott. Their greeting was barely finished before Scott said, "Adrien, your son…unless you say otherwise, I'll keep my words few to spare you revived pain. Know that I am grieving with you."

"Those words are more than sufficient," Adrien answered. A moment of silence was given before Scott took them on a brisk walk.

Adrien and Sam stood with Scott as he lowered his spyglass and continued to stare up the Mississippi River. Then he said, "Go tell the men, Private, that they can all stand on the bank downriver."

The private saluted and ran across the fort to where Scott's men were being confined for the cholera. He stopped abruptly, adjusted his uniform, came to attention, and shouted, "Black Hawk's comin'!" He was addressing the remnant of the general's force that was once a thousand men strong when it left the East for war. The cholera had killed nearly six hundred of his men, in the midst of which many others deserted out of desperate fear for their lives. Only 220 troops remained, all of whom were resting in quarantine at Fort Armstrong having marched miles through death across Illinois. Scott lost more men in the Black Hawk War than all the other commanders, all of the settlers, and all of the Indians combined without ever seeing or engaging in a single battle.

A sergeant jumped to his feet and asked, "Where's the general, Private?"

"On the riverbank, waitin' for his boat to be readied," the private answered. "We must hurry if we want to see Black Hawk. He's comin' downriver now."

The soldiers quickly formed up into double columns and marched to an isolated spot at the river's edge.

"Your boat is ready, sir," the general's aide said.

As Scott handed his spyglass to Adrien, he said, "This damn war never should have happened. Black Hawk did not want war. Blood should have never been spilled. Untrained militia is no way to engage a conflict." Then he followed his escort to a small boat, which he boarded to drift out midriver to greet Black Hawk.

Black Hawk was enjoying light conversation with his charge officer, First Lieutenant Jefferson Davis, a West Point graduate who came from the south to partake in his first war. But the conversation soon became heavier.

Black Hawk looked to the east as the steamboat moved downriver toward Rock Valley. Davis listened respectfully while the great chief reflected, "This was the land of my fathers, the land where I grew up and became a chief. It is my home. The Great Spirit told my grandfather to bring his family to this land. At the same time, the Great Spirit also told the son of the French king to come to this land. The young French chief honored my Grandfather with loyalty and gifts. Even the Spanish were close by in St. Louis, and their chief was a great father to our Sauk Nation. Our only problems came from our enemies of old: the Osage, the Cherokee, and others who wanted the land of our fathers. I watched my father die nobly in a battle with the Cherokee trying to prevent any loss of our land, and we succeeded. It was not until the Americans came that real problems for the Sauk began.

"Your nation has many great fathers and chiefs. I am no longer a warrior but am reduced to a civil subject. There is no one now to lead my people, and just as I have pleaded with your leaders over the years to make right the Treaty of 1804, I will spend my remaining days pleading again for the protection of my conquered family."

They were interrupted by a command. "Lieutenant! Bring the prisoner to the deck!"

"Yes, sir!" he answered. Davis brought Black Hawk to the upper deck of the steamboat placing him in full view of Fort Armstrong. They could see Scott stopped in the middle of the river waiting on their approach, but the steamboat did not slow down.

"Why are we not stopping?" Black Hawk asked. "The War Chief must board."

"The cholera took nearly all of the general's men. He cannot board due to the present danger of spreading the disease," Davis said.

As the boats got closer to each other, Black Hawk said, "The War Chief looks well. News spreads that he tends to his dying men without any harm from this disease."

Davis said, "The boat captain will not take the chance."

Black Hawk scowled and said of the boat captain, "Coward."

Davis straightened his stance and saluted General Scott as the steamboat passed closely by the small boat. Scott saluted back; then he exchanged observations with Black Hawk while his depleted unit quietly watched the steamboat float by en route to Jefferson Barracks, Missouri. Meanwhile, Adrien and Sam took turns watching through the spyglass without speaking.

When Scott returned, Adrien and Sam joined him in his quarters where the two seasoned men seemed to continue in conversation where it left off years before. They dined and drank and remembered. Sam listened and learned.

Scott asked Sam, "What do you know of your father-in-law's service during the War of 1812?" Sam looked at Adrien who did not look back at Sam. "That's what I thought." Scott laughed. "He never was one to boast." Scott thrust his finger at Adrien and said, "This man should be dead. A man who walked into a small enemy camp of some very fierce British and Indian men to single-handedly rescue two young American soldiers should do us all the honor of boasting." Scott and Sam stared at Adrien and waited.

Finally, Adrien began, "They were just kids. They belonged to my company, and I was responsible for them. When I sent them to spy, they were captured, and because they were Irish and considered by the British to be deserters, we were sent word that they were going to be executed for treason. On the same day, I received a letter from my wife telling of the birth of my son, and I think I went blind. I had to get those boys back. I didn't consider the danger, really."

Scott pushed Adrien for more. "Tell him how you did it." When Adrien hesitated, Scott took over. "Ah, it would be faster if you would just write it down." Scott turned to Sam and continued describing Adrien's heroic feat. "He left his own camp without word. No one knew where he went or if he, himself, had been captured. He left his uniform coat and hat behind to conceal his rank and identity. He snuck up to the enemy camp, which was rather confident at the time due to recent victories, so they were relaxed. He came up with his plan while sitting in hiding and watching the British commander shave. He threw a few rocks as far as he could to make some noise in the distant trees to distract the guards and the aide, and it worked. They mistakenly left the commander alone just long enough to give Adrien time to sneak up on the commander and put a pistol to the back of his head." Sam pulled his chair in a little closer. "That's right. He simply walked into that camp, and then he whispered, 'You have two American prisoners, and you will release them to me immediately.' Just then, the guards and the aide returned, and upon seeing their commander being held hostage, they aimed their muskets. Adrien rammed his pistol so hard against the commander's head that it made him bleed. The commander quietly ordered them to drop their weapons and get the prisoners. He walked out of the camp with the commander and the two Irish soldiers. He went a short distance, gagged and bound the commander, and left him there. Then he brought his two Irish boys safely back to his camp, which gained him fierce respect and loyalty from all of his men for the rest of the war and even beyond it."

"Isn't this heroic act captured in war events somewhere?" Sam asked while looking in awe at his father-in-law.

Scott replied, "Very few heroic acts of any war are captured, shared, or even remembered. Very few. For every one that is written down, a thousand more are not." Then he asked Adrien, jokingly, "Where was your bravery when I was held prisoner?"

"Once is bravery. Twice is stupidity," Adrien said with a slight smile.

"I read of your imprisonment," Sam said to Scott.

"I remained with the British for a solid year. But I was exchanged for British prisoners and back in the war thereafter within hours," Scott answered. "After three years of fighting the most powerful military on earth, the very same army that defeated Napoleon, it ended with nothing gained or lost."

Adrien said, "Not exactly. Twenty-two thousand men died, mostly American. The White House and Capitol building were burned, Indian nations suffered more defeats, and the Battle of New Orleans catalyzed the political career of Andrew Jackson."

Scott nodded in acknowledgment, and he said, "True, yet regardless of what one might think of President Jackson, no one can dismiss the military courage and successes of General Jackson."

Scott walked his guests to their horses where Adrien asked, "What now, Winfield?"

Scott looked out at the terrain beyond the fort and around the inside of the fort, and he answered, "If I don't die here with the rest of my men, I suspect I will answer the next call of duty."

In the weeks that followed, Scott fearlessly provided direct aid and care to his men that were dying of the cholera, including the young private that summoned the troops to the riverbank to catch a glimpse of Black Hawk.

*****

"Illinois is described as being a sick place to live!" Charles Mueller complained to Adrien and Sam over his beer at the tavern. "Look here." Charles showed them the newspaper. "The cholera moved from Canada to the Great Lakes region, and it traveled with the army in this damn war against Black Hawk right here to Illinois!" Charles pointed to other articles about misery, fear, isolation, abandoned homes, death, too many flies, and not enough caskets.

"Many thousands have died in Europe, and we are on the brink of the same." Charles read some more. "Hundreds have already died in Baltimore, and New York, having lost count, simply estimates a hundred dead a day. And now nearly two hundred more have died on Rock Island, many of them General Scott's men. It has already made its way down the Mississippi to New Orleans. Running is useless; where can anyone go that's safe? It's everywhere. It says here that one minute you're having a drink with your friends; the next, you're depleted of all fluids and left debilitated with a nasty shade of gloom. The nation is encircled by death." Charles looked at Sam and Adrien with fear in his eyes.

Adrien had seen enough panic in his lifetime to resist becoming so now, except perhaps for the article on the back side of Charles's paper titled *Bank War*, which covered the debate about the closing of the Second Bank of the United States. President Jackson was becoming insistent on shutting it down upon the expiration of the bank's charter, if not sooner. *What was the president thinking?* Adrien wondered. The bank had its problems, but it also provided economic security for the country. And what did the president mean by saying that the holdings would be distributed from the Second Bank to select state banks? While Jackson argued reasonably that the Second Bank of the United States was biased toward the industrial north and overlooked, if not omitted entirely, loans to lesser populations, ambitions, and Southern states, closing it posed great risk to the nation's stability, which left Adrien troubled.

Sam, on the other hand, did panic as he imagined how the cholera had spread through the army and militia while advancing on Black Hawk. Would Nathan have fallen to this enemy if not to the one he met? Sam managed to escape the war, but would he be able to escape the grip of this disease? What of Jane and Adrien? He remembered the scene of panic at the hotel in St. Louis. Could similar panic happen in Edwardsville? Sam took another drink and changed the subject.

"All of my mares were in season last week," Sam said. Charles and Adrien were taken aback by Sam's odd contribution to the conversation. "My stallion was quite busy." Sam smiled.

Adrien laughed, raised his mug, and said, "To your stallion."

Charles shook his head and conceded. "Yes, to your stallion." Their mugs met, and then they drank.

*****

Summer was quickly coming to an end. Jane and Sam spent every spare minute they had at their property working with the builders and clearing sections of land to plant corn and other crops. Jane thought she knew what hard work was until she combined a full day hoeing with the scorching heat. She had spent more than her share of time in a garden but never like this. Even after tilling, the ground resisted her. Her hands were raw from several days of battle, and the pain in her back never seemed to let up. She thought about the thousands upon thousands of slaves that faced the fields day after day, year after year, and she forced herself not to complain. As she held on to the hoe for support and arched backward seeking some relief, she was frightened by a shadow on the ground that did not come from her.

"I'm sorry. I didn't mean to scare you," said an elderly black man. "I'm Joseph, your neighbor."

"Ah, Mr. Pope! Of course." Jane laughed with her hand over her heart. "My husband told me to be prepared to meet you. Evidently, I did not listen! I'm Jane."

"Well, it's nice to finally meet you. I'm here with an invitation. It's hotter than normal this time of year, and my wife is putting a nice lunch together. Thought you and Sam might want to come by and join us when you're ready for a break."

"I hope you won't find it inappropriate of me to say thank God. We would be delighted," Jane answered. Sam was relieved when Jane told him of the invite. By the time the sun reached its noon position, they were both already worn out.

Joseph and Vivian's quarter section of land had become under-worked and overgrown, other than what they needed to sustain themselves. They were in their early fifties, and their only daughter was grown and gone, maybe even dead. They couldn't be sure. Joseph was happy to accommodate Sam's request to rent out grazing land, as the added income was deeply needed. Their home was humble, and the adjacent barn seemed too large for the minimal farm life it now housed. A few chickens, a hog, a cow, and two horses were all that remained from what once was a lively and vibrant setting. Hot days, like this one, reminded them both that they were tired, and they were silently waiting on the Lord to bring them home. But Sam and Jane disrupted that somehow.

Vivian's home was comfortable, but she and Joseph had not had guests in years, and she was nervous. She was concerned that her new neighbors would look down on her, but that concern vanished upon meeting them. Jane, too, was worried. She was a mess from working the hard ground, and there seemed to her to be no sufficient recovery to her appearance.

Vivian and Joseph both showed signs of wear and tear. Vivian still had a curvy figure, which left a lingering hint of her more attractive, younger years, but her walk was a bit bent and strained. Her hair was gray, and she had eyes that seemed to want to tell of the situations she had endured and survived. She normally pulled her short, coarse hair into a tight simple bun. But the events of the day revived her interest in making the effort to return to her teased, smoothed, gathered, and pinned hairstyle. It might as well have been a day for church.

Joseph had the kind of handsomeness that men acquired with age. He was fit and healthy, and he still deeply loved his wife. He concealed his resentment that he could not do more to make a better life for himself and Vivian, and he was hopeful that Sam's grazing plan would ensure a few extra dollars to spend on her for special occasions.

He had been a slave, but it was hard to tell, and his freedom had come with planning and preparation. Though educating slaves was illegal, his owner did it anyway. Joseph could read and write, and he had numerous skills, but his freedom seemed to be met with such societal resistance that he could never secure a strong foothold. The only reason he had not given up was Vivian.

Lunch lasted long and became supper as they all enjoyed the company. Joseph and Vivian shared some of their wisdom and experience with Sam and Jane.

Joseph used to make furniture, and he took Sam to his barn and offered him use of any tools he needed. He displayed his carving collection to Sam and demonstrated the use of a few choice pieces, much to Sam's interest and fascination. He showed Sam a chair he made and described other pieces like tables, desks, wardrobes, four-post bed frames, and more that he sold off and on well enough to prevent him from ever entering into debt for maintaining his land, as so many of his colored neighbors had suffered and consequently lost all they had.

He took Sam on a wagon ride around his acreage and discussed good grazing options for Sam's horses. He told Sam they could cut a section out of the fence on their border and put in a gate for easy access when rotating the horses.

Meanwhile, Vivian rubbed a soothing ointment on Jane's hands, which brought her instant relief. She introduced Jane to many remedies for home and health. Jane was intrigued, and she made no attempt to prevent Vivian from sharing her long list of must-haves and needs-to-know.

As the sun was dipping down, Joseph observed that Sam and Jane lost any remaining opportunity for work, and that was met with genuine thanks from his guests.

"I don't know what the highlight of this day has been: the wonderful lunch or the joy and comfort of getting to know our neighbors," Jane said. "I look forward to repaying your kindness." Sam agreed with appreciation.

"How much longah 'fore you settled?" Vivian asked.

"Settled? Years, probably," Sam confessed. "But the house is almost done. So we'll be moving in, in a few weeks. I think I'll take your advice on that fence gate, Joseph."

"You just say when, and I'll be there to help," Joseph said. And Jane and Sam pulled away in their carriage.

Chapter 15

S am went to his property early to start work on a small corn-crib, which would be placed adjacent to the barn to hold the anticipated annual harvest. Before he left, he kissed Jane, who spent half of her time at her father's making bedding and preserving food for the winter and the other half of her time working the land of her new home.

"I'll be along later. I'll bring you something to eat," she said as he left, which was her routine. When she arrived and saw his work in progress, she thanked God for his skills and determination to meet their needs, which inspired her to keep up a good pace in doing her part.

After a few days of work, the crib was finished with just the right space between the slats for the corn to get air. It was late in the evening when Sam put all his tools away. Jane smiled at the crib's perfect design, and she took her husband home. He washed after a quick meal, and he fell into bed beside Jane completely worn out, which made him wonder why he couldn't sleep.

When he forced his eyes closed, images of the crib kept coming to his mind, and he tossed to the left, and then to the right, onto his back, onto his front; then he repeated it all over, somehow managing not to wake Jane. Finally, he fell asleep, but he woke abruptly from a dream that he was trapped alive in a coffin.

The dream scared him. He couldn't shut his mind off from the feeling of being trapped. He became angry, and as each moment passed, he became angrier. But he didn't know why. Enraged, he got up, went back to the property, stared at the corncrib, and aggressively tore it down.

When Jane arrived in the morning, she saw the pile of wood that only hours before belonged to a beautifully constructed storehouse, and she sank in worry. Neither she nor Sam made mention of it.

A few days later, Sam began to rebuild the crib, but he couldn't complete it. It made him physically ill, and it sat unfinished. One day, he stood again before the partial construction, which conflicted and angered him to the core. He turned away, but he came upon another obstacle: Jane was standing there watching. Unable to look at her, he closed his eyes and turned his head.

"What is it? What's troubling you?" she asked.

"I just can't make it right," he said. He walked away leaving her terribly confused.

Later, she found him working again on the corncrib. She left him alone except to say that she would come back with dinner, if he liked. He simply shook his head and kept working.

As she pulled away in her carriage, she prayed, "Lord, free him now from whatever has him in bondage. Please, Father. Whatever it takes. Do not delay. I'm so afraid." All the way home, she petitioned with tears streaming down her face.

Sam finished the crib just as it was starting to get dark. Jane had not returned, and he became angry again. He gritted his teeth and looked at the structure with contempt. He wanted to tear the whole crib down again, but something made him acknowledged his spiritual and mental disturbance, and he controlled himself.

While taking a few deep breaths, he noticed a raised nail head on the floor. He stepped inside and began to hammer it down causing the crib to rock the door closed. Sam turned to the sound of the latch falling into place, locking him inside. He dropped his hammer and tried to get the door to open, but it was no use. His construction was too good.

He looked between the slats in hopes that Jane would arrive soon, in spite of his opposing request. Nothing. He pushed on the door again and again. Then he yelled for help, hoping someone would hear him. No one did. He picked up his hammer and tried to pound the slats loose, but they would not give. He gritted his teeth again and threw the hammer as hard as he could. It bounced off the wall and hit him in the shin. He let out a yell of pain, fell over, and held his leg, which bled through his pants and onto his hand. He lay there alone, trapped, wounded, helpless, and feeling buried alive.

He looked between the slats until the sun went down. Jane did not come, and he heard a voice in his head say, *Why would she? You can't keep pushing her away and expect her to keep coming back.* Regret consumed him.

Minutes felt like hours. He could hear the crickets and see the dense star patterns in the clear night sky. He said aloud, "Come on! Someone has to hear me!" And he yelled again for help. Nothing. Then he yelled to heaven, "God, can't you send someone to free me from this prison?"

Sam heard in his mind, *I did,* and it jolted him. His eyes were wide open in the darkness trying to see the light. He scooted to the wall of the crib for support, knowing he wasn't going anywhere.

"Okay, you got me here. What is it you want me to know?" he asked. He heard nothing. So Sam listed truths from Jesus's teachings, as if verifying what he understood and accepted as gospel. "You are the way. You are the light. You tell the truth. The way is narrow. Faith like a mustard seed can move mountains." He went on and on reciting scripture from book to book, almost with anger. "I know these things, Lord. What else do you want me to know? Why do you have me in here?" He sat in silence alone with his thoughts for a long time. Then he shouted, "And if I know these things, then why isn't it enough? Why I am I still so angry?"

Sam waited and waited. Still no answers. Then he whispered, "Yeah well, there are a few things I want you to know too. I'm right to be angry. Where were you? When I was beaten for being loved by my mother, where were you? When I was being beaten for just being born, where were you? When Amos was whipped in my place, where were you? When I couldn't have friends because of him, where were you? I didn't do anything wrong. I was just a child. I didn't ask for this. Amos was just a child, and he still is. He didn't ask for this. Mother was just a gentle woman whose good was returned with evil. Why? Where were you?"

As Sam wept, he remembered one more scripture: "Jesus wept." He wiped his eyes and nodded in understanding.

"You were right there with me, right there beside me, and I know you are with me now." He came to his feet and walked around, ignoring the pain in his leg from the hammer. He continued to share, "What else do you want to know? Do you want to know that I am still lost? There's so much I don't understand, and that scares me. Please keep teaching me. Do you want to know my darkest thoughts? That I hate him? That I passionately want him to suffer deeply? That I want him to pay for what he did to us? That I think about that all the time? Do you want to know that I still long for him to see me, to approve of me, to love me? And even worse than all that, I am terrified of becoming him? Please don't let that happen. God, don't let that happen. Whatever the cost, sift me thoroughly so that I don't become like him. Help me become like you, instead." He took a break for a few minutes. He lay down. Then he said, "I know how Jane feels. I don't want to hurt anymore."

I won't hurt you, Sam heard. Comforted, he talked to Jesus until he was empty. Then he fell asleep.

*****

It was very late. While Adrien and Jane were driving to the property to find Sam, Jane was convinced that she was wrong to ever doubt him, and Adrien was convinced that he was right all along.

Jane said, to assure herself, "I'm sure he is just overworked and worried about how much he has to carry for us. There is still so much to do. Surely, you remember when you and Mother were building your home together. It couldn't have been easy."

Adrien silently remembered that it was hard enough with a clear vision. How hard will it be without one? He pulled the carriage to a stop. Sam's horse was wandering around. They looked all over the property, but he was nowhere to be found. Adrien was furious, but he didn't show it to Jane.

"He's not here. We'll leave his horse in the barn in case he comes back here and he needs it," Adrien said gently, but he was seething inside over his hatred toward Sam for confirming his old prediction.

Jane's heart was pounding. "Father, where could he have gone? I'm so worried."

"Could he be at Joseph's?" Adrien asked.

Jane gasped. "Yes, I'm sure you're right. Can we go and see?"

Sam woke to a sound, and when he looked between the slats, he saw Adrien and Jane driving away. He yelled, but he was too late; they could not hear him. He closed his eyes, laughed, and said, "Okay, what else should we talk about?" And he and the Lord went another round.

*****

In the morning, Sam felt surprisingly rested. The sun streaked through the slats, and he stretched and sat up to find the door to the crib open. His brow narrowed as he looked around.

He rode up to the Pruitts' and entered through the kitchen where Jane stood over the table seating Esther, Pierre, Danny, and Reverend Hunt.

"Sam!" Jane said, and she rushed to him. They wrapped their arms around each other. Everyone was happy to see him. Just then, Adrien entered having returned from an early morning start of his day. Jane continued, "Where have you been? Father and I came out to the property to find you, but you were not there."

"I was there. I fell asleep in the corncrib," Sam explained. Jane sighed and smiled in relief. Sam placed his hands on both sides of Jane's face to make her look at him, and he said, "I'm sorry. I'm really sorry. Please forgive me." She nodded. Adrien lowered his head, nodded, and smirked as if in his own conversation.

The reverend had no idea what was going on, but he knew God's ways such that he said, "Sam, I'm glad to know you are all right. Come by for a visit later."

Sam assured, "Oh, I will."

As the reverend left, Esther slapped her hand on the table and said, "Well, looks like we can all git back to work," and she and Pierre left too.

Jane said, "Let's stay here today. I will go make a bath for you."

Danny got up and stared at Sam. Then he said in disgust, "Who falls asleep in a corncrib when he could come home and sleep in a warm bed beside his wife? You' a damn fool."

Sam laughed as Danny walked out. He turned to pour himself some coffee but stopped pouring upon hearing Adrien ask, "How did you get out?"

Sam turned around with the pot in one hand, his cup in the other, and he looked at Adrien curiously, knowing he had said nothing about being locked in the crib. Then he came to a realization and said, "It was you. You opened the door."

Adrien answered, "Did you think God did it?" Sam returned to pouring his coffee, a bit annoyed. "Don't be too hard on yourself. Early in my marriage, I once prayed in anguish for God to relieve my financial strain. We had just built our home, and my business wasn't moving as fast as I had planned. I was desperately broke, with only seven dollars in my safe. That was it. And I prayed on my face for a miracle." Sam leaned against the counter and drank his coffee as he listened to Adrien confess. "Soon thereafter, I came to my office, opened my safe, and there sat two thousand dollars in addition to my seven. I was shocked. And I praised God for multiplying my funds. I told my wife all about it. And though God did answer my prayer, he did multiply my funds, it wasn't quite the monetary procreation I had imagined. My new wife explained that she had delivered to me, by way of surprise, her dowry of which I knew nothing. She saved it for a time such as the one we were in and only after she knew confidently that I was not lazy.

"Though I felt rather foolish, it occurred to me that God allowed it all, especially the timing of it. I was brought to a point of complete dependency on him, so he had me right where he wanted me." Adrien paused and Sam remained curious. Then Adrien asked, "How long did you wrestle him last night?" Sam was quiet. "All night? Who won?" Sam smiled softly. "He trapped you, all right. And make no mistake, he also set you free, just like moving the stone from your tomb to raise you from the dead." Sam stopped drinking his coffee and listened carefully. "You can be sure it was God who opened that door. I know because he raised me last night, as well.

"I was angry with you over your recent behavior, and my fears of you revisited me. And I wrestled with a lie that brought me to shame, once again, because I listened to the wrong voice. I began believing that I was right after all, that you and Bishop are the same. I was trapped, just like you, until I chose instead to wrestle with the truth, to which I lost the fight. That's a fight God always wins. And here is the truth: you are Samuel Callahan, not Bishop Callahan." Tears started to run down Sam's face as Adrien moved closer. "And I will never allow myself to be confused about that again. That's when I got up and went back to find you. When I found you locked in the crib, I knew it was God's doing." Adrien put his hand on Sam's shoulder and said, "Yours is not an easily won battle, son. But I am with you and for you. I know you can do it."

Adrien released him, and as Sam nodded and wiped his tears, Jane walked in. She stopped abruptly, not knowing what she was walking in to. Adrien said, "That's just one story about my wife. Hopefully, the next one will make us laugh instead of cry." And he left.

*****

Weeks later, Jane straightened the white tablecloth over her dining table and pushed the chairs in with uniform space between them. She placed a candle at the center of the table and lit it. Then she set the table for two, stepped back, and looked. The first meal in her newly finished home was about to be served.

The Callahan home was a two-story farmhouse with four bedrooms upstairs. Downstairs were the kitchen, the dining room, a sitting room with an enormous fireplace, and a small separate area for office space. The house was raised, as it was not uncommon for the Mississippi River's floodwaters to reach several miles beyond its banks, and this made for a large storage space that reached well under the house. The home had a covered porch on both the front and the back. The barn was near the house with a separate twenty-stall stable and a corral beyond to accommodate Sam's anticipated growing herd of horses.

Four each of apple, plum, pear, and sour cherry trees were planted, and Sam estimated five years to the first harvest. The garden, though, would provide a source of free food starting in summer, weather and pests permitting.

Sam rubbed Crimson's nose as he looked at her and then at his other stabled mares, and he wondered if their time with his stallion had taken. It could still be months before he would know if any of them were pregnant, and he would not permit a foal to leave its dam until at least six months old, preferably longer. Sam calculated that the soonest he could start selling any horses would not be for another fifteen months, and even then, only foals. He still had plans to expand his numbers by at least another dozen, to include specifically, Morgans. He wondered why anyone would come all the way to Edwardsville for a horse.

"Help me, Lord," Sam prayed as he committed all his labors to God. He washed his hands and face in a barrel of cold rainwater and shook off the excess on the way to the house. It was getting dark and a little chilly on this early October day, and he could see smoke rising from the chimney and warm lantern light glowing through the window. He stopped at a distance and watched Jane as she walked back and forth between the kitchen and dining room. He was finally home.

Jane served supper and sat down. She and Sam had been married for almost five months, but it wasn't until now that it felt like it. Sam took Jane's hand and lowered his head.

He prayed, "Father, who are we that you should be mindful of us? Regardless of what others choose and regardless of our circumstances, we commit ourselves to you, Lord. We pray that you will bless this home, bless this meal, and lead us to be ever mindful servants of you. Amen." And Jane echoed.

He took a bite, raised his head, and closed his eyes as he enjoyed the flavor of Jane's fine cooking. He looked at her from the corner of his eye and smiled. She was pleased that he liked his meal.

"Something tells me Crimson is pregnant," Sam said. "Maybe it's just wishful thinking, but I'm pretty sure."

"Me too," Jane said and smiled.

"Really? You think so?" Sam was surprised and a bit excited by the validation. "Does she seem different to you somehow?"

Jane did not answer. Instead, she stopped eating, placed her fork on her plate and her hands in her lap, and she looked deliberately at Sam. He waited for her answer and was confused by her stare. Suddenly, he jumped to his feet, which knocked his chair over. Then he got down on his knees and reached for her as though he was afraid to touch her.

"It's all right, Sam. I won't break," she said with a warm smile. He took her into his arms and kissed her again and again.

Jane stayed close to home during the months of her pregnancy, as was the tradition for expectant women. Public appearances exposed the intimate cause, which was highly protected as private. More common, instead, were visits to her home. Rose, Esther, and Vivian were regular guests. They helped Jane sew blankets and clothes in preparation for the arrival of what was deemed miraculous, as were all gifts of life. Interestingly, Adrien had consistent timing of showing up when Rose did. Jane wondered about it but she never asked.

Suppers with family and neighbors were frequent in the new Callahan home, and Sam felt himself establishing very deep connections. But he also felt the pull of his younger brother, and he saw himself as negligent for doing nothing. Now the joy of fatherhood was counterbalanced with the painful delay it would cause in bringing Amos to Edwardsville. When Adrien left for Pennsylvania, Sam ached.

Chapter 16

oles swirled his glass of cognac, smelled it, chimed his glass against Adrien's, and raised it in the air before sipping. Adrien, too, sipped; then he gazed into the fire and asked, "Whatever became of that letter you wrote to President Jefferson?" Coles raised his head in thought. "The one urging him to end slavery in Virginia," Adrien clarified.

"How do you know about that?" Coles asked.

"I was working in your office one day when I overheard you talking to your lawyer about it. I have never stopped wondering about it."

Coles walked to his desk, thumbed through his files, and pulled out two letters. After reading silently the one Adrien referenced, he handed it over and Adrien read it aloud.

Washington, July 31, 1814

Dear Sir,

I never took up my pen with more hesitation or felt more embarrassment than I now do in addressing you on the subject of this letter. The fear of appearing presumptuous distresses me, and would deter me from venturing thus to call your attention to a subject of such magnitude, and so beset with difficulties, as that of a general emancipation of the Slaves of Virginia, had I not the highest opinion of your goodness and liberality, in not only excusing me for the liberty I take, but in justly appreciating my motives in doing so.

I will not enter on the right which man has to enslave his Brother man, nor upon the moral and political effects of Slavery on individuals or on Society; because these things are better understood by you than by me. My object is to entreat and beseech you to exert your knowledge and influence, in devising, and getting into operation, some plan for the gradual emancipation of Slavery. This difficult task could be less exceptionably, and more successfully performed by the revered Fathers of all our political and social blessings, than by any succeeding statesmen; and would seem to come with peculiar propriety and force from those whose valor wisdom and virtue have done so much in meliorating the condition of mankind. And it is a duty, as I conceive, that devolves particularly on you, from your known philosophical and enlarged view of subjects, and from the principles you have professed and practiced through a long and useful life, preeminently distinguished, as well by being foremost in establishing on the broadest basis the rights of man, and the liberty and independence of your Country, as in being throughout honored with the most important trusts by your fellow-citizens, whose confidence and love you have carried with you into the shades of old age and retirement. In the calm of this retirement you might, most beneficially to society, and with much addition to your own fame, avail yourself of that love and confidence to put into complete practice those hallowed principles contained in that renowned Declaration, of which you were the immortal author, and on which we bottomed our right to resist oppression, and establish our freedom and independence.

I hope that the fear of failing, at this time, will have no influence in preventing you from employing your pen to eradicate this most degrading feature of British Colonial policy, which is still permitted to exist, notwithstanding its repugnance as well to the principles of our revolution as to our free Institutions. For however highly prized and influential your opinions may now be, they will be still much more so when you shall have been snatched from us by the course of nature. If therefore your attempt should now fail to rectify this unfortunate evil—an evil most injurious both to the oppressed and to the oppressor—at some future day when your memory will be consecrated by a grateful posterity, what influence, irresistible influence will the opinions and writings of Thomas Jefferson have on all questions connected with the rights of man, and of that policy which will be the creed of your disciples. Permit me then, my dear Sir, again to intreat you to exert your great powers of mind and influence, and to employ some of your present leisure, in devising a mode to liberate one half of our Fellow beings from an ignominious bondage to the other; either by making an immediate attempt to put in train a plan to commence this goodly work, or to leave human Nature the invaluable Testament—which you are so capable of doing—how best to establish its rights: So that the weight of your opinion may be on the side of emancipation when that question shall be agitated, and that it will be sooner or later is most certain—That it may be soon is my most ardent prayer—that it will be rests with you.

I will only add, as an excuse for the liberty I take in addressing you on this subject, which is so particularly interesting to me; that from the time I was capable of reflecting on the nature of political society, and of the rights appertaining to Man, I have not only been principled against Slavery, but have had feelings so repugnant to it, as to decide me not to hold them; which decision has forced me to leave my native state, and with it all my relations and friends. This I hope will be deemed by you some excuse for the liberty of this intrusion, of which I gladly avail myself to assure you of the very great respect and esteem with which I am, my dear Sir, your every sincere and devoted friend.

Edward Coles

Adrien finished but continued to read it again to himself. "This is a masterfully written request. I fear my next question."

Coles answered Adrien before he had a chance to ask by handing him Thomas Jefferson's response. And Adrien read it aloud, as well.

Dear Sir,

Your favour of July 31, was duly received, and was read with peculiar pleasure. The sentiments breathed through the whole do honor to both the head and heart of the writer. Mine on the subject of slavery of negroes have long since been in possession of the public, and time has only served to give them stronger root. The love of justice and the love of country plead equally the cause of these people, and it is a moral reproach to us that they should have pleaded it so long in vain, and should have produced not a single effort, nay I fear not much serious willingness to relieve them & ourselves from our present condition of moral & political reprobation. From those of the former generation who were in the fulness of age when I came into public life, which was while on paper only, I soon saw that nothing was to be hoped. Nursed and educated in the daily habit of seeing the degraded condition, both bodily and mental, of those unfortunate beings, not reflecting that that degradation was very much the work of themselves & their fathers, few minds have yet doubted but that they were as legitimate subjects of property as their horses and cattle. The quiet and monotonous course of colonial life has been disturbed by no alarm, and little reflection on the value of liberty. And when alarm was taken at an enterprize on their own, it was not easy to carry them to the whole length of the principles which they invoked for themselves. In the first or second session of the Legislature after I became a member, I drew to this subject the attention of Col. Bland, one of the oldest, ablest, & most respected members, and he undertook to move for certain moderate extensions of the protection of the laws to these people. I seconded his motion, and, as a younger member, was more spared in the debate; but he was denounced as an enemy of his country, & was treated with the grossest indecorum. From an early stage of our revolution other & more distant duties were assigned to me, so that from that time till my return from Europe in 1789, and I may say till I returned to reside at home in 1809, I had little opportunity of knowing the progress of public sentiment here on this subject. I had always hoped that the younger generation receiving their early impressions after the flame of liberty had been kindled in every breast, & had become as it were the vital spirit of every American, that the generous temperament of youth, analogous to the motion of their blood, and above the suggestions of avarice, would have sympathized with oppression wherever found, and proved their love of liberty beyond their own share of it. But my intercourse with them, since my return has not been sufficient to ascertain that they had made towards this point the progress I had hoped. Your solitary but welcome voice is the first which has brought this sound to my ear; and I have considered the general silence which prevails on this subject as indicating an apathy unfavorable to every hope. Yet the hour of emancipation is advancing, in the march of time. It will come; and whether brought on by the generous energy of our own minds; or by the bloody process of St Domingo, excited and conducted by the power of our present enemy, if once stationed permanently within our Country, and offering asylum & arms to the oppressed, is a leaf of our history not yet turned over. As to the method by which this difficult work is to be effected, if permitted to be done by ourselves, I have seen no proposition so expedient on the whole, as that as emancipation of those born after a given day, and of their education and expatriation after a given age. This would give time for a gradual extinction of that species of labour & substitution of another, and lessen the severity of the shock which an operation so fundamental cannot fail to produce. For men probably of any color, but of this color we know, brought from their infancy without necessity for thought or forecast, are by their habits rendered as incapable as children of taking care of themselves, and are extinguished promptly wherever industry is necessary for raising young. In the mean time they are pests in society by their idleness, and the depredations to which this leads them. Their amalgamation with the other color produces a degradation to which no lover of his country, no lover of excellence in the human character can innocently consent. I am sensible of the partialities with which you have looked towards me as the person who should undertake this salutary but arduous work. But this, my dear sir, is like bidding old Priam to buckle the armour of Hector "trementibus aequo humeris et inutile ferruncingi." No, I have over lived the generation with which mutual labors & perils begat mutual confidence and influence. This enterprise is for the young; for those who can follow it up, and bear it through to its consummation. It shall have all my prayers, & these are the only weapons of an old man. But in the mean time are you right in abandoning this property, and your country with it? I think not. My opinion has ever been that, until more can be done for them, we should endeavor, with those whom fortune has thrown on our hands, to feed and clothe them well, protect them from all ill usage, require such reasonable labor only as is performed voluntarily by freemen, & be led by no repugnancies to abdicate them, and our duties to them. The laws do not permit us to turn them loose, if that were for their good: and to commute them for other property is to commit them to those whose usage of them we cannot control. I hope then, my dear sir, you will recon-

cile yourself to your country and its unfortunate
condition; that you will not lessen its stock of
sound disposition by withdrawing your portion
from the mass. That, on the contrary you will
come forward in the public councils, become the
missionary of this doctrine truly Christian; insin-
uate & inculcate it softly but steadily, through
the medium of writing and conversation; associate others in your labors, and when the phalanx
is formed, bring on and press the proposition
perseveringly until its accomplishment. It is an
encouraging observation that no good measure
was ever proposed, which, if duly pursued, failed
to prevail in the end. We have proof of this in
the history of the endeavors in the English parlia-
ment to suppress that very trade which brought
this evil on us. And you will be supported by the
religious precept, "be not weary in well-doing."

That your success may be as speedy & complete, as it will be of honorable & immortal con-
solation to yourself, I shall as fervently and sincerely pray as I assure you of my great friendship
and respect.

Thomas Jefferson

It was quiet for a long time. Adrien scanned the letter again. "I
confess, somewhat shamefully, that I am a bit overwhelmed by my
own rushing feelings. I am convinced by his position, yet angry. I am
full of admiration, yet contempt. He understood clearly the scope
of the matter and affirms slavery as evil, yet he left it for posterity to
bear. He was old, indeed, when he wrote this, yet he was of sound
mind and strong body. He lived another twelve years and did so as a
slave owner."

Coles answered, "Rather ironic, isn't it, that he did so much
to end the expansion of slavery, and because of that, I urged him

on. He had the power alone to rally support to end this birth defect that came with our independence, just as Adams did in stirring the colonists to revolt against the king. I can't quite make sense of his inaction toward addressing emancipation lest I enter into judgment of the man's motives and the personal comforts achieved through the holding of some six hundred slaves over his lifetime with more than one hundred upon his death. I dare not enter into such speculation."

Adrien added, "To his credit, he raises attention to pertinent emmancipation obstacles, such as laws preventing a slave's freedom and no meaningful transition from slavery to freedom, but it is simply insufficient to leave it there. And while he is certain it will come to an end, he disengaged from any effort to that end other than prayer. Does God not call us to action, as well?"

"Indeed," Coles answered. "The next course of action is to change the laws. I shrugged off the defeat that this letter left with me and chose, instead, to let it serve as a catalyst toward my original pursuit. I wanted to tell him how wrong he was for insisting that a freed slave was incapable of taking care of himself. Certainly, being deprived of access to education, to worship, and to independence would hinder any man or woman's ability toward self-care. 'Give the man a chance,' I wanted to shout. And I still do. But to whom? While there is enough evidence on Prairieland alone to cause the argument in Jefferson's letter to fall like a house of cards, there is not, like he said, an interested body. How I wanted them to come to Prairieland and see for themselves the ignorance supporting the doctrine of paternity over what has been defined as some helpless group of children in need of great paternal care by one called a master. It's an evil excuse for this ongoing inhumane enterprise. Had they come to see, as I had hoped, the proof before them would have convicted them to cease and desist. That, my friend, is why no one would come. They don't want proof. They don't want to cease and desist.

"So I endured and still do as an old man who resists Jefferson's notion that this is a problem for the young." Coles paused in reflection. Adrien paused in wonder of this warrior and friend, Edward Coles. "A root has been planted, and it is deep, causing its branches to spread. I am thankful to God that he has given me strength to endure and persevere against much resistance since defying my family, since my first letter to Jefferson, since governing Illinois, and now working beside Jefferson's grandson to end slavery in Virginia."

Adrien said, "Edward, please know and understand that your sweat and labors to end slavery have been blessed, and you are not alone. The battle continues. God willing, we will see not only an end to slavery but also an end to Black Codes." Coles nodded in appreciation and agreement, and he sipped some more brandy. "You know, I often imagined you as president," Adrien added. "Had Illinois permitted governors to run for consecutive terms, you most certainly would have won, and you would have been on a direct course to the White House. Your family ties, your long service as private secretary to President Madison, and your friendships with Jefferson, Monroe, and so many others would have made you a likely and strong candidate. Is it offensive for me to ask why you exited politics?"

"You don't know?" Coles asked as he watched the fire's dancing flames through his snifter. "The game changed. When I ran for a second term in '32, I realized I was no contender because I am not a party man. I am a principled man. I believe in presenting a case based on truth and using truth to appeal to our countrymen. I could not compete on that and I accepted permanent defeat."

"President Washington warned us with intense concern of the detriment brought on by party politics. You left for honorable reasons," Adrien said, and he raised his glass.

Coles paused. Then he asked, "Tell me, how is Robert? His letters tell of Prairieland's struggles but little of himself."

Adrien adjusted to the transitional question. "Robert is among the best of all of Edwardsville's residents. He leads with precision, and his farmhands follow him willingly. And he is rising in his church. He is a good friend, well-respected, and loyal to you."

"Thank you for that. I truly miss him." He refilled their snifters, and they moved to plush chairs in front of the fire. "Forgive me, Adrien, for subjecting you to suffer my intrusion, however well-intended, as I ask of Nathan. If you can endure it, please explain how he met his tragic end and how you manage such a loss?"

Adrien took his time gathering his thoughts, and Coles waited patiently. "The army has no official version on how he died, only that he died bravely. His throat was cut by an unknown source shortly after Stillman's men were slaughtered by Black Hawk's band. So I live with the unknown. But what can be done? I manage by having learned a hard lesson with the loss of my wife. Her death disabled me for years, such that I had to repent of my selfishness and faithlessness. How my children managed, I'll never know. I would not have survived without Pierre and Esther." He rested between thoughts as Coles absorbed Adrien's explanation.

Adrien lifted the discussion on a positive note. "I also manage out of thanksgiving for what I still have. Jane is such a blessing, and she and Sam deserve my attention to their joy."

"Samuel Callahan is now your son-in-law. Everyone anticipated that except you." Coles laughed. "What a fine young man he is. It gives me hope."

Adrien laughed, too, and said, "It was my fierce resistance that shaped him to the man he is today."

"Oh! Is that what did it?" Coles laughed again.

Adrien smiled and said, "Well, it comforts my ego to think so. Seriously, though, Sam is"—Adrien searched for the words—"perfect for Jane, and I have come to respect and admire him. Somehow, that makes the loss of my son more manageable." Coles got his answer, and Adrien looked away slightly until the water in his eyes retreated.

*****

The next day was busy. Coles had reentered high society since moving to Philadelphia, and he had planned an intimate gathering at his home with some rather high-profile guests.

"Adrien," Coles said, "allow me to introduce to you Miss Sally Logan Roberts."

Adrien hesitated a moment before kissing the hand of the beautiful young woman. She was only slightly older than Jane and just as strong, well-spoken, and graceful. But who was she? Adrien wondered.

207

"Mr. Pruitt," she said as she put her arm under his and led him to the table, "please sit by me. I have heard so much about you, and I count it a privilege to learn more."

Coles stood at the head of the table and made introductions. Among the eight guests were James and Dolley Madison and the late-arriving Thomas Jefferson Randolph, Thomas Jefferson's oldest grandson. Adrien appeared comfortable, but he felt like a foreigner.

"Thomas! You're just in time! Dinner is just being served." Coles welcomed his guest, and everyone stood briefly upon his arrival. "It's been far too long!"

Madison asked, "Tom, is it time to celebrate?" He appeared concerned.

Thomas smiled with his lips pressed tightly together, seemingly about to burst, and then he did burst by saying, "Yes! It is time to celebrate! Monticello is sold! Mother is now free of the burden and visiting my sister in Boston. Four years of searching for a buyer. It's like having the rope of an anchor cut from my leg and being able to surge to the surface for that first breath of air." Thomas's smile dropped as he looked into the eyes of the stunned guests. He lowered his head and said, "Forgive me."

"Nonsense!" Coles replied. "You're among friends. Monticello was left to Martha with joyless weight. Who among us could have carried it? You stood by your mother through and through. And we stand by you. Now you can turn your attention to other interests. Praise God."

"Here, here!" the other men exclaimed. Dolley affirmed the men by clapping her hands purposefully and tipping her head to Thomas. And Sally reached her hand across the table and placed it on his.

Adrien raised his glass and said, "So let's celebrate. To Mr. Randolph and to Monticello." And everyone joined in for the toast. Coles smiled at Adrien.

Dinner was lively but orderly. Coles masterfully included each person individually in conversation and subtly presented highlights about their greatness and with equal consideration. As the evening looked like it was coming to an end, he stood and said, "I asked you all here tonight for a reason, and I waited for Adrien to arrive to make this night complete." He extended his hand to Sally, and she took it. "Sally and I are going to be married." Sally looked up at Coles with genuine love in her eyes as she smiled at his announcement. After a moment of shared surprise among the guests, the evening's momentum was revived until nearly midnight.

The Madisons and Thomas stayed particularly late while Dolley and Sally retreated to talk alone, and the men settled in Coles's study for brandy. James Madison knew he was in trusted company when he opened the conversation.

"Edward, I have been agonizing over my desire to free my slaves, but how can I? I must know that Dolley will be cared for when I am gone. I simply cannot leave her destitute."

Coles answered, "I am compelled to dispute the economic advantage of slavery."

"As am I," said Thomas. "My grandfather opposed slavery, but the institution was forced upon him when he inherited not only his father's slaves but all of his father's debt, as well. He was saddled and bridled from the beginning. And if slavery were that beneficial, why are so many slave owners in debt?"

Adrien added, "If I may, my observation is that slavery is often desired or perceived to be needed to achieve a certain status in society, yet it is very costly in every way, especially economically, morally, and spiritually."

"True," Coles added, "the very cost of owning one or many slaves exceeds the overall benefits. You said so yourself. If you recall, James, it was you who inspired in me a vision for emancipation."

Thomas continued, "The highest cost comes upon selling them. My mother could not free them because of the debt her father left to her. She will grieve that to her death. And what of the question of how this burden came to be in the first place? Her father was a former colonist, a revolutionary who proclaimed and fought for freedom. He wrote almost single-handedly the Declaration of Independence and became the third president of the United States. He also wrote acts preventing the expansion of slavery yet left to his daughter the gross burden of selling his slaves to help pay off his massive debt. Between advocating freedom for all, including slaves, yet owning them into the hundreds and acquiring financial hardship on a frightening level, the legacy he left is rather confusing. What will posterity say?

"And let me add this: a greater grief, short of the death of one of my own children, I cannot imagine than what was endured upon breaking up slave families who had been with my grandfather for decades. Slaves that built Monticello, slaves that tended his home and gardens, and slave children that made nails for his business were all left hoping for his grace upon his death. Instead, they remain in bondage, and many of them carry the excess weight of never being able to see their loved ones again! Knowing what I know now, I would argue, sir, that destitution is far better than that, and God will honor such a choice."

"That is why, James," Coles continued, "Thomas and I are working tirelessly to bring an end to slavery in Virginia. When we bring together the words of Thomas Jefferson and the antislavery acts of him and George Washington and impose them accurately against this immoral practice of human bondage, we can tear it down once and for all."

Madison answered, "It's not just Dolley I am worried about. If I free my slaves, what's to become of them? What of the morality of freeing a slave whose only future prospect is poverty? What hope is there for my elderly slaves? What of my slaves who are married to slaves of other owners, who will never see their loved ones again once free? I am responsible for them as slaves as well as for what happens to them once free, am I not? Frankly, I have an excess of labor now, but if I free them, the demise they will face, given our present social conditions, is unspeakable."

"Yes, James, a responsible transition to freedom is morally paramount. Prepare your slaves now for freedom, as I did, so they can prosper in it. Two years ago at your home we discussed this fully, and you committed. Have you changed your mind?" Coles said.

James answered, "No. I am still committed. What has me at a loss is how."

Conversation stalled, though Coles could have gone on until dawn, much like the apostle Paul when giving testimony to would-be believers.

In transition, Thomas reached into his satchel and pulled out three books. He handed one to each of his friends. It was called the *Virginia Housewife*. "My Aunt Mary, God rest her soul, wrote this. It has become wildly popular, and I thought you might like it as a gift."

Adrien combed through the beautiful book, which was full of efficient and tasteful recipes. He looked at Thomas and handed it back, saying, "Mr. Randolph, I cannot accept this treasure, knowing that you don't even know me."

Thomas smiled. "Oh, but I do, Mr. Pruitt. Keep it, I insist. I brought it for you, and may it bless your home."

*****

While Adrien prepared to leave after nearly two weeks, Coles said, "You could stay, you know. This invitation was somewhat intended to tempt you, I shamefully confess."

"Though temptation is raging through me, it must be satisfied with occasional visits and correspondence. My home, my family, and my life are in Illinois. And then there are also my business affairs that continue in St. Louis," Adrien answered with raising his brow.

"Our business is still related, and those same affairs can be accomplished from here," Coles assured.

"Better, perhaps, that you take it on from the east, and I take it on from the west, pressing it to the middle. Success could be realized. No?" Adrien proposed.

Coles smiled and conceded. "Return soon, then, and bring Jane and Sam."

"Another invite that I cannot refuse," Adrien said as he nodded to the driver to open the carriage door. But then he added, "Edward, your Sally is lovely. You're happy and peaceful. I have never quite seen you this way, and your joy is an answered prayer. I am thankful to you for the invitation and that I had enough sense to accept it." Upon parting, they shook hands firmly, and all the way home, Adrien contemplated what was left of his future.

Chapter 17

Late 1832 was quiet in Illinois. The Indians were all gone, having been moved successfully west of the Mississippi or imprisoned for warring against the United States. The war was now a memory, and Black Hawk and his minor chiefs were in confinement at Jefferson Barracks in St. Louis. Lieutenant Jefferson Davis was already being publicly praised for his reverence and kindness amidst the public's full admiration and recognition of the brave and desperate finish of the Indian warrior and his tribe. And with the cholera epidemic being over, Jane's nerves eased. As she gathered and bound pine stems into a Christmas wreath for her front door, she grew in confidence that the world would be peaceful enough to allow her child to enter into joyful times.

Jane's house was becoming a home, but there was still so much to do. She had numerous bare spots and three empty bedrooms. In spite of the fact that she and Sam worked with diligence to get settled, it would still be months, maybe even longer, before they would feel like they could rest. Were it not for the help of her father and their friends, they would be in panic. Even so, by the time winter came, large sections of their land still needed to be cleared. Fruit trees needed to be planted. Jane's garden space was minimal and covered by just two large sheets as it waited under the snow for spring, which could not come soon enough. She needed a cradle, a rocker, and more blankets. Her lengthy list ran on and on through her mind. She had to stop herself from entering into a state of worry.

She thought about her mother and father; they moved to Illinois when it was a territory, and they had no one to help them. They were barely settled when Mrs. Pruitt became pregnant with Nathan and Mr. Pruitt left for war. How brave they were to move into untamed Indian territory. So many burdens, so few comforts, so much opportunity for something to go wrong. No wonder her parents were so tightly bonded. They would not have survived without each other, and they had endured so much together. Jane realized that she knew more about her mother now than she ever did when she was alive, and she missed her. She rested her hand on her unborn child and gave thanks for everything she had.

Sam was at his desk with his Bible open and was writing in another book when Jane wrapped her arms around him from behind and whispered in his ear.

"I love you, Sam Callahan. Come to bed." He quickly closed his book. "What is this?" Jane asked as she reached for it.

"Just some notes." He put the book under his Bible, stacked them together on a shelf, and followed her upstairs. "Jane, I've written Bill Garvin. I'm asking him to send me another mare. Can you adjust the budget?"

"Of course," Jane said while her mind was still on the book.

Sam got into bed and came up on his elbow to face Jane. He gently caressed her face.

"My God, Jane, you are more beautiful by the hour." She pressed his palm to her lips and kissed it. He moved his hand to her belly and asked, "Are you at all scared?"

"Yes." She smiled with a nod. "You?"

"Terrified," he confessed with a light laugh. "We have taken on a lot, Jane, and I know things are a little rough right now, but in a year or so, we'll be stable." Sam's assurance was just as much for himself as it was for her. It was one thing to own land or breed horses; failing there would be a setback but manageable. It was quite another to be responsible for people's lives. At twenty-one, he was already a husband and soon to be a father. Saunderman didn't teach him anything about that.

He thought about the number of women who entrusted themselves, their children, and their futures to men—women who were fiercely dependable and devoted to men who could not or would not provide and who eventually abandoned their families, leaving their wives to figure out how to survive. He thought about the number of men who succeeded because of tireless support from their wives versus those who failed because they received no support in their efforts. Then he thought about Saunderman again, who was somewhere out there in the mountains bypassing any such responsibility to himself or others, including possibly Rose. Maybe he had already been down the path Sam was on, and life led him to avoid it again. Sam now understood the relief that could come with the life of a mountain man. But there would be no relief for him if it meant a life without Jane.

Failure. The word beat inside his head with the rhythm of his heart. Or was it more like a thorn in his flesh that forced him to remain fixed on God, as Reverend Hunt explained? *Stop worrying,* he told himself. *Where is your faith? God was with you when you were lost. Don't you think he will be with you now?* He watched Jane's eyes look at him with complete confidence. She had no doubt in his abilities, and he loved what that did to him. But after Jane fell asleep, Sam got up and went to the barn and stayed there until just before dawn.

*****

The spring of 1833 was remarkably pleasant. It was wonderfully warm with consistent light rains, such that everything bloomed early, including Jane's garden. A flood of newcomers entered the state, and there was a boom to goods, services, and property value. Surely, some of them would need horses too.

Sam resumed clearing the remaining sections of his property and was able to plant more fruit trees and a few walnut trees. He asked Jane to restrict herself to light gardening and focus on interior demands, to include the finances. Sam would work on the property until noon; then he spent the rest of the day in Joseph's barn.

Sam commissioned Joseph to help him build furniture for his home. They built a cradle, a crib, a guest bed, wardrobes, chairs, tables, and bookshelves. Joseph found himself wondering where Sam would put it all. Sam spent weeks in Joseph's barn measuring, cutting, piecing together, and staining. Danny would show up from time to time, which helped to move things along. When Vivian would fail at attempts to draw them into the house to eat, she would bring trays of food out to them. She had not seen Joseph this interested in anything in years, and she often just sat to the side and watched him work.

Joseph taught Sam and Danny the differences in qualities of wood and the differences in qualities of furniture building: what wood and designs would endure time and what wouldn't, what wood was hard to work with and what was agreeable, how to bevel and embed designs, and how to pull out grains or hide them with finishes. And Joseph loved explaining and demonstrating the use of all his tools, especially how to use them in unintended ways, which ensured Joseph left a signature mark on his work. He was not just a master in the trade; he was also an artist.

Sam pulled some money out of his wallet and started counting out his payment to Joseph for the furniture they built together and several other pieces Joseph built alone. As Joseph counted silently along with Sam, he became confused.

"Sam"—he laughed—"I think you lost count. That's far too much." Sam handed him the money without word and walked around the different pieces he bought, and he shook his head.

"What's wrong?" Joseph asked after watching Sam for a while.

"There's something I don't understand," Sam said. Joseph and Danny waited. "You can't find furniture like this in Madison County unless it's brought here from the East." Joseph became a little defensive and started cleaning up. Danny found himself agreeing with Sam.

"That's true. Why don't you sell your furniture?" Danny asked. Joseph didn't answer.

"Joseph, you could make a pretty good living—" Sam began to say.

Joseph stopped Sam in midsentence. "Black folk can't afford to pay even what it costs me to build it." He threw some tools in a toolbox. He was visibly agitated. Sam and Danny glanced at each other.

"Well...who said anything about black folk?" Danny asked cautiously.

"Whites don't like buying from a black man," Joseph declared.

"I'm white," Sam stated the obvious.

Joseph glared at him. "Well, that's different," he said.

"How?" Sam asked.

Joseph started to make his way out of the barn. "I think that's enough for one night," he said.

Danny asked, "Joseph, what happened? Was it something bad?" Joseph stopped but kept his back to him.

Sam said, "You can trust us, no matter what it is."

Joseph turned around, walked back toward Sam and Danny, and rubbed his hand over his chair before he answered. "At first, it was good. Too good. When our master—" He stopped. "I don't feel right calling him a master. He was a friend. Anyway, when he died, he set us free. I opened a shop there in St. Louis, sold my furniture, and we were doing pretty good for a while. But one family hated us. They did everything they could to run us down to the ground. Nothing worked. Then one night, my son was in the shop with me helping out as best a four-year-old child could. We lived right next to the shop, and I left to go get something from the house. I didn't think about it at the time, but I should have brought him with me. It took a little longer than I thought it would. When I came out of the house, the shop was engulfed in flames. They just wanted me out of business. When they saw me leave the shop, they set the fire. They didn't know Jacob was in there. Nonetheless, he died." Danny turned his back, shaking his head. "Shortly thereafter, Vivian and I moved here. Tried to start over. I made a few pieces, but I never had the heart to make furniture like that again."

"Until now," Sam said with compassion.

Joseph thought about it. "Until now," he confessed.

"I'm sorry, Joseph, truly. I can't imagine…" Sam walked around a bit, finding it hard to move beyond what Joseph described, but he said, "It's up to you, but there are several ways you could go about it if you wanted to sell furniture again, everything from doing what you did before with a shop here on your land to having a shop in town or even selling to a dealer. Maybe even all three. You think it over.

"And by the way, I didn't overpay you. Five of those pieces are going to Charles Mueller. He saw the desk you helped me build, and that was all it took. He'll be by for his pieces tomorrow, and if you recall, I didn't help build any of those, so all that money goes to you. I gave him a price based on what I saw for a similar piece in St. Louis, and that's what he paid you. Pretty nice to get paid for your efforts, don't you think? Joseph, he's white, and he knows you're black." As Sam started to leave, he said, "Word is going to get out. If you don't want the business, like I said, that's up to you. I'll come by next week with a wagon for my pieces. Jane is going to love them. She still thinks she has no cradle for the baby."

From the time of Charles Mueller's purchase, Joseph had steady business.

*****

Adrien noticed that the graves of his wife and son had been groomed and blessed with fresh flowers. He looked around wondering who had done it. As he adjusted his hat and turned to leave, his eyes landed on a woman at a considerable distance. She was standing up from a grave having just removed old flowers to replace them with new ones. It was Rose. Adrien waited.

As Rose strolled back to the cemetery's gate, she gazed at the springtime sky and the budding trees, and it was when she looked up from smelling some flowers that she noticed Adrien noticing her. He offered his arm to escort her out. She almost looked back toward her husband's grave but stopped herself. She walked toward Adrien, smiled, and took his arm.

Adrien led them toward their carriages and kept going. Rose said nothing. He said, "My plots have been tended. Was it, by chance, you?"

Rose answered, "No. It wasn't me. I find myself tempted, but I worry that it would be an intrusion."

"Rose," Adrien said, "I've been wondering."

"Tell me, Adrien, about what?"

"What you would say to being my wife," he said, and he kept walking. She was shocked but also relieved because she had been in love with him for years. He finally stopped and looked at her. "Perhaps I should take a knee. You certainly deserve it."

"No," Rose said. Adrien looked up and away, trying to mask his disappointment. "I mean no, you should not take a knee." Rose realized what she had said and laughed as she rested her forehead on his chest.

Adrien gently wrapped his arms around her. "You nearly gave me a heart attack," he said, smiling in relief. "I've been feeling rather sure of myself."

"I'm sorry," she said, still laughing.

"Which brings me to what is probably a fact; not to cast a dark cloud over the request, but I am much older than you. Surely, you realize the likelihood that you will bury a second husband."

"Not too soon, I hope," she said.

"It's something to consider, Rose. Seriously. You have other options. You must be aware."

"I do? Enlighten me to these other options. Perhaps I should weigh them," she said in fun.

Adrien smirked and said, "Many, Rose. Many."

"Hmm, if that's true, they might make fine husbands...for someone else," she stated.

He lightly brushed the back of his fingers across her ivory cheek and said, "Rose McGregor, I love you and have for quite some time. Be my wife. I will fill your days with happiness and adventure."

"Yes, Adrien. I would love to be your wife," she said. Adrien kissed her.

*****

"Rose!" Jane hollered as she welcomed Rose into her home. "I've missed you! Has business been that good?"

"Yes, actually! I have had to turn people away and hire some help," Rose said. "I have never seen so many people come through town at once."

"Who is helping you?" Sam asked, trying to imagine the bustle of his former home.

"Hannah Mueller," Rose said. Sam pulled his head back as if dodging a slap. "I know what you're thinking," Rose said, "but she has been a wonderful blessing. She is a natural in the house and with the guests. The only reason I'm able to be here is because she is there!"

"Supper is almost ready. Will you stay?" Jane asked.

"I confess, I was hoping you would ask. I need a break from my own cooking," Rose said, and she sat down at the table. "I will be enjoying even more help soon." She clearly baited Sam and Jane, and they both bit. "I have fancied a man for a long time now, and he has finally come asking for my hand in marriage."

"When did this happen?" Jane asked somewhat defensively, trying to recall the last time she saw her father with Rose. Sam quietly watched both women.

"Two days ago, actually," Rose said. "And rather suddenly. He likes the social setting of the boardinghouse, and he is going to sell his own property. When we marry, he will move in with me." A glass slipped out of Jane's hand and hit the floor, breaking into pieces.

"Oh, my goodness," Jane said as she bent down to pick up the pieces.

"I'll get it, Jane," Sam said.

When she looked at Sam, she was upset. Just then, Adrien arrived. Jane became very nervous and wondered if he had already heard the news.

"Well, that didn't take long," Adrien said upon entering the kitchen. "Hello, Rose." Rose smiled and stood to greet him.

"What, Father?" Jane asked.

"I already have a buyer for the house. Two families made offers and nearly got into a fight on the porch!" He laughed.

"You're selling the house?" Jane had difficulty imagining her childhood home going to other hands.

"When I was offered a price that exceeded the property's value, how could I refuse?"

"Well, where will you li—" Jane started putting two and two together. Rose joined Adrien by his side, and Jane dropped another glass.

*****

Adrien had been meaning to move the piano to Jane's house. Now he had no choice. Many items went to Jane's home. Many items went to Rose's home. Many items moved on to other homes. Room to room, he packed and purged memories with the help of all his family and friends who supported him more than they could ever know.

"Are you sure this is what you want?" Rose asked. "We could live here, if you prefer. I can't bear the thought of you living with regret."

Adrien answered, "Want? Yes. And need. I was sure before I ever asked you to marry me."

Nathan's room was the hardest for him. He had spent many nights sitting in Nathan's room thinking, remembering, longing. He and Jane collected a few memories in a box. Pierre, Danny, and Sam burned all that remained, sparing Adrien and Jane of torment. Esther and Rose did the final cleaning.

Everyone waited outside while Adrien made one last round through all the rooms of the house that he built with and for his wife. He heard the voices of his family in each room and from each year, and they followed him all the way to the front door until he closed it upon leaving. He held on to the doorknob briefly before letting it go. He looked out across the yard and remembered days when his children played and laughed, especially the ones with the Callahan boys. He took a deep breath, stepped off the porch, joined Rose in his carriage, and did not look back.

Chapter 18

As Jane's delivery neared, Vivian told Sam to raise a flag over his roof to signal her when the time came. Rose was making daily visits to the house to put herself within reach of helping. Esther was intent on being there for the birth of Mr. Pruitt's first grandchild, and she counted on Danny for regular updates on Jane's condition. Everyone was ready.

Jane was basting a roast for supper when Sam walked by and kissed her on the back of the neck. She was startled and it made her laugh. Then both she and Sam looked toward the floor where they heard water dripping from underneath Jane's dress. She suddenly winced and bent over as she grabbed her belly and called out to Sam. He rushed to her, swept her up into his arms, carried her upstairs like she weighed nothing, and he put her in their bed.

"Rose will be here soon. I'm going to go raise the flag for Vivian," Sam said with urgency.

"Sam, no!" Jane reached for him. "There's no time!"

What does that mean? Sam wondered. He had delivered many foals, so he was distantly aware of Jane's condition and what would happen next, but it was not customary for husbands to be in the room during childbirth, so he was not prepared for there to be *no time.*

Jane let out another loud groan and began pulling up her dress. "Help me!" she yelled at Sam.

Sam broke from his paralyzed state and went to work. He frantically prepared Jane. He gathered sheets, blankets, towels, and splashed water into the basin. He hated his helplessness while Jane endured the pain of childbirth. When reaching for her hand to comfort her, she pulled it away. He ran a cool damp cloth across her forehead, but she tapped his hand and told him to stop. His failed attempts to comfort her went on between her screeches, and he began to worry. He kept looking out the window for Rose hoping she would rescue him and do whatever it was that women did to help with childbirth, but Rose did not come. When Jane let out her final painstaking yell, Sam was there to help his child out of the womb.

Jane sank into the bed and wiped her brow with her forearm, but she regained her strength and ignored her pain when she heard Sam take in a deep breath.

"It's a boy," Sam said in amazement while shifting his eyes back and forth between Jane and his son. He heard a carriage pull up. He covered Jane and the child and went to the window.

"Rose! Come up. Hurry!" he yelled out the window.

Adrien entered the bedroom with Rose, but when he saw blood, he immediately retreated. Rose rushed to Jane's side, who could not take her eyes off Sam. Then Rose saw that the baby had already come.

"Thank God you're here," Sam said as he wiped off his son's head. Rose realized that Sam aided Jane in the birth and was astonished. She joined Sam at the foot of the bed.

"Well, the hard part is over," she said. "How long has it been?" Sam didn't know what she meant. "Since he was born? How long?"

"Less than five minutes, I think," Sam said.

Rose looked at the boy and saw that, though he was not crying, he was breathing well and his color was good. She reached in her basket and pulled out a pair of scissors. As she cut and tied the umbilical cord, Sam became bothered at the sight of more blood.

"It's normal," Rose said with a gentle smile. She cleaned and wrapped the child in a blanket and carefully handed him to Jane, who only then took her eyes off Sam. Morgan Samuel Callahan was born on April 25, 1833, in less than an hour.

Rose told Sam that there was more work to do and that he should leave it to her. He washed his hands in the basin, kissed Jane on the forehead, and met Adrien downstairs.

Adrien was staring at the small book collection in the sitting room when Sam walked in. Sam found it odd that Adrien seemed noncelebratory and did not turn around to greet him. But then Sam remembered.

"Adrien, you're a grandfather," Sam announced gently, "and both your daughter and grandson are fine. Better than fine, actually. They're beautiful." Adrien still did not turn around. He simply closed his eyes and nodded.

Upstairs, Rose took Morgan from Jane and placed him in his cradle. She finished with cleaning the effects of the birth, and then she helped Jane get comfortable. She washed Jane's face, brushed and braided her hair, and changed the bedding masterfully while Jane continued resting. Then she dampened a cloth and washed Morgan. As she swaddled him in a blanket sewn by his mother, he began to cry, so Rose placed him in his mother's arms and gave instruction on nursing.

"How is it, Rose, that you know so much about childbirth?" Jane asked.

Rose smiled. "Years of running a boardinghouse. I've been on hand for many births, but never one like this! I think it's time to hand things back over to Sam."

When Rose entered the sitting room, Sam left.

"Are you all right?" she softly asked Adrien.

"Is she all right?" Adrien asked for confirmation about Jane's condition. Rose nodded yes.

"She couldn't be better. She's already thinking of others, as she does. She asked me to tend to her roast so the company will have something to eat. Ah, to be young again," she said to Adrien who was seventeen years her senior. He rolled his eyes in return, and she laughed.

Morgan slept in Jane's arms. Sam knelt on the floor beside the bed and watched them both. He took Jane's hand in both of his and kissed it.

"Sam, I've always thought you would do anything for me, but now I know for sure." She smiled.

"Please don't ever do that again," he said softly, but he only partially meant it, which was revealed by his smile. He played with her wedding ring on her finger, and he could see she was starting to doze off. He took Morgan from her, placed him in the cradle, and joined her in bed.

Hours later, Sam was still awake. He kept rewinding the scene of Morgan's birth through his mind. It was perhaps the most incredible experience he had ever had. But he also knew how dangerous childbirth could be and how fortunate he was that Jane's delivery was completely free of incident, unlike her mother's. What if something had gone wrong in his hands? He thought of what Adrien endured and thanked God for sparing him from tragedy again.

He got up and prayed over Morgan while he slept in his cradle. Sam studied his small face, his tiny fingers, and his remarkably full head of hair. He thought of Joseph and what losing his son did to him. Then he thought of his own father and wondered if losing his son did anything to him. Eventually, he joined Jane and fell into a peaceful sleep.

*****

Jane let Sam sleep in as she nursed Morgan from her new rocking chair. When he fell back to sleep, she went to the barn for eggs. She saw Sam's Bible lying open on his workbench. It was severely worn from having been read and reread. Then she noticed an open book lying near the Bible, and she picked it up. It was full of Sam's notes. She flipped through pages about their property and how Sam wanted things laid out. She read his best guesses about the horses and potential profits. She scanned furniture sketches and prices for the items he and Joseph made for her, and it made her smile.

As she gazed away briefly while connecting herself to Sam's written thoughts, the pages flipped past many blank sheets to a place in the book where Sam had been keeping separate notes, ones that were much more personal. Jane was captured. There was a list of dates corresponding to the letters that he had sent to Amos and his mother. He also had written thoughts about what Amos would be doing at his age, how he would be enduring Bishop, and what effect it might be having on him. Sam wondered what Amos might think about partnering with him in his business. And there were many prayers. Some of Sam's thoughts were broken but seemed to expose his concern with going to Washington to get Amos because of the demands he faced at home. And there was more. Page after page after page revealed his incessant hatred for his father.

Sam opened his eyes from his sleep. Jane was on the edge of the bed, and she reached for his hand. He was surprised that she was already up, dressed, and moving about with no expressed discomfort.

"I think it's time," Jane stated. Sam rubbed his eyes and started to get up, feeling a little guilty. Jane laid him back down and finished her thought. "To bring Amos here."

Sam's demeanor changed, and he was quiet for few minutes while thinking about Jane's proposal. *Why now?* he wondered. "You've been reading from my journal," he said, and he felt a little violated.

"Yes. It's one thing to keep a record of your plans and even your struggles. It's another to think I would not understand. Don't you know, Sam, that I know you? Don't you know how much I pray for you? Trying to lead a separate life, even in your thoughts, is pointless. God will always expose you and your needs to me so I can love you as he loves you. Please go get Amos and bring him home. We'll be fine here."

Sam had already calculated that a trip to Washington and back would take nearly two months. How could Jane and her newborn son possibly be fine? What of his mares? They were all due to deliver soon. Danny could handle it, but he wanted to be there, and he was concerned about the timing of a departure. *Another delay*, he thought.

"Okay, if you're sure," Sam yielded. "My mare from Bill will be here in a week or so. I'll make plans to go after that." Jane leaned over and hugged him. "Thank you," he said.

Jane said in his ear, "And while you are there, destroy your idol before it destroys us." She released him to find his expression of confusion, which was met by her expression of solid intent, and she left him with his thoughts.

*****

Sam was at the hotel waiting for the stagecoach to arrive, which was bringing him the new addition to his breeding pool. As the stagecoach pulled up loaded with passengers and cargo, Sam could see two horses tied to the rear. The driver hopped down and began helping passengers out and untying luggage straps. Sam remained on the hotel porch, waiting patiently.

"Your horse, Mr. Callahan," Sam heard the driver say from a distance. But the driver wasn't talking to Sam.

"Thank you," the driver heard back, but it wasn't Sam speaking. Sam looked around for the voice and walked toward the back of the stagecoach to find Amos reaching for his horse's reins from the driver. Sam could hardly move.

The driver asked as he turned his attention to Sam, "Are you Sam Callahan?" Sam just stood there, staring at Amos.

"No, my name is A—" Amos said but stopped short when he looked up and saw Sam. Then he smiled. Sam slowly moved toward Amos in near disbelief, but Amos lunged at Sam and hugged him.

"You two brothers?" the driver asked.

"Yes. I'm Sam Callahan and that's my horse." Sam signed for the horse, then he and Amos resumed their greeting. Amos looked good, Sam thought. Really good. They both had so much to say that they kept running over each other's words.

"I can't believe you're here. I was heading out tomorrow to come find you," Sam said. Amos looked at Sam skeptically.

"I'm thirsty," Amos said. "Is there someplace around here a man can get a drink?" Sam led the way.

They sat in a quiet spot in the tavern talking over their beers. Amos explained the trip he just took across the completed section of the National Road and the various sights he had seen. Soon, though, Amos's mood shifted downward.

"Why didn't you write?" Amos asked. Sam's suspicions came true; Bishop must have intercepted the mail and kept Sam's countless letters from Amos and his mother.

"I did write, Amos, a hundred times!" Sam said with grief.

"Father," Amos said conclusively.

"Yes. *Father*," Sam agreed, bitterly. "And what of *Father*? Has nothing changed?" Amos looked at Sam and pain rose in his eyes. "What is it, Amos? What's happened? Is it mother?" Amos struggled for a long time before he could speak.

"Mother is dead," Amos said. He was becoming distraught but held himself together, mindful that he had little privacy. Sam's expression became wrenched as he waited for Amos to explain. "Father's dealings caught up with him, and his reputation eventually slid so low that no one would offer him work. For the last year there has been very little money. Father was forced to start selling off valuables, and there was just not much left. The weight of the situation was becoming unbearable, and his temper rose far more often.

"Things were getting out of control, and mother pulled me aside and gave me nearly a hundred gold coins to exchange for cash. I assumed I was to return home with the money. As I left, I could hear Father yelling at her. He was asking her where she had sent me and told her if it had anything to do with giving away more of their fortune, he would kill her. She told him that he had killed her a long time ago. Then I heard a gunshot." Amos paused. "Sam, she shot herself in the head right in front of him."

Sam's eyes could not focus. Pictures of the horrific scene blurred his vision, and he felt that familiar sickness that always came with being anywhere near Bishop.

"I should have stayed," Amos said, now losing his composure. "I knew how bad things had become, and when she gave me that money, I knew what it meant. I never should have left that night."

"Stop it! You should have never been placed in that situation! If anything, I should have kept you here with me, but we both know how that would have ended," Sam said. He was angry. "You're here now. That's what matters. And you cannot carry the weight of their broken lives with you. You won't be able to stand under it. Do you hear me, Amos?" Amos tried to agree, but he didn't know how to do anything but carry their weight. It was all he knew.

"Where's Mother? Was she buried?" Sam asked.

"Yes, in the family plot," Amos said.

"Where's Father?" Sam asked.

"He was arrested. The police think he did it," Amos said.

"You didn't tell them?" Sam was disturbed by Amos's answer.

"After the shot, I ran back inside and upstairs. There she was, on the floor, with the gun in her hand and Father standing over her in shock. Then I left as fast as I could, and I never went back, not even for mother's funeral." Amos was now slumped over the table, and all he could do was shake his head.

"You did the right thing, Amos. You did the right thing." Sam sat back in his chair thinking as he looked around the tavern. "Let's talk about something else." Amos sat up as he tried to transition his thoughts elsewhere. They were both silent for a while.

"So what are you doing here? Jane?" Amos asked assumingly.

"Jane," Sam confirmed.

Amos asked, "Did Nathan finally go to college?"

"No. Shortly after Father took you and Mother back East, Black Hawk tried to resettle his tribe in Illinois."

"Yeah, I know about Black Hawk. I saw him in Washington right before I came to Edwardsville."

"You saw Black Hawk?" Sam was sidetracked by Amos's news.

"Yeah. After President Jackson released him from Jefferson Barracks, he paraded him all over town like a trophy. Baltimore and New York too. There were other planned stops, but"—Amos laughed—"Black Hawk was so popular everywhere he went that Jackson was in his shadow. Can't have that now, can we?" Amos shook his head and took a drink.

Sam was captured by the images Amos just painted for him. "What was he like?" Sam asked, having only seen the great chief by spyglass at a far distance.

As Amos thought about it, his expression transformed to that of awe. "He was a warrior. Just like you'd think a warrior should be. It was hard to believe he could have been conquered. No wonder people were fascinated by him. It was really something to see. People came from all over to see him," Amos said. "So, you were saying?"

Sam returned to his memory. "Well, I joined the militia, and—"

"You were in the Black Hawk War?" Amos leaned halfway across the table eager for confirmation.

"If you want to call it that. Anyway—"

"Hold it!" Amos closed his eyes and waved his hand back and forth slightly in front of Sam. He opened his eyes again and grilled Sam. "You? You were in the Black Hawk War?"

"Shhh. Keep your voice down." Sam looked around to make sure they weren't drawing any attention. Annoyed, Sam said, "Yeah, I was in the Black Hawk War. There are reasons I don't talk about it, one being that Nathan died there."

Amos was crushed. He could hardly ask, "H-how?"

Sam answered, "His throat was cut. No one really knows what happened. And I'm leaving it there. You do the same. Are we clear?" Amos didn't want to leave it there, but he did. Sam smiled gently and said, "I married Jane, and we have a son, Morgan." Amos dropped his jaw, smiled, and then raised his beer. Sam was reminded of how Amos had a gift for being able to rebound quickly from pain, but he also knew that Amos's pain was deep. "It's good to see you, Amos. Let's go home," Sam said.

Jane saw three horses turn from the road onto the property. Two of them were mounted. She watched as they came closer, but she could not arrive at who was with Sam until they dismounted and walked up to her.

"Jane, you remember—" Sam started.

"Amos!" Jane threw her arms around him, pulled back to look at him, and threw her arms around him again. Sam was relieved that his brother was met with such invitation, but a concern lingered in the back of his mind on what this would mean to the harmony he had established in his home, which made him think of Adrien.

Amos was relieved too. However, Jane's welcome left him feeling uncomfortable. He wondered how long it would last.

That night, Sam went to the barn after Jane fell asleep and returned before she woke.

Chapter 19

Sam put Amos right to work. He wondered how Saunderman managed to be so patient with him as he now put Amos through the same work routine he suffered under Saunderman. Danny wanted to kill Amos on more than one occasion, and Sam worried that his brother was beyond reach.

It was a hot day in June—too hot in the house, and too hot in the sun. Rose and Adrien were sitting in the shade on the porch with Jane as she rocked Morgan. Amos was hanging around the house, which, on this particular day, suited Sam and Danny just fine because Amos's motivation to work was still unpredictable, and neither of them were in the mood. Sam could hear Jane greet unexpected guests who came bearing gifts for the new addition to the community. He met the Muellers as their wagon pulled up, and Amos helped Julia and Hannah down. Amos was immediately captivated by Hannah's inviting smile. Sam looked at Rose and began to recall the day he met Hannah.

"We heard there was cause for celebration," Charles said of Morgan. Adrien was torn by a conflicted hope; did Charles bring brandy or not?

Gifts were delivered by the Muellers, dinner was served by the Callahans, and bonds between families were tightened.

That same night, Crimson went into foaling in a nice slow manner, which was encouraging. Sam and Danny anxiously monitored her on alternating shifts until the final stage, hoping she would not suffer another stillborn birth. Amos was ordered to stay close and learn.

Near 4:00 a.m., Crimson lay down and was losing fluids quickly. Sam tapped Danny and Amos to wake up. They joined Sam just in time to see the foal's front feet, and they watched while leaning against the birthing stable fence. Within another couple of minutes, there was a head, and the foal showed signs of life. Sam dropped his head on his forearm in thanksgiving.

Crimson moaned as she pushed. She adjusted her position as best she could as she endured the next phase of birth. A few minutes passed as the foal was caught between the womb and the world. Suddenly, the foal escaped the canal in one swift exit, and its head ripped through the sac and began looking around. It was a colt. Crimson got up and immediately began cleaning her first successful delivery. Her colt shook a little as he faced his new environment. He was chestnut, like his mother, but he had his father's white dagger on his head. Before long, Crimson was walking around her colt until at last he came to his feet with his legs spread out to support himself.

"That never gets old," Danny said. Sam could not stop smiling. Amos was mesmerized.

*****

Amos looked forward to church, but Sam knew it was for reasons that had nothing to do with God.

"Hello, Miss Mueller." Amos bowed slightly upon greeting her. Charles grunted and stepped around them as they spoke briefly before the start of service.

Reverend Hunt reminded everyone during his announcements about the social coming up but also cautioned his congregation not to overindulge in a setting prone toward excess and misconduct. Jane and Sam skipped the event, but Amos could not wait.

*****

When Charles Mueller showed up at the Callahans' house very late the night of the social, Sam came out to greet him. But when Charles pointed his rifle at him, he stopped in his tracks. Sam could see that Charles was pulling a horse behind him with Amos strapped to it, belly down.

"One chance, Sam. That's all he's getting." Charles was furious. Sam raised his hands to show he was yielding. Jane and Danny walked out of the house and stood on the porch, watching and listening.

"What happened, Charles?"

"I'll tell you what happened. This brother of yours took advantage of my daughter. She's been smitten with him ever since he came into town, couldn't stop talking about him. He showed up at the social tonight, and they danced and danced. Never seen her so happy. Then they were gone. By the time I found them in a nearby barn, he was drunk and handling her in violent ways. Tore her new dress, called her names only fitting for hell, and I got there just before he aimed to hit her. My girl was a mess." His chin shook as his anger stirred. He leaned over his horse and pointed his finger toward Sam. "The only reason he's not dead is that you and I are friends. He comes around again, he won't get a second chance." Charles threw the reins to Amos's horse down to the ground, and he rode off before Sam could say anything.

Sam looked at Amos, took a handful of his hair, and lifted his head. Amos moaned. Sam let go, and his head dropped. Jane and Danny began walking toward Sam, but Sam told them to go back in the house. He walked Amos's horse to the back of the barn. Then he untied the ropes holding him to the horse and let him fall to the ground, causing Amos to start coming back around to consciousness. He grabbed the back of Amos's shirt, pulled him up to a stand, forcefully walked him to the empty corncrib, and threw him inside. Amos collapsed again. Sam opened the back doors to the barn and sat within view of the crib, waiting.

He immediately began to pray in sheer obedience, "Jesus, help me. Intercede, Lord. You warned me of Amos's pain. Take me through this your way, not mine. And be swift. Spare him. Release him. Use me to achieve your will. Plant yourself right in the middle of this situation. Take over completely. Don't permit me to move to the left or the right of your word. All for the glory of you. Amen."

After a while, Jane came out with two blankets. She handed one to Sam, and as she was beginning to lift the latch to give Amos a blanket, Sam stopped her. "He doesn't get a blanket," Sam said. Jane looked at Amos and felt sorry for him, but she did not oppose Sam. He said, "He needs to find out right now just how cold the world can be."

Amos began to stir. He came up on his hands and knees and saw the crib floor. Was he still in the barn with Hannah? He didn't know. He rubbed at the pain on the side of his head where Charles hit him, and he came to his feet. He was still very unstable as he looked around and realized where he was. He pulled on the slatted door to find it locked and then pulled it harder and harder as he began to yell.

"Hey. Hey! Let me outta here. Sam? Let me out!" Amos continued to yell and pull on the door. Then he spotted Sam through the slats. "Sam, why am I in here? Let me out!" Sam came to his feet.

"You should go," Sam said to Jane and kissed her on the cheek. She understood and left, but Danny was in the shadows, watching. Amos saw Jane leave; then he looked at Sam wondering what he was going to do.

"Sam, you gotta let me out. We can talk about this man to man."

"Man to what?" Sam asked. "Do you know what you did tonight, Amos? Or were you too drunk to remember?"

Amos's eyes moved around as he tried to think. He pulled on the gate again. "Let me out, and we can talk about it," Amos yelled. "That girl isn't hurt. You're making a big deal out of nothing," Amos protested.

"Make yourself comfortable, Amos. You're going to be in there for a while, unless the corn harvest comes first." Sam sat back down. Amos moved to the back corner of the crib and sat down too.

Sam was startled by a noise in the barn. It was Danny coming to join him. Sam handed Danny the other blanket and wondered what motivated him to stay. Was it in support? Was it just to see how things would unfold? Was it to save Amos if things got out of hand? Or was there something within Danny that made him understand what caused Amos to unravel? Whatever it was, Danny did not leave Sam's side that night.

Sam woke up to see Jane standing at Amos's door with a Bible and reading scripture in a soft voice. Between scriptures, she prayed for the chains on Amos to be broken. Sam rubbed the sleep off his face and remembered that Danny stayed. He looked at Danny, who had clearly been awake for some time. Danny wondered what would happen next, but he didn't ask. Jane finished with a silent prayer, and then she walked to Sam as he came to a stand.

"Breakfast is ready. He's not going anywhere. You should come inside and eat," Jane said. Then she looked at Danny to make sure he heard her too. "Should I feed him some slop?" Jane gestured toward Amos and looked at Sam disapprovingly.

"You read my mind," Sam said. Jane became irritated and turned to leave. "Jane." Sam stopped her.

"I'm not saying there is any excuse for what he did, but I can't see how this is the answer," she said.

"Please trust me. I know what I'm doing," Sam said. Danny wondered if Sam really did know what he was doing. Jane yielded but still disagreed. "I'll be in shortly," he said.

Sam walked to the crib and saw Amos sitting in a slumped position against the back wall, still out.

"What now?" Danny asked.

"Time," Sam answered. "What's keeping you here, Danny? Curiosity?"

"Yeah, curiosity. I'm wondering what he's fightin'. You bes' be wonderin' too."

Sam did know what Amos was fighting, but he still asked, "What do you mean?"

"I think I understand Amos. When the world's been unfair for so long, it makes you crazy. And the crazier you get, the righter you think you are. That's not God. That's Satan. On the other hand, God might have him right where he wants him," Danny struggled to say because he knew that he was talking just as much about himself.

"So what are you saying?" Sam asked.

"I'm saying that you can't expect him to understand you. The only way you' gonna reach him is if you understand him. Jus' like the Lord. He takes us as we are, right where we are, and he helps get us untangled 'cause he can see the knots inside us, why they' there, and how they got there. If you take Amos as he is, right now, you might be able to help him get straight."

Sam's eyes moved back and forth thinking about what Danny meant. He nodded and said, "I see your point. Thank you."

*****

It didn't take long for news to hit the streets of Edwardsville that Sam's brother was a vicious drunk that beat the young and fair Hannah Mueller. Whispers varied from folks not believing a word of it to flat lies that further tarnished both Hannah and Amos. Talia Green was all but celebrating over her afternoon tea with the ladies at her mansion.

"It seems the Callahans have a blemish after all! One enormous one called Amos!" She laughed and laughed, and the ladies joined in, even one against her better judgment.

Vincent overheard Talia and he entered the room. "That's enough for one day, Talia." Talia scowled at him for violating her privacy. "Tell your friends to go home."

"I most certainly will not," Talia protested and turned to her friends and laughed.

"I said the party is over," Vincent said calmly. Talia gritted her teeth and went to stand, but Vincent put his hand on her shoulder and pushed her back down in her seat. Her guests all quickly gathered their things and left. Then Vincent said, "You and I need to talk," but she got up abruptly and ran out of the room growling.

*****

Reverend Hunt came by to visit the Callahans and offer prayer. Jane explained that Sam had Amos confined to the corn crib and was going on a second day. Reverend Hunt walked to the barn and overheard Amos's continued plea to be let out. Sam saw the reverend and met him outside.

"You have an interesting method of correction, Sam," said Reverend Hunt. Sam sensed his disapproval. "Be careful. It might just break his spirit."

"We can only hope, Reverend," Sam said firmly.

The reverend considered Sam's meaning and asked, "Any progress?"

Sam looked back in the barn and let out a deep breath of fatigue and answered, "No, not yet."

Reverend Hunt did not protest. Rather, he prayed for a long time as he walked around the barn and the crib. Then he left and went to the Muellers to check on them. Charles welcomed him in and they spoke privately.

"I've just come from the Callahans," Reverend Hunt said. Charles pursed his lips and began to breathe hard.

"I hope they have that animal penned up," Charles said as he began to pace the room feeling more and more like an animal himself.

"Then you've heard," Reverend Hunt said.

"Heard what?" Charles asked.

"That's exactly what Sam has done," Reverend Hunt said. Charles stopped pacing and looked questioningly at the reverend. "Charles, Sam is horrified over what has happened, and he is taking it very seriously. Amos is not the kind young boy he was when he left here with his family. He is torn apart inside. He did not intend to hurt anyone, but he has to be intent not to hurt anyone again. Sam knows that. And it would be good for Hannah to know that what Amos did had nothing to do with her." Hannah was standing nearby and listening.

*****

Amos walked around in his limited space. It was already getting dark again, and he dreaded the idea of sleeping in the cold for another night. He pulled on the door. Then he kicked it, but it was useless. He was at the mercy of Sam, who was working in the barn.

Amos yelled, "You're no different than Father. You think you're better than he is, but you're just like him!" That hurt a little, Sam confessed to himself.

"I can see why you would say that, Amos. But it's not true," Sam answered as he kept working.

"Yeah? You lock me up like a prisoner. I haven't even done anything to deserve it. How much longer before you pull out a whip?" Sam ignored him. Amos was quiet for a while but only verbally. His mind was raging. There was so much noise in his head that he couldn't think straight.

"I hate you, you bastard," Amos admitted. Sam started to respond but held back and just listened. "You left me. You abandoned me, your younger brother, even though you knew what life for me would be like. You stayed here and never gave me a thought. You took care of yourself, though. Look around at your empire."

"I can see why you would think that too. I would probably think the same way. But it's not true. And I think you know it's not true," Sam said over his shoulder as he blended feed for the animals.

"It is true. Look at you. You care more about your horses than you do for me," Amos yelled again.

"I care about the horses, Amos, because of you," Sam stated. Amos didn't want to hear it. Nothing was said while Sam put feed out for the chickens. "I'll be back with your supper."

Sam came back about an hour later. He pried loose and removed one slat of the crib, and when he tried to slide the plate of food between the slats, Amos pushed it back, knocking it out of Sam's hand and to the ground. Sam was beginning to lose his patience with Amos and wondered if it wouldn't speed things up to just beat the hell out of him. Sam kicked the plate aside and began to lift the latch. Amos watched with hatred in his eye and prepared to lunge at Sam. But Sam stopped himself and left.

"Sleep well, Amos," Sam said. Amos kicked the door again.

Jane was finishing up in the kitchen when Sam slammed the front door, waking Morgan from a sound sleep. Jane met him in the entryway with her head tilted in frustration as she heard Morgan's cries.

"I'm sorry, Jane," Sam said

"Sam, please come help me." Jane led Sam upstairs to Morgan's crib. She picked up her child who was in need of her care, and he immediately stopped crying. Sam watched as she rocked Morgan in her arms for a few minutes, and when he fell back asleep, Jane laid him down and covered him in a blanket, tucking him in on all sides. She said, "Sam, I understand your concern and need to protect our family, but your hatred and anger toward Bishop have left you fearful that he will one day cross our threshold. They have become idols that you have not destroyed, which begs for caution over the potential for hypocrisy as you punish Amos for being in the same condition as you. You say you know what you are doing, but I have to ask, are you sure? Frankly, it appears as though you don't want him here." Jane waited patiently for his reply, which took time.

"You're wrong in saying that I don't want Amos here. But you're right in saying that I hate Bishop. And you're right in saying that my hatred and anger are idols, ones that I both worship and battle daily. You're even right in saying Amos and I worship the same idols. The difference, Jane, between me and Amos is that I see it and he doesn't. If he can't see it, he can't know that he needs to destroy it. And if he doesn't know he needs to destroy it, then he can't stay here. And I want him to stay here."

Jane was startled upon reaching understanding, and she conceded. But she added, "Nonetheless, it grieves me to see you so harsh. Can you soften your heart somewhat?" And she handed him another blanket. "I'll be along later to check on you two."

Sam took another plate of food to Amos and gently handed it to him. This time, Amos did not refuse it. Sam also pushed the blanket through the slat.

"Amos, let me be candid. For you to believe that you did nothing wrong to Hannah is frightening. I'm asking you to open your eyes and do it soon." Sam moved to his chair, pulled his blanket over himself, and waited. He woke to hearing Amos wailing on the floor of the corncrib.

"Amos?" Sam called to his tormented brother.

"I can't fight it, Sam," Amos cried. "It's like an animal inside me trying to get out, and it can't find the way." Amos paused. Sam listened. "Sometimes, I think I get it under control, but I never know when it's going to attack again. It catches me off guard, and eventually, I can't fight it anymore," Amos cried some more. Sam got up and moved to the crib. "So I don't. I just let it consume me. That's when someone gets hurt." Sam sat down with his back against the gate.

"I know, Amos," Sam confided.

Amos slowly sat up and looked at Sam through the barrier slats. "You know?" he asked.

"Of course, I know. Why wouldn't I know? We fight the same demons, and it's centered on not becoming what we hate," Sam waited while Amos calculated. "Amos, everyone battles this."

"How do you do it? How do you win?" Amos asked as if looking for a magic formula.

"You don't. You lose if you're smart. In fact, you make a point of losing." Sam smiled while Amos frowned. "Pray, Amos. That's how you win. Pray."

"You pray?" Amos asked.

"All the time." Sam laughed, knowing it was hard for Amos to understand. "I pray every day that I will lose my fight with God. Then I wake up the next day and do it all again. Losing yourself to God is how you win."

They sat for hours talking about their upbringing, exhausting their memories of Bishop, and embracing their memories of Charlotte. They recalled their times together at the Pruitts' home and how different it was from their own home. Sam shared his memories of courting Jane and how his fear of her father was far different than his fear of Bishop. But what Amos wanted to understand the most was how Sam escaped their upbringing unscathed.

"I didn't," Sam answered. "Nowhere near it." He paused as he crafted an explanation. "I remember one time when I was sitting behind a family in church. A brother and sister were fighting, and the sister was really mad. Her father told her to be quiet and get over it. I kept thinking about the father's solution: get over it. Could I just get over it?" Sam looked at Amos doubtfully. "You don't just get over eighteen years of life with a man like Bishop Callahan, Amos. It's been over a year of diligent purging, and I still fight the animal.

I still hate my father. That's not something you just get over. That's something you get rid of. All that hatred has to go. And I get rid of it over and over again. Do I pray? Hourly. That's how I make sure I don't become him. I'm not passing what Father experienced with his father and what you and I experienced with our father on to my wife and children. That legacy ends with me. I made that decision during that one minute that Father gave me at dinner. I prayed to God to help me, and from that night forward, he has never left me. So pray, Amos. Clear your head and listen to his voice and only his voice. Look at me. You were never forgotten. Everything I have done has involved finding a way to bring you here."

"And Jane?" Amos asked through his tears. "Is this what she wants too?"

"More than you know," Sam said.

Amos asked, "Why? Why would either of you want me here?"

"Because we love you, Amos," Sam answered.

Amos started to cry, and he said through his tears, "I don't hate you, Sam. I hate myself. Especially now. I can't believe what I have done, and I've been thinking that it might be best for everyone if I just leave," Amos said.

Sam answered, "Amos, you see yourself though the wrong set of eyes. Don't look at yourself through Bishop's eyes, or mine, or Jane's, or anyone else's. See yourself through God's eyes only. That's how I see you. But you have to work to empty yourself of your hate because it's destructive to yourself and others. You think this crib is a prison, but it's nothing compared to the prison of hatred. You have to ask yourself, are you going to settle on how the world has shaped you? Or are you going to take charge of how you shape the world around you as a servant of God?"

"I want to. I really do. But I don't how, and I can't face anyone after what I've done," Amos admitted.

"The only one you have to face is God. Once you've done that, facing everyone else is easy. And I'll be here to help. Okay?" Amos nodded. Sam smiled, stood up, and opened the gate. He waved Amos forward to come out of the crib and said, "Welcome home, Amos."

Jane rushed back to the house unnoticed by Sam and Amos that she had been there. Sam went straight to bed and lay down with one hand under his head and the other across his chest, thinking about all that God had done to prepare him for this day. No one understood, and despite doubt from his family and friends, he stayed the course that God had put him on even though he really did not know what God was doing. He was thankful that he was given wisdom and strength to trust and endure it.

Jane sat down on the bed beside him and ran her fingers through his hair. Her breathing was shallow, and her eyes were wide and overwhelmed. Sam took her hand to steady her and asked, "What is it?"

"I trespassed. I didn't mean to. I came out to the barn to check on you and Amos, as I said I would. But you two were talking and rather than interrupt, I thought I would wait for an appropriate break in your discussion, but it didn't come. I should have left, but I'm not sorry because I saw deep inside you, and..." Jane pulled her lips in and lowered her head.

"I have no secrets, Jane," Sam said.

"Maybe not. But you've not always been an open book, Sam. You are now, though, and the best one I've ever read. I can't wait to find out what will happen next," she said with a smile and a breath of relief that came with her honesty. And she took a moment to look into his green eyes before she leaned in to kiss him. And Sam untied the lace ribbon on the back of her gown.

*****

It was late in the morning before Sam knocked on Amos's door; he wanted to let him rest after their long night, but Amos did not answer. He was gone.

Sam struggled throughout the day wondering where Amos was, and Jane struggled in her attempt to console him. Danny tried, too, but Sam kept to himself and his work. Sam couldn't even begin to think where Amos would have gone or why. Was he coming back? He searched for a note, but there was nothing. It was dark when Jane, Sam, and Danny quietly sat down to eat; then the front door opened.

"What's for supper?" Amos asked. Sam was shocked and caught between being relieved and wanting to hit him, but Jane simply placed another plate on the table and smiled. Danny stood to greet Amos with a handshake. Amos immediately dug in, seemingly starved.

"I've been thinking, Sam," Amos said, "it's time I take on more with the horses. I admit that I have not been very interested in the business, but I'm coming around." Amos continued eating. Sam did not question what Amos did all day.

After dinner, Jane played the piano softly, and the men in her life sat quietly and listened to her nurturing sound.

Chapter 20

"Amos, will you drive us to town?" Jane asked. "I need to run some errands, and I want to bring Morgan along." Amos was happy to accommodate Jane's request until he learned that their first stop would be at the cemetery. Jane was surprised again to find the gravesites groomed and blessed with fresh flowers. She took a deep breath and looked around.

"What's wrong?" Amos asked.

"Well, nothing really. It's just that someone keeps caring for the graves, and I can't figure out who." She pulled two bunches of flowers out of her basket and handed one to Amos. "I suppose we will just add these to the ones already here." She knelt down and placed the flowers on her mother's grave. When she stood up, Amos had yet to move. She placed her hand on Amos's arm and said, "I know this is your first time at Nathan's grave, and I know you have never been to your mother's grave. It's important that you learn to deal with death because life is filled with it, but if you're not ready, it's quite all right."

Amos looked at the graves, and he could not hold back his tears. He knelt down beside Nathan's resting place, remembered him, and nestled the flowers next to the others. Then he looked at Mrs. Pruitt's headstone and pictured one with his mother's name. He walked around to the other side, knelt down again, repositioned the two bunches of flowers, and cried harder.

Jane bent over him and whispered, "You take your time." And she walked back to the carriage.

Amos sat next to the graves with his knees bent and his arms across them to support his head as he wept. It took him just as long to regain his composure as it did to purge his sadness, but he finally returned to the carriage and simply said, "Thank you."

He drove Jane to visit Rose at the boardinghouse and her father at his office, and by the time she reached the grocer's for food, fabric, and newspapers, Amos was worn out, as planned.

*****

Talia Green had spotted Jane with Morgan. Envy was unbecoming on Mrs. Green.

"I want a child!" she barked at Vincent in his study. Vincent ignored her while he continued working at his desk. She came to his side and screeched in his ear, "Don't ignore me when I'm talking to you. I said I want a child. I have waited long enough!"

Vincent stood up and looked down at Talia. "I wouldn't have a child with you if my life depended on it." He moved her out of the way so he could leave his study for better air.

"Well, we'll see about that. If your reputation is your life, then your life might just depend on it."

"Meaning what?" Vincent challenged.

"I have proof that you and Senator Norwood's daughter are involved. Not that I care really, aside from the fact that, that information is quite useful to me as it should be all the leverage I need to gain your, shall I say, understanding?" Talia partially turned her back, then looked over her shoulder at him as if to say, "Checkmate."

Vincent ran her words through his head. "What is it you think you know?" he asked her.

"She was seen going into your office just last week, as if it were common. You should learn to be quieter. Your playful affair could easily be heard by passersby. Really Vincent! The senator is a close friend of your father. The impact would be shattering for you and your parents. I must thank you for that."

Vincent laughed. "That's it? That's what your leverage is?"

"More than sufficient, I should think!" Talia raised her chin. "Your reputation will be ruined, which will also take down the senator, and you will lose your job. Your father will be so disappointed in you, but the family money remains. That's all that matters."

Vincent seemed paralyzed, and though his contempt for her was screaming inside his head, he simply stared at her silently.

Talia walked to him seductively and leaned against him affectionately. "There now. That's better. Let's set the evening aside for ourselves, Vincent. It might be fun." Her smile was demonic.

Vincent smiled agreeably, but then he stepped away causing her to lose her support and balance. "Do what you have to do, Talia. There will be no child." He closed the door quietly as he walked out. Talia stomped the floor with her feet. She picked up a book from the sofa table and threw it across the room, smashing a glass-paned cabinet door.

*****

Talia sat at her favorite table in the restaurant, which she reserved for herself and her friends each Wednesday for tea since the last episode at her home. As she and her friends were finishing their time together, she saw Senator Norwood and his daughter being escorted to a table. She told her friends to go ahead without her, and she calculated her strategy as she watched her friends walk out. Then she rose and approached the senator.

"Pardon me, Senator. I have something most unpleasant to discuss of an urgent matter," Talia began.

"Mrs. Green," the senator said as he stood, "do we need privacy? We can retreat to a quieter setting," he offered.

"On the contrary, Senator. I mean to make this public. You see, I have been offended and deeply so. Your daughter is having an affair with my husband. She was seen entering his office last week and was clearly overheard enjoying his intimate company, if you know what I mean. I want it to stop immediately, whatever the cost."

Talia made no effort to lower her voice. Guests were now looking on, but the experienced senator ignored them. His daughter remained quietly seated and perfectly still except for her glance at her father and Talia. The senator stared into Talia's eyes, and she stared back. Then the senator smiled. Then he laughed softly. Then his laughter built to a roar that caused the watchful guests to follow suit.

Talia's expression revealed her discomfort and confusion as she looked around the room. "This is hardly a trivial or humorous matter, Senator Norwood. I demand correction to this injustice," she stated.

"As you said, my dear, whatever the cost. Yes, my daughter was in your husband's office last week. I know because I was in your husband's office, too, the entire time. We had long boring business ahead of us, which I knew would keep my beautiful daughter waiting for an unpredictable amount of time. So I bought her a puppy. While your husband and I retreated to his inner office, she waited in his main office and enjoyed the company of my gift to her. I would hardly call it an intimate setting, but"—he laughed again—"that is subject to one's opinion!" The guests all joined the senator for another good laugh. Talia gritted her teeth and her face turned red. "Go home, Mrs. Green. And appreciate that your husband's impeccable reputation remains intact." He took his seat and the waiter handed him a menu, which the senator began reading as a message to Talia that the discussion was over. Talia was blinded with fury but composed herself as she left the restaurant.

*****

Sam walked by the front window and saw Jane rise to her feet from praying. She tucked something behind some pillows on the sofa, wiped her eyes, and moved to the kitchen beyond Sam's view. Sam came inside quietly and pulled several newspapers from Jane's hiding place. News of another spread of the cholera dominated every paper. Numerous articles focused on Ninian Edwards, the only governor of the territory of Illinois and the third governor of the state. The news highlighted his political, legal, and land victories for Illinois and the country overall. Edwardsville was named for him.

Sam joined Jane in the kitchen and placed the papers on the counter. He took her in his arms and held her close. Jane started to cry again.

"Ninian Edwards is dead," she said with shortness of breath and under the embrace of Sam's arms. "He was just trying to comfort the sick in Belleville, and the cholera took him almost immediately. What hope is there, Sam, if we cannot even comfort each other in such a dark hour without becoming victims ourselves?"

She picked up one paper after another, flipping through them. "Quincy, Jacksonville, Carrollton, Galena, Belleville, Rock Island, and now Springfield. It's in our backyard, Sam. One in three who contract this disease dies. One in three! One family lost nearly all its members. Neighbors cannot even depend on friends who now hide in fear that one might contract it from the other."

"Jane," Sam said as she cried some more.

"I can't bear it, Sam. I cannot lose you or Morgan. God help me, I can't. And the thought of leaving you two alone without me to provide you with the love and support you both need is unbearable."

"Jane, listen to me." He raised her head and wiped her tears. "You know too much to let this rule you. Can I lose my mind thinking about death at our door? Of course. All we can live for is today. We will worry about tomorrow, tomorrow. Right now, we have our family. And as you said, not everyone does. We must be thankful." Sam said no more than the simple truth, and eventually, Jane showed signs of being comforted. He wiped the last of her tears and kissed her.

That night, Sam found Jane in their bedroom sitting and holding their sleeping child. Sam took Morgan out of her arms and gently put him in his cradle. She watched him change into his nightclothes and pick out a gown for her. He helped her stand up. Then he undressed her and put her in her gown. He unpinned her hair, sat her at her vanity, and brushed her long curls with gentle strokes. He knelt down beside her, took her hands, and prayed for her, their son, their families, their friends, their home, their community, and the less fortunate. He turned down the bed, laid her down, moved in beside her, and held her all night.

The next day, more panic was in the air. Sam, Jane, and Rose talked back and forth for some time before Sam noticed how quiet

Adrien had been during supper. After supper, Adrien discreetly signaled Sam to engage privately outside.

"Something's wrong," Sam said.

Adrien looked at Sam affirmatively. "Indeed," he said. "President Jackson officially shut down the National Bank, and he has begun to move all the funds to select state banks of his own choosing."

"How can he do that?" Sam asked.

"Illegally, that's how. His treasurer refused to follow his orders, so he fired him. He hired another one who also refused. He fired him too. The next treasurer agreed, and all federal funds are being moved from the Second National Bank to these pet banks with seemingly no governance in place to protect national resources."

"I confess, Adrien, I am not sure what this all means," Sam said.

"It means the entire nation's economy is on thin ice. National revenues in the hands of state banks? Banks that Jackson handpicked? It's an impeachable act. It's hard to blame Jackson for his suspicion and resentment of the bank's dealings, but his response is ignorant and prideful, at best!"

"Let me rephrase my question. What does this mean to me?" Sam asked. Adrien paused to think.

"What does it mean to any of us? Time will tell. In my opinion, when the bottom falls out, many people will suffer, and severely so. The poor will take it the hardest, as always, and they are the very people Jackson means to protect. It will probably even reach Europe. It's hard to say what the value of money will be. And if that's not enough, the federal government wants only gold or silver for land sales, yet state banks have been printing paper money recklessly. If it becomes useless…" Adrien could not bear to finish his thought. "We will just have to keep our eyes open. In the meantime, I am going to convert my money to silver and be very cautious with my investments and spending. I suggest you do the same."

*****

A one-year-old child wouldn't know to be afraid of heights. So, when Sam sat Morgan into Crimson's saddle for the first time, he only smiled. Sam walked beside Crimson and held on to Morgan's britches to secure him in the saddle while Danny led with the reins. Jane preferred not to watch.

After a bit of a walk, Sam said to Danny, "Let's go for a ride."

"A ride? You sure? We got a lot to do yet." Danny glanced at the still undeveloped property.

Sam gazed at the spring day and then answered, "There will always be a lot to do. This day is too nice to pass up." He rubbed Crimson's neck and said, "You're coming, too, girl." Crimson was Sam's favorite broodmare, and he rode her only to give her exercise. Today, it would be for pleasure, the first of such times since bringing her to Edwardsville from St. Louis.

Sam looked at the house where he knew Jane was already consumed with her work, and he told Danny to hang on. After overcoming some resistance, Sam convinced Jane to join them, and she packed a light meal for the outing.

Jane was used to being in carriages, not in saddles, and Sam had to acquaint her with her new seat. Because Sam had no sidesaddle for her, she had to ride astride, but she came to love it and learned no other way. She straddled Sunny, her Palomino, and her only real challenge was adjusting her dress to cover her legs. Unlike Morgan, she was nervous about being so high and in an unpredictable situation. What if her horse did not respond to her commands? What if she fell?

After adjusting and settling, Sam, Danny, Jane, and Morgan began their first of many such outings, which exposed them to various spots of Illinois's beautiful countryside where streams and groves seemed untouched by human hands.

Chapter 21

It was a fine summer morning and still dark when Sam finished reviewing his journal in the barn. He closed it, contemplated, and tossed it aside. He went back to the house where Jane was just getting up, and he said, "It's time kill my idol." She understood.

In Amos's room, Sam said, "Amos, wake up. You need to pack."

"Pack? Where am I going?" Amos was groggy.

"We're going to Washington," Sam stated. "Hurry. I want to get an early start."

"Washington?" Amos said to himself because Sam had already left his room.

Amos rubbed the sleep off his face, packed, and came downstairs to the kitchen to find Jane serving breakfast. He quietly sat, ate, and listened to Sam go over again and again with Jane that Danny would be there daily, that Joseph was next door, that her father and Rose and a list of others would be close by if she needed anything.

Sam finished up inside by holding Morgan and telling him he was now the man of the house. Outside, he held Jane in his arms for a long time.

"Sam," Jane whispered, "God has gone ahead of you, and the way is already prepared. We'll be fine. And so will you. I have prayed, and this trip will exceed your expectations." Sam held on a few more seconds. Then he released her. As he left, he looked over his shoulder numerous times until the house was no longer in sight. And when Sam was no longer in her sight, Jane went back inside and broke down.

*****

Averaging thirty miles a day, it was nearly two weeks before Sam and Amos reached Columbus, Ohio, at which point they took the National Road all the way to Baltimore. Taverns and inns were available roughly every ten miles, and they were typically lively as the traffic on the road was high and diverse with horsemen, wagons, stagecoaches, livestock, and even people on foot. Sam took comfort in having constant road companions but only to a point as it made for slow progress at times. It also made him realize just how many people were pouring into the newly settled and Indian-free Mississippi Valley. He was reminded of Adrien's prediction that Indian removal from the frontier was still to come, and he winced.

Many stopping points were surprisingly well-equipped minicities where the taverns were surrounded by larger hotel accommodations, businesses, stores, blacksmiths, cartwrights and wainwrights, livestock traders and sellers, grocers, post offices, restaurants, and sometimes an opera house. Money changed hands in excess. The Callahan family took this road three years earlier, and with exception of the extended length of the road, little had changed. Amos had just traveled this route on his way to Edwardsville, which provided some fresh insight on desirable quarters and good beer, though his consumption was considerably lower since his tragic night with Hannah Mueller.

Zanesville, Ohio, was their next destination. The town was once Ohio's capital and was named for Ebenezer Zane. With the tasking and blessing of Congress, he surveyed and cut Zane's Trace, the original road that ran west from Wheeling, Virginia, which further opened up the territories for settlement. By now, Zane's Trace had been largely replaced with the National Road.

Zanesville could not come soon enough. When the sky fell with relentless rain and darkness closed in, Sam and Amos were regretting their decision to push the fifty-five-mile stretch from Columbus. They had already passed three perfect rest stops in favor of gaining ground, but the price was becoming too high.

"How much farther do you think?" Amos yelled through the storm to Sam. Just then, lightning struck a tree not far ahead of them, startling both horses and throwing Amos into the middle of the road. Sam was caught between watching Amos's horse run off and noticing that Amos was not moving.

"Damn it!" Sam said as he struggled to see. He jumped off his horse, and as he approached Amos, he heard a stagecoach coming. Before Sam could prevent it, his horse jerked the reins from his hand and also ran off. He turned to his brother, who was now coming to his feet, and he threw himself into Amos, tackling him to the other side of the road just seconds before the stagecoach passed. Sam and Amos found themselves sitting in a pool of cold water between the trees and the road.

"Are you all right?" Sam asked Amos.

"I think so. The only thing hurting is my pride," Amos said. Sam got up and reached out to Amos to help him to his feet. "I thought Jane said she prayed for us. Did she forget to tithe or something?"

Sam laughed. "I don't know how you do it, Amos! Aside of that stage missing you by a hair, things could not be much worse. And you just…," Sam said, smiling as water dripped from the rim of his hat.

"What?" Amos asked, smiling back at Sam.

"Nothing bothers you! You must know what a gift you have. It's incredible!"

Sam turned his attention back to his horse and whistled, but he did not come. He whistled again and again, but he still did not come. Sam was starting to panic. He and Amos walked only a short distance before finding Amos's horse. They rode together as Sam continued to look for his horse, but it was useless. Another hour or so of rain and cold caused them to stop short of Zanesville in favor of the shelter and heat they found at the newly constructed Rock Cliff House, an enormous and comfortable tavern. There was one room left. Sam handed the room key to Amos and turned to leave.

"Where do you think you're going?" Amos protested. "Wait until tomorrow. There is no possible way you'll find your horse tonight." The Rock Cliff owner came around the corner.

"It can't wait, Amos! I have to find that horse!" Sam barked.

"Did you lose a horse?" the owner asked.

"Yes!" Sam replied with a tone meant to say that he did not appreciate having it rubbed in his face.

"Well, you might be in luck. A horse was dropped here tonight by a stagecoach. Come take a look." The owner gestured Sam to come outside. Sam looked at Amos in disbelief.

"She did pray," Amos said and smiled.

The owner led Sam to the barn, and from a distance, he was able to recognize that it was, indeed, his horse. He checked all the bags, and everything was still there. In relief, he thanked God, Jane, the owner, and the honest stagecoach driver who secured his possessions.

Both Sam and Amos packed well enough to have a dry change of clothes. And the chill through their bones was eased by the fire in the dining room along with some stew, bread, and beer; the combination was like medicine. Amos raised his mug and Sam smiled. Sam reflected on how close the two of them had become in such a short time. He was thankful for this trip with Amos and was just about to say so, but Amos shared first.

"It's not true," Amos stated. Sam was unsure of what Amos meant, and his expression spoke for him. "Lots of things bother me." Sam remained quiet to allow his brother time to complete his confession. Amos pushed his plate forward slightly as if to make room for what was coming. After a moment of preparation, he began.

"Certain memories, for example, bother me a lot. Not just the obvious ones, but ones that might not seem worthy of leaving a mark, like clinging to every chance I got to go to the Pruitts' home with you. That's how much I hated being at home alone. Mother's silence. I hated her for that. The emphasis placed on your future while none was placed on mine. You hated all the studying you had to do, but I envied you. Someone was investing in you. And by the time I should have entered tutoring, all the money was gone. Things like that. Lots of things like that. And then there *are* the obvious ones, like watching you leave. That's actually a good memory, but it bothered me because you were the only source of sanity I had. So, that one runs through my head over and over. Hannah—that will always bother me. And then there are memories yet to come. I mean, what's at the end of this trip, Sam? I'm not sure what you are trying to achieve, and that really bothers me."

Sam was still logging the painful list Amos gave him. His eyes rocked as he searched for the right words. "Clean hands," Sam finally said.

Amos looked at Sam with a bit of confusion. Sam went back to eating. After a moment, Amos nodded and pulled his plate back in to eat.

Sam, Amos, and their horses rested for two days at the Rock Cliff House. They had their clothes washed, boots cleaned, and horses groomed before moving on. They rode straight through Zanesville, but Sam took time to examine the town's famed Y-bridge, a construction feat shaped like a *Y* to accommodate crossing the confluence of the Licking and Muskingum Rivers. Amos dismounted and gazed out over the flow of the two merging rivers and made no attempt to rush Sam who rode his horse back and forth several times looking at the design and structure of the bridge. When he reached the other side of the bridge, he stopped and looked back. Amos waited.

"That's a lot of water," Sam released from his deep thoughts.

"It reminds me of a spot where the Missouri and the Mississippi rivers meet near Hartford right where Lewis and Clark had their winter camp. The river swells there and seems like it's standing still, but underneath it's a raging force."

Sam knew the spot, and he wondered about its importance to Amos. Sam got off his horse to get a closer look at the bridge's design, bending over the railing, squatting, and gazing beyond.

"What's on your mind?" Amos asked.

Sam answered, "I'm thrilled when I can build a chicken coop. So when I look at this bridge, I am fascinated." Sam laughed a little. "But I'm also disturbed. It wasn't that long ago that there were no settlers west of these rivers. But they endured these rivers even before bridges. There's little left to slow them down now. And with no right, settlers are crossing the Mississippi and Missouri Rivers into Indian territory that our government has promised to protect. What is it that drives mankind to go the next distance, and what do we think we will find when we get there?" After a moment, Sam mounted, turned his horse east, and resumed riding. But he noticed that Amos did not follow. He turned and looked at Amos inquisitively.

Amos answered, "Why do you think Lewis and Clark endured Jefferson's *great commission* to explore navigable routes to the west? Adventure? No. Property ownership. And that equals money. And money equals power. That's what drives mankind, and it always has. Going west, they call it opportunity, but what they really mean is money and power. Europeans have been fighting over this continent's territory for centuries, and it *will* fall to one of them. The French are all but gone. The Spanish too. Now it's down to the Americans and the British, and the US government will exhaust all its power on making sure the British leave too. This country will be settled from the Atlantic to the Pacific. It's all they talk about back home. Jackson's Indian Removal Act is just a small part of the plan." Amos looked back across the river. "Don't think I don't share your sentiment. I hate the thought of it. But there's a storm coming, Sam. And there's not one Indian nation or one unified group of compassionate Native supporters—no matter how strong, no matter how brave—that can weather it. It's coming, and there's no stopping it. The best we can do is try to soften the blow." Amos kicked his heels into his horse and rode past Sam, and Sam acknowledged the disturbing reality of times to come and his own resistance to facing it.

*****

The weather was good during the day, and Sam continued to study the bridgework along the way. The stretch beyond Zanesville had several S-bridges made of stone that added a pleasing touch to the already picturesque countryside. By nightfall, as was typical, the weather turned sour. Cambridge, though, was just up ahead, and this time, Sam and Amos arrived at their destination dry.

Conversation broke out across the dining room while Sam and Amos were finishing their meals, and it was hard not to overhear.

A refined man on the other side of the fireplace said, "Every time I take this National Road, there are hundreds more travelers, new booming towns, sometimes endless lines of freight wagons moving goods with the labor of eight oxen. But the accidents are what shock me the most." A group of men had gathered around a guest's table and shared their observations of the evergrowing commerce along the evergrowing road.

Sam and Amos looked at each other upon hearing the word *accident* and shuddered a little. They had been so consumed with recovering and making up time that they had not given much consideration to how close they had come to death. They listened as the refined man continued telling of his experiences.

"Just yesterday, I saw a lad lose his footing and fall over right in front of a team of horses pulling an overloaded wagon. When the driver tried to stop, his load buckled and tipped over. The lad survived, but the driver was crushed and died instantly. He had a wife and three young children and no family traveling with them. Quite horrifying."

"What happened to the family?" another man asked. By now, Sam and Amos had finished supper and politely joined the men.

"A group of us managed to get the wagon up and going again. We left some of their goods on the road to make room for the dead man, and the devastated mother and her children rode on to the next town. I can't say what happened af—"

Suddenly, the tavern door flew open by the force of a man who, like Sam and Amos two nights before, was drenched from the rain. He struggled to make his way to a table, and he sat down alone with his eyes wide open. He rubbed his hand over his mouth again and again. Everyone watched him.

"Mercy, my good man! You look as though you have seen a ghost!" another man said. The soggy man pulled himself away from his traumatizing thoughts and looked into the eyes of each man looking at him.

"I have," he said. Then he turned away. After a pause, many of the men let out belly laughs. But not Sam or Amos or the refined man describing the accident. They all came to his side.

"What do you mean you have seen a ghost?" the refined man asked the weary traveler.

"What's the use? You won't believe me," he growled in defeat.

CROSSINGS

"Try me."

A barmaid was watching and listening as she served more rounds. The man's glossy eyes looked up again desperately wanting to ease his own mind.

Hesitantly, he began to explain, "It was just outside of Morristown that I lost the sun behind the dark rain clouds. I still had hours to go before getting here. There was thunder and lightning in the distance, which was frightening but also helpful because it provided some much-needed light, for the road bends often in this area, and I was moving at a good pace." He rubbed his mouth again. "All of a sudden, there was someone riding beside me. It was a woman on a high-spirited horse." He paused and looked at the refined man very seriously. "She was just an apparition, and she had no head! I stopped so quickly that I almost fell from my horse, and then she and her horse vanished." He turned away again.

The refined man signaled the barmaid to bring this troubled man a drink, and he sat down to join him, concerned. Amos was very attentive to the man's story and could hardly move. Sam, though, was not afraid of ghosts, at least, not that kind. When the barmaid delivered the beer, she engaged.

"It was that girl from Wheeling that you saw," she said. "She died there two months ago from a broken neck when her carriage flipped on one of those tight bends. She was running away to join the love of her life in Fairview against her parents' wishes. They thought he was beneath her, you know. You saw her, all right. Lots of people do." She confirmed with a nod before moving to the next table.

Sam rested his hand on the man's shoulder briefly and tipped his head meaning to wish him well. Then he and Amos sat down at another table.

"Morristown is our next stop," Amos said, somewhat concerned, "and we won't get there until dark." Sam rolled his eyes before flagging down the barmaid for another round.

*****

It would take ten hours to get to Morristown at a walking pace, not including stops, and Sam wanted a slow pace for the sake of the horses. Much faster would require additional rest time for the horses, and it would lengthen the trip, and Sam did not want to repeat his mistake from Columbus to Zanesville. Amos kept trying to speed things up, but his brother was no help. He glared at Sam, and Sam just smirked.

"I think we can make it to Morristown before dark. I suggest we stay at the Black Horse Inn," Amos said. "Good food and drink and very comfortable. If we want a room, we had better hurry." Amos led his horse to a trot. Sam's horse walked. A bend was up ahead, and Amos rode out of Sam's sight. When he looked back for Sam, he was not there. Amos stopped and called out for him.

"Sam, stop messing around! It's going to be dark soon, and we need to get to Morristown!" Amos felt a raindrop. Then another. Then a steady flow. "Sam!" Amos yelled. Frustrated, he rode back to where he last saw Sam, but there was no sign of him, and now with the rain, Amos could find no tracks. He waited. Then he looked at his surroundings and became very nervous. He thought he heard something in the woods, and he called out to Sam again somewhat cautiously. He struggled to see through the trees as it was getting darker and wetter, and the tightness in his chest was becoming uncomfortable. When he gave up and turned his horse around toward Morristown, Sam was right in front of him, and he screamed.

"You bastard!" Amos yelled. "Now I really do hate you!" Amos rode past Sam in anger, but he stopped suddenly and waited for Sam to join him to ensure there would be no more mischief.

"Ghosts, Amos, are for the dead, not the living," Sam claimed with a smile.

Each day came with thirty to forty miles before reaching the next stay. Each stay came with the same routine of getting cleaned up, enjoying supper and conversation, and making a point of falling asleep quickly only to face the next cold and damp morning. It seemed a major accomplishment to cross the border from Ohio to Virginia, only to face another long journey across Pennsylvania before reaching Maryland, which should have been a welcome sight. But Sam was back in familiar country, and it made him feel heavy.

"I have a stop or two to make in Baltimore," Sam said. Amos had resumed his demeanor of being unbothered, and he did not even inquire to Sam's demand. They got a room at a hotel, and Sam left Amos there for several hours. When he finally returned, he sat Amos down and handed him a small strong box. Amos opened the box with a key and found inside thousands and thousands of dollars.

"What's this?" Amos asked in shock.

"Remember what mother gave me that last night I saw her?" Sam asked. Then he explained to Amos the entire experience in St. Louis and that this was now his share. "You will have plenty of time on this trip to think about how you want to build a life for yourself with your inheritance. I have already been robbed once. We will have to be very careful with this."

"That's why you were so panicked over losing your horse," Amos said. Sam nodded.

*****

Amos had to guide Sam through the capitol because so much had changed since leaving there for Illinois in 1830. As they rode down Pennsylvania Avenue, Sam's attention was locked on the White House and the decisions made therein until he heard someone scream. He looked over his shoulder to see a slave auction in progress within plain view of the White House and Capitol Building. Sam redirected their course to that sound.

The scream came from a woman whose young son was being forcefully taken from her arms. She was naked and made to resume her position back on the block for other buyers. The auctioneer whispered something in her ear, which prompted her to regain her composure in spite of the tears pouring down her face from watching her son being pulled away by his new owner. His screams for her lingered, but she stood at attention. Sam could only guess that the auctioneer made some kind of horrible threat to her. He pictured Morgan being ripped from Jane's arms. He rubbed his jaw and blinked the water from his eyes.

Amos watched the scene a bit more objectively. Slavery in America was the consequence of poisoned hearts that produced a severe clash and contradiction within the country's freedom experiment. God would render justice and deliverance, someday.

Sam then examined the buyers. He watched them as they studied their purchasing options. Then he laughed in disgust and shook his head.

"What?" Amos asked. Sam paused on that loaded question. Then he looked deliberately at Amos.

"Just a few short years ago, Father drove us in his carriage past scenes like this, and it had no impact on me. Had we stayed here, what's to say that I would not now be a slave owner?" Sam's breathing became shallow.

Amos contemplated the possibility but rejected it. "God had other plans, Sam."

Sam nodding both affirmatively and apprehensively. *What plan?* he asked silently.

"Why couldn't they just keep them together?" Amos asked painfully.

"Greed," Sam said.

"Let's go. I'm feeling ill," confessed Amos.

Sam agreed, but their next stop was no better. Sam and Amos arrived at the prison before visiting hours began to ensure a chance to see their father, but the news from the guard posed a setback.

"I'm sorry you traveled all this way, gentlemen," said Sergeant Unger, "but Bishop Callahan is not taking visitors."

"He'll see me. You tell him Sam is here, and I'm not leaving." The sergeant looked blankly at Sam. "Tell him," Sam demanded.

After a long wait that tried Sam's patience, Sergeant Unger came out and led Sam and Amos to the busy visitors room behind tightly secured doors where loved ones and lawyers met with men held back from access to the free world. Sam and Amos both absorbed the setting.

Bishop came and sat down across a table from them. He was thin and balding, and he looked much older than he was. Sam was surprised by his father's condition and had to work up an expression of neutrality. Bishop stared at his boys and raised his thick eyebrows as if to say, "Get on with it."

"We need to get you out of here," Sam simply said. Bishop now had to work to hide his own expression of surprise. He expected to be condemned further, and he was puzzled by Sam's sense of loyalty.

"Why?" Bishop asked.

"Because you didn't do it," Sam said.

"So? I thought you hated me. Why come to my rescue?"

Your rescue? Sam asked.

Bishop took a minute to calculate Sam's meaning. "Ah, I think I understand. Afraid of the dark, are we?" Bishop chided with sarcasm.

"Father, let's not chase the ghosts of why," Sam said. There was a long period of silence during which Sam acknowledged that these were the kinds of ghosts that scared him, and Bishop wondered about the kind of time it would take to chase those ghosts, the kind of time he didn't have. "To clarify, Father, our attempt to right a wrong is in response to God's command to extend grace. I will not let bitterness take me over. I'm afraid of the dark enough to prevent that." Bishop was quiet for a couple of minutes. Sam waited.

"How do you know I didn't do it?" Bishop asked.

"Amos heard the whole thing. And he will be your witness."

"My witness? Amos missed his chance. Mighty kind of you, by the way," Bishop said to Amos. Amos lowered his eyes, still governed by his overpowering father. "And besides, I've already been judged." Bishop laughed knowing that the sentence he had received came from a judge much higher than man.

"We can get the verdict reversed with Amos's testimony," Sam insisted.

"You don't understand." Bishop raised his voice. "I might just as well have done it. Leave it alone."

"Father, I did not come all this way to deal with lies! If you have something to say, say it. Just tell me the truth!" Sam demanded.

"The truth? Are you sure?" Bishop leaned across the table exposing his nature of aggression, but Sam did not move. When Bishop saw a guard close in, he backed off.

"Yes, I'm sure! The truth," Sam demanded again, but he also wondered if he was sure.

Bishop looked to the left. Then he scanned the room of visitors and inmates as he looked to the right. Then he looked at the guards, at his boys, and into his soul. Finally, he began to speak of his childhood.

"I was twelve when I met Charlotte. So was she. We were both very poor and living in rotten, hopeless conditions. She was a beauty, and in that beauty, I saw promise in the future. She told me if I ever wanted to be with her, I had to be rich, that she wouldn't live as we had been living, and she would not bring a child into this world if it meant living like pigs. That's all I have to do? I thought. Become rich? Seemed easy enough to me. I spent the next several years of my youth doing every job I could get my hands on. They started off legal, but the illegal ones paid better.

"With my earnings, I would buy her things to keep reminding her of me while I rose to the top. By my late teens, I set my sights on politics and being in the government. Wanting to make a name for the Callahans and lift up our heritage, I took lessons to improve my reading and writing, my manners, my speaking. I was becoming *polished*. Then I put Charlotte through the same lessons so that she would be comfortable in American aristocratic settings. She fit like a glove. She was everything I wanted—stunningly beautiful and attentive to me. Then *you* came along," he said to Sam with contempt. "And then you," he said to Amos. "You stole her from me. I tried to win her back—a mansion, furs, jewelry, high society, trips. But I never could get that edge again. I learned I had a temper. I punished you as a way of punishing your mother for pushing me aside." Bishop looked away.

"Is that why mother never tended to us? Because it led to our punishment?" Sam asked. And Amos felt tremendous guilt for hating his mother.

Still looking away, Bishop answered, "Was that the truth you were looking for?" Sam closed his eyes. Amos widened his. "Doesn't matter, really. The police know I didn't do it. I'm not in here because of what happened to your mother."

"What?" Sam winced.

"I've been taking bribes for years, handing out just as many too. They said I had...sticky fingers"—Bishop wiggled his fingers—"and blood on my hands. Didn't you ever wonder how I made such a comfortable living as a government worker? Well, my enemies did, and they were all too eager to help lock me up and throw away the key. That Pruitt fellow knew too. He had me pegged the moment I opened my mouth. Your mother reported my *habits* to the police. That was my punishment. She arranged for them to come at a specific time, and she sent Amos to sell off what little we had left, knowing it would start a fight. Then she took her life just before they arrived." Sam was overwhelmed by the horror of his father's story. So was Bishop, as he dropped his head and pressed his fist to his teeth.

"But they gave you a life sentence," Amos said.

"People get hurt in the midst of extortion. That comes with a price, and now I'm paying it." Sam didn't know what to say. "I have had a lot of time to think in here. Seems I recreated the very life I ran from. I couldn't see that being on top didn't make you any different than those under you. What makes you different, regardless of where you are, is knowing who's in control." Bishop looked up as if to acknowledge God's sovereignty. "Your mother told me that I killed her. And I suppose she was right," he said somewhat emotionally. "I belong in here. Even if you could get me out, I wouldn't want you to. I can see clearly in here. Out there"—Bishop waved his hand as if he saw the world in front of him—"there's too much temptation for a man like me."

Both Sam and Amos were thrown by Bishop's words. Amos began to cry. Sam tried to speak but couldn't find the words. Bishop got up to leave.

"Don't spend your lives trying to figure out everything from your past. It's not worth...*I'm* not worth...the trouble. Just look ahead. I left a letter for you two with the guards in case one of you ever came. Ask for it on your way out." He looked at his sons and nodded goodbye. As Bishop Callahan vanished among the other inmates, he said so everyone could hear, "The devil may play, but God has the last say."

Sam sat back in his chair sorting through in his mind what just happened. What was it Jane said about this trip exceeding his expectations? Or did it only change them?

Amos wiped his tears and looked around hoping no one saw him crying. He said, "I'm not sure what redemption looks like, but I think we just witnessed it."

Of all the things Sam heard during the visit, Amos's words stunned him the most. A guard tapped Sam on the arm with his billy club and gestured to the exit saying they had to leave now.

Sam stopped by the guard's desk and inquired about the letter. Sergeant Unger told Sam to take a seat and wait. Sam and Amos sat for a long time waiting and without speaking. Finally, Sergeant Unger came out and handed an envelope to Sam. Amos read silently over Sam's shoulder.

> Sons, there's nothing left. The government con-
> fiscated everything. Even the house. You were
> good sons even though I was a bad father. Still, I
> knew enough to be proud of you. I can't ask for
> your forgiveness, but you can't withhold it either,
> unless you want your souls to rot, as mine did.
> Move on and don't look back.
>
> Signed,
> Bishop.

Sam looked toward the dark hallway leading to the iron bars that separated him from his father. Then he turned to face the exit doors where sunlight was shining so brightly through the glass that it was blinding. And he and Amos walked out.

To be continued…

Bibliography

Primary Sources (content is directly taken from the following):

1984. *Thomas Jefferson Writings; Letter to Edward Coles.* New York: Literary Classics of the United States.

Black Hawk. (2008). *Life of Black Hawk, or Ma-ka-tai-me-she-kia-kiak.* (G. J. Kennedy, Ed.) New York: Penguin Books.

Coles, Edward. n.d. *Letter from Edward Coles to Thomas Jefferson (July 31, 1814).* https://www.encyclopediavirginia.org/Letter_from_Edward_Coles_to_Thomas_Jefferson_July_31_1814.

Herndon, W. H., & Weik, J. W. (1888). *Abraham Lincoln: The True Story of a Great Life* (Vol. I). A Public Domain Book.

Herrick, Jennie Mellin, interview by T.M. Ward. 2015. *The Morgan Horse* (May 4).

Leitchtle, Kurt E., and Bruce G. Carveth. 2011. *Crusade Against Slavery: Edward Coles, Pioneer of Freedom.* Carbondale and Edwardsville: Southern Illinois University Press.

Miller, Bern, interview by T.M. Ward. 2014. Bridgeport, NE, (September).

Miller, Bern, interview by T.M. Ward. 2015. *The Morgan Horse* (September).

Supporting Sources:

Alchin, Linda. 2014. *Irish Immigration to US Timeline.* September. http://www.datesandevents.org/us-immigration-timelines/irish-immigration-america-timeline.htm.

Anderson, Neil T. 2000. *The Bondage Breaker.* Eugene: Harvest House Publishers.

Anderson, Neil T. 2000. *Victory Over the Darkness.* Ventura: Regal Books.

Baker, Donald G. 1967. "The History of Entrance Examinations." *Improving College and University Teaching* 15 (4): 250–253.

Beschloss, Michael. 2015. "The Near Death, and Revival, of Monticello." *The New York Times,* February 7. https://www.nytimes.com/2015/02/08/upshot/the-near-death-and-revival-of-monticello.html.

Cooperman, Jeannette. 2010. *Take Care, and Don't Take the Cholera.* June 25. https://www.stlmag.com/-ldquoTake-Care-and-Don-rsquot-Take-the-Cholera-rdquo/.

Ehle, John. 1989. *Trail of Tears, The Rise and Fall of the Cherokee Nation.* New York: Anchor Books Editions.

Farshler, Earl. 1933. *The American Saddle Horse.* Louisville: The Standard Printing Company.

n.d. *Governors of Illinois; Ninian Edwards.* http://www.onlinebiographies.info/gov/il/edwards-n.htm.

Hainesworth, Lorna. 2011. *Historic National Road; An All American Road.* December. http://marylandnationalroad.org/wp-content/themes/mnra/pdfs/Historic-National-Road.pdf.

n.d. *The History Box | The Panic of 1837.* Accessed October 10, 2015. http://thehistorybox.com/ny_city/panics/panics_article5a.htm.

1882. *History of Madison County Illinois.* Edwardsville: W.R Brink & Co.

Kotar, S.L. and Gessler, J.E. 2009. *The Steamboat Era, A History of Fulton's Folly on American Rivers, 1807–1860.* Jefferson: McFarland & Company Inc.

McAndrew, Tara McClennan. 2016. *Illinois Issues: Slave State.* Edited by Jamey Dunn. NPR Illinois. October 20. http://www.nprillinois.org/post/illinois-issues-slave-state.

1832. *Muster Roll of Captain A. Lincoln's Company of the 4th Regiment of Mounted Volunteers.* University of Chicago. May 27. http://pi.lib.uchicago.edu/1001/cat/bib/4904596.

Norton, W.T. n.d. *History of Alton Township, Madison County, IL (Part 1)*. Edited by W.T. Norton. The Lewis Publishing Company. http://history.rays-place.com/il/madison-alton-1.htm.

Olson, Greg. 2017. *The Cholera Epidemic of 1833 in Illinois; Plague on the Prairie*. January 15. https://drloihjournal.blogspot.com/2017/01/the-cholera-epidemic-of-1833-in-illinois.html.

Prucha, Francis Paul. 1994. *American Indian Treaties; The History of a Political Anomaly*. Berkeley and Los Angeles: University of California Press.

Randolph, Mary. 1832. *The Virginia Housewife*. Baltimore: Plaskitt & Cugle.

Slattery, Thomas J. 1988. *An Illustrated History of the Rock Island Arsenal and the Arsenal Island, Part One*. Rock Island: Historical Office, U.S. Army Armament, Munitions, and Chemical Command.

Urofsky, Melvin. n.d. *The Sale of Monticello*. The Thomas Jefferson Encyclopedia. https://www.monticello.org/site/house-and-gardens/sale-monticello.

n.d. *Western Saddle Guide; History of the Western Saddle*. The Lariat Group. http://www.western-saddle-guide.com/western-saddle-history.html.

Whitney, Ellen M., ed. 1970. *The Black Hawk War 1831–1832* 1, Illinois Volunteers. Springfield: Illinois State Historical Library.

Young, John Richard. 1954. *The Schooling of the Western Horse*. Norman: University of Oklahoma Press.

CPSIA information can be obtained
at www.ICGtesting.com
Printed in the USA
FSHW011519010420
68707FS